The characters are fictitious. Any similarity to anyone, living or dead, is coincidental and not intended by the author.

No part of this book may be reproduced, or stored in a retrieval system, or transmitted in any form or by any means, electronic, mechanical, photocopying, recording, or otherwise, without express written permission of the publisher.

ISBN: 9798332682537

ONE IN EIGHT

Ash Kade

CHAPTER 1

07:30, Saturday 2nd June 2063

Unless you've been there yourself it can be difficult to understand. "For god's sake, snap out of it," she would say, as if being joyful and buoyant was a simple choice and I could alter my mood at the flick of a switch. The fact of the matter is it's all down to chemistry. If you don't have the serotonin then happiness can be a physiological impossibility, even if you could find the motivation to try. "Man up" was her other helpful suggestion. But that was even more difficult to comply with, and ridiculous given our predicament. The meaning of 'man' was not the same as when that phrase was coined. Possession of a Y chromosome is one definition at a biological level, but beyond that I had long lost all sense of the word's value.

I hadn't always been that way: useless, pathetic, so full of self-loathing. I was once a man of stature. Someone who commanded respect. A man amongst men. In the dysfunctional chaos that society had become, it was my career that had anchored me. More than that, it had defined me. So when that was taken away, my identity went with it, along with the incentive to live. The gradual deterioration into darkness began. Day after day of meaningless existence takes its toll. I had attempted to escape the torment once, but that wasn't something we talked about.

"The kids are fighting, get up."

She hadn't always been that way either. We used to love each other deeply. I still did, even then. She was a brilliant woman, and I couldn't be more proud of her. I thought she still loved me, locked away somewhere deep down inside. At least, I hoped she did. I saw something in her eyes from time to time. That tiny glint of how things used to be, when she would look at me as if I was everything to her. It's just... things had changed. She had become a product of her environment, that's all.

"Jack, I said get up." A sharp elbow jabbed into my rib cage.

I had barely slept, as I rarely did. I was often grateful of that fact, as the nightmares that followed did not make it worthwhile. It was hot and I was tired. I wanted to bury my head in the pillow and pretend the world didn't exist, but I wasn't going to risk an argument. I never won them, even when I thought my case was watertight. She had this ability of making everything seem my fault. I could never work out if I was being manipulated, or always in the wrong. Whichever it was, I never came out on top.

The cotton sheet that covered me was damp with sweat and humidity and stuck to my bare skin as I peeled it back and reluctantly pushed myself out of bed. I stepped across to the open window, taking shallow breaths as putrid air was sucked into my nostrils. The edge of the raging summer sun was just visible above the silhouetted roofline of the houses opposite, a tiny speck of burning white light, bringing with it the arrival of another day in hell. I watched it rise for a moment. As the speck grew larger, the intensity of the heat beaming down increased, like the power being cranked up on an enormous laser in the sky. Down on the pavement below, a festering mound of household waste was piled six feet high; a giant stack of black plastic bags, humming with the smell of death, attracting multiple species of vermin. It wasn't ideal conditions for anyone to be hauling rubbish into the back of a truck, but that fact was irrelevant. The bin men wouldn't be coming either way. I closed my eyes as I stood there, concentrating hard, trying to perceive the slightest breeze to offer some relief and cool my clammy skin. But the air was motionless. All I could sense was the rustling of rats, the buzzing of flies and the distant screams of someone in distress.

"What are you doing?" Zoe said, pulling me back into the room. "It sounds like World War III is going on down there." World War III would have been a welcome distraction, I thought. Vaporisation might even be preferable.

"Closing the window," I replied, as I pulled it shut. "That smell is making me sick. I need to freshen up, then I'll go sort them out."

I rummaged in the drawer of my bedside table until I found what I was searching for, a small, clear, plastic pot. I took it, headed for the bathroom, and locked the door. I may not have been useful for much, but the one thing of value I had was my genetic code, and the powers-that-be wanted my DNA. Tall, broad-shouldered, blonde hair, blue eyes; I ticked all the boxes of sought after characteristics. They paid me for it, quite generously in fact. Not because it was the right thing to do, but because sperm was one of the few things that could not be extracted from a man using threat of violence. The filled pot locked with a click as I tightened the lid. I scribbled my name and date of birth in marker pen.

Jack Wilson – 04/05/13

Icy water rained down as I opened the valve on the shower, its coldness intensified by the contrast to the heat radiating from my body's surface. I took a sharp intake of breath as my skin constricted, squeezing me inward from all directions. It was torture, but I relished it, soaking up the suffering on my own terms. I used to do the same in the army, but for different reasons. Mind over matter. Mental toughness. Make discomfort the norm and everything else becomes easy. But that day at home I wanted something, anything, that proved to myself that I was in control.

I towelled off, pulled on a pair of shorts and a t-shirt,

and headed downstairs. Sunlight forced its way through the drawn curtains, casting a surreal yellow glow in the kitchen. I opened the fridge. The interior remained dark, so I deposited my sample pot and shut the door to keep the cold air trapped inside.

The source of the disturbance became immediately obvious. Cora, our twelve-year-old daughter, sat cross-legged on the floor of the living area in spotty pink pyjamas, hunched over her portable music player. Her long blonde hair fell messily around a pair of headphones that were blasting out some awful music. She had my colouring, but not my temperament; as feisty as they come, like a bossy little gremlin. Zach, our fourteen-year-old son, was the spitting image of Zoe. Chestnut brown hair that had been hacked at with blunt scissors by father-come-barber. A smattering of freckles across his button nose. Rarely seen dimples that sunk pits into his cheeks when he smiled. Meek and timid, he would speak only when spoken to, and even then, it would be brief. Another one who was a product of their environment. He was curled up on the armchair with his face buried in a book about history's female scientists.

"You didn't run the tap long enough," Cora yelled without looking up. "This water is warm and disgusting. Get me another one."

"I'm sorry," Zach replied. He placed down his book, dashed into the kitchen, and then shuffled back towards his sister, head bowed, clutching a fresh glass of water two-handed, like he was presenting a precious gift to a princess. Cora snatched the glass without making eye contact or uttering a word of thanks, and Zach retreated to his chair, picked up his book, and awaited his next order.

I took a deep breath and lifted one side of Cora's headphones. "Listen, you're shouting very loudly. You've woken mum and she's not happy. Please, can we tone it down a bit? And a little please and thanks wouldn't hurt. Or you could get your own water the way you like it."

"Shut it, Dad," Cora replied, snatching her headphone back down. "Why don't you go and do something useful. There's a good boy."

My cheeks flushed red with shame and stifled rage. I knew I shouldn't let her speak to me that way. I should have dragged her upstairs and made her sit in her room. Confiscated her music player. Anything. But that wasn't how things worked. The dynamics of society had shifted. As a grown man I could take it on the chin, but it broke my heart to see Zach behave that way, intimidated by, and subservient to, a girl two years his younger. But that was the intention of the system, to put boys in their place from day one.

So I did as Cora told me, cleaned up after dinner from the night before, took the rubbish out - making the pile even bigger - and mopped the floor until the bumping above my head told me that Zoe had decided to wake up. My watch said 09:30. Her busy week had obviously worn her out. The bumps moved across the ceiling and then came down the stairs. A groggy Zoe emerged.

"Morning. That was a long sleep." I attempted my duty of greeting my wife with a kiss, but it landed on a cheek that she turned by looking away.

"Not long enough," Zoe replied under a yawn.

"You've certainly been putting the hours in this week. Must be close to the finish line though," I said.

"It would be nice if I didn't have to think about work as soon as I've woken up," she replied.

"Ok then..." That stumped me. "Come and sit down. Do you want some breakfast?" I said, pulling out a wooden chair for her at the kitchen table. "What can I get you?"

"Just a coffee."

Just then the lights clicked on, the microwave beeped, and the fridge began to buzz and whirr. "Good timing," I muttered to myself, as I dithered with the kettle and mugs.

The awkwardness that hung in the air was so intense that it almost solidified. Zoe's work was her life. If she didn't want to talk about that then I didn't know what else to say. I had no interesting stories to tell. I placed a mug of the synthetically flavoured caffeine drink that we had become accustomed to calling coffee in front of Zoe and pulled out the seat next to her. Her dark brown eyes, usually so big and bright that I often felt I could fall into them, were sunken and bloodshot. Her brunette bob was sticking out in all directions like it had been ruffled by an overzealous grandparent. But the freckles that covered her nose radiated cuteness that shone through her exhaustion. She was as beautiful as the day we met, probably more-so. She had matured gracefully into the confident and intelligent woman that was trying to rid an entire nation of a curse that had been inflicted upon it. I reached out to take hold of her hand, but she pulled it away.

An eternal minute of silence.

"So, what's on the agenda for today?" I eventually said.

"I need to write up some lab notes from yesterday and then Grace is coming over. She called me last night in a right state."

"Did she say what's up?"

"No."

"Is she bringing... him?"

"Didn't say. Just make sure we have enough food in. And not penne pasta again. Use your imagination."

"I need to pop out this morning to take in my sample. I'll go to the shop at the same time."

Grace was our eldest daughter. She had turned twenty-two six months prior and marked the occasion by moving in with her boyfriend, Logan. He didn't have much between the ears and I never warmed to him, but the traditionalist in me was pleased she had gotten together with a boy, even if he had an IQ lower than his shoe size. But Grace had experienced anguish that a girl of her age should not, and I had a bad feeling forming a heavy knot in the pit of my stomach. Call it father's intuition. I had already made it clear to Logan that if he ever hurt her, there would be a bored househusband who had been trained to kill a man in fifty different ways lurking around every corner. I didn't have much else to occupy myself, so I hoped for his sake he listened.

"I'll be back shortly," I called out as I stepped out into the cul-de-sac. I circled around the horseshoe of red-brick houses with their patchy brown lawns and single driveways, all identical other than which of the windows were boarded up, and the burnt-out car that rusted away outside number six. Roots from untamed trees forced their way through the pavement making it too uneven to walk on without risk of tripping, so I stepped out into the road and meandered around the cavernous potholes that led down to the centre of the earth. I held my breath as I passed that pile of rubbish.

Up ahead, I could see Patrick from number one doing something in the garden, so I slowed my steps. I wanted him to go away so I didn't have to plainly ignore him. I couldn't work out what he was doing, but he was wearing only his boxer shorts and kept moving back and forth while staring at the ground, like he was searching for something. My delaying tactics didn't work. Once within twenty feet, I shifted strategy and quickened my pace to a borderline jog. Better to get the encounter over and done with as quickly as possible. He didn't look up as I passed, just carried on pacing up and down, like his body was vacant and on autopilot. An empty shell of a man. Or a man who had lost the plot. From the corner of my eye, I could see he had a thick lip and bruising around his face. My mind threw up the memory of the scream I heard earlier that morning. I couldn't be sure it was him, but it was possible. The curtains in his living room twitched. Someone was watching. The soldier in me demanded that I help him, but that part of me had grown small and weak. I knew I couldn't risk stopping.

Fifteen seconds later my cowardice was validated as a police van screeched on to the estate and came to a stop outside Patrick's house. Three black-clad police officers jumped out and battered Patrick to the ground with truncheons. He made no effort to defend himself, lying flat out on the lawn accepting blow after blow, as if they were welcome. A kick to the ribs. A stamp on his knee. Then a truncheon blow to the head was his final release and his body ceased all response. He was bundled into the back of the van and then they were off, driving slowly past me with the window wound down, as I kept my gaze focussed on my feet.

The Highstreet was a scene from a disaster movie. It always was, but the absence of other humans perpetuated the war-torn zombie apocalypse vibe. No doubt everyone else was hiding away from the relentless heat. I had never known a summer like it. My first stop was the pharmacy that collected the samples. I sometimes wondered how many children I had, and whether I had ever seen one without knowing. When I signed up to the donation program, they told me that the maximum number of children a man could father was twenty, and these would be spread nationally to reduce the likelihood of siblings accidently partnering up. But I had been dropping off samples almost every week for close to ten-years without anyone telling me to stop. Probably a sign of the exponentially increasing demand. A steep decline in natural conceptions along with a high rate of female homosexuality meant the waiting list for IVF was long. The rules must have been relaxed at some point.

"Are you registered with us?" the girl behind the counter said. The same question I get from the same person, every time I visit, a short, impish goth, with spiky black hair and thick glasses. The fantasy role-play type.

"Yes, I am," I replied with a sigh.

"Name?"

"It's Jack. Jack Wilson. I'm a regular here."

"I'll need to see your ID card."

"Here," I said, handing over my ID. She tapped some information into her computer.

"Says here your last deposit was over a month ago."

"Yes, my wife has been busy at work. I've been a bit distracted."

"There is a note on your file to say your fee has gone up fifty percent, did you know about this?"

"No, I didn't. But that's good news. Thanks."

"Nothing to do with me. Comes from central office. Put your sample in the plastic bag and seal it."

I swapped my sample for a fistful of notes and turned to exit. I hadn't noticed the raggedy guy standing behind me enter the store, silently creeping around like some sort of homeless ninja, but I smelled him before I saw him. He spotted the cash in my hand and then looked me up and down with wide-eyes and a gaping mouth. Cutting off supply for a while had paid off, even if unintentionally. A warm sensation I had not experienced in a while pulsed in my gut. I felt pleased with myself. It was nice to know that I was needed.

Not penne pasta. Zoe's voice rang in my ears as I entered the supermarket. I picked up a basket and began the pointless search for food on the bare shelves, fluorescent tube lights flickering overhead.

Use your imagination.

If she had done the shopping occasionally, she could see for herself what a challenge it was. Pasta, potatoes, bread, tinned beef. Wheat flakes for breakfast, sometimes porridge oats. These were the things that you were pretty much guaranteed to find. Anything else was potluck, depending on our position on the rationing rotation. There was no point in writing a shopping list, it was a case of being satisfied with whatever there was. Like the hunter-gatherer days, you ate what you found. I strolled past the stacks of empty plastic crates in the fruit & veg aisle until I reached the potatoes. Next to them was a tonne of muddy parsnips, and a few shrivelled beetroots. Being fussy wasn't an option, but the thought of putting beetroot in my mouth sent a shiver down my spine. Parsnips I could stomach. I was glad to discover spaghetti in the pasta aisle, which met Zoe's demand of *not penne pasta*, if only by a technicality. I approached the empty fridge where the fresh meat should have been. It had been weeks since we had fresh meat of any kind. You had to be queuing up at opening time to even stand a chance. I wasn't disappointed as I had learned not to get my hopes up. I crouched down to peer at the back of the fridge, just to make sure, and my heart skipped as I spotted a lonely packet of minced beef wedged almost out of sight. Somehow it had been missed by everyone else, but I wasn't going to question it. Feeding Zoe something that she wouldn't complain about would save me an earful of grief. I reached into the fridge to claim my prize and was hit by a pungent yet oddly familiar smell. Then a filthy hand snatched out from behind me and grabbed the packet I was holding. It was the stealthy hobo guy from the pharmacy. He scowled his dirty face as he yanked at the packet, trying to pull it off me. Two decades of hand-to-hand combat training is not easily forgotten. It becomes ingrained, like an instinct, reacting involuntarily when faced with a threat. My free hand flashed out and grabbed hold of his wrist, bending it back towards his elbow. He yelped in pain as he released his grip and the meat tumbled to the ground. He grimaced, showing rows of fossilised teeth. He had a face that was older than his age. A matted brown beard with flecks of grey. Leathery, sun-damaged skin camouflaged by a smear of grime. Deep black eyes that were brimming over with sadness and desperation. A fellow man at rock bottom, scavenging what he could, doing what he must to survive. And there I was, fighting him for it. But he wasn't my enemy. I let go of his wrist and stepped back, horrified by my behaviour.

"I'm sorry," I said. "Here, you take it." I picked up the meat and handed it to him. He reached out slowly, like a suspicious animal, unsure whether it was a trap, then snatched it and scuttled off without a word.

Spaghetti, corned beef, parsnips. No doubt it would earn me the cold shoulder for the rest of the day, but I was beyond caring. Maybe *she* could use *her* imagination, and pretend she was eating something different.

If only I dared to say that to her face.

CHAPTER 2

Alobar holoprosencephaly is the technical name. It's the most serious form of a condition where the brain fails to separate into the right and left hemispheres during foetal development. The result is severe facial disfigurement and a one-hundred-percent mortality rate. Cyclopia is the name more commonly used, as foetuses that are allowed to develop have a single eye in the middle of the face. It doesn't often get to that point in the developed world, as the condition will get picked up during the first trimester scan and the foetus will undoubtedly be aborted. Under normal circumstances the incidence rate of Cyclopia is less than one in ten thousand conceptions. In Britain, ever since 2023, it was occurring in precisely 87.5% of pregnancies, but only where the mother was carrying a boy. In 2063, forty years after it all began, the ratio of men to women in Britain was roughly 3:7. This imbalance would increase until all the men born before 2023 had died, when the ratio would plateau, at 1:8. The reason for the sudden increase in the condition remained unknown for several months until researchers at Oxford University identified a novel, gene-editing virus, but its origin was a mystery. The virus spread its way through the British female population in a matter of months and caused a genetic mutation that led to the random absence of a protein that was linked to brain development during pregnancy. All women became affected by the mutation, but its effects did not manifest consistently, so just because a mother delivered a healthy son once, did not mean she would do it again. For each pregnancy, the woman played the same game of Russian Roulette as every other mother-to-be. Worst of all, the mutation was hereditary, passed down from mother to daughter, generation after generation. The affliction became known as The Gaea, derived from Greek mythology where the Cyclopes were sons of Gaea, mother of the earth.

As the asymmetry in number increased, so did the asymmetry in power.

Grace sat at the kitchen table, a sobbing wreck of mascara-stained tears and streaming mucus. It didn't look like she had been near a shower or changed her clothes in days. Zoe stood behind, stroking her greasy auburn hair.

I paced the kitchen like a caged lion.

"Pregnant?! Again?" My state of apathy had given way to rage. I was furious. No, I was incandescent. Logan had made the wise decision to stay at home. If he hadn't, he would have been short of a few teeth.

"Jack, for god's sake, be quiet. Leave this to me will you," Zoe said, pushing me aside and sitting down in front of Grace. "Sweetie, are you sure?" she said, switching her tone to mothering sympathy. "Have you done a test?"

"Of course I have done a test, Mum. I have done four tests and I've missed three periods. I'm pregnant."

My teeth sank into my bottom lip.

Zoe continued, "You were supposed to be using protection, after last time. You know the risks and you know what happens if you have a boy."

"That's it though, we were using condoms, but they didn't work. Logan has been trying to persuade me to stop using them. He wants a baby. Part of me wonders whether he made this happen on purpose."

"I'm going to kill him!" A thunderous explosion of anger erupted from my mouth. "I'm going round there right now, and I'm going to kill him."

"Dad, no!"

"Jack, stop it!"

Their synchronous replies hit my ears in stereo.

"Gracie, you went to hell and back with that last abortion," I said. "I'm scared of what might happen if you have to go through that again, physically and psychologically."

Grace burst into tears again as Zoe tried to lift the mood by reframing the situation with her rational thinking.

"Let's not get ahead of ourselves. Look at it this way. You have a one-in-two chance of having a girl and a one-in-eight chance of having a healthy boy. That's greater than a fifty percent chance of having a little bundle of joy. This could be exciting."

"I guess so." Grace sniffed through stifled tears.

"How far in are you? Three missed periods must be, what, fourteen weeks?" Zoe said.

"I think it's about that."

"First thing is to get yourself to a doctor and get checked over. By now, they will be able to tell you whether there is a problem during the scan. We can take it from there, okay?"

"Yes, thanks Mum."

"Do you want me to come with you?"

"Yes please."

"See when they can fit you in and I'll make sure I'm free."

By the time Zoe had brought the situation under control it was early Saturday evening. Grace had decided to stay for dinner, and I was halfway through making little balls of canned meat with my hands. It was oddly cathartic, and I could feel my blood pressure returning to normal as I squished the brown paste between my fingers. My t-shirt had a wet triangle pointing downwards on my chest and beads of sweat formed streams down the middle of my back. I wiped my leaky brow with the back of my forearm as I scooped another handful of meat from the tin and rolled it between my palms.

It was the first Saturday of the month which meant the evening in our house would be spent like it would in most other households around the country, watching The National Address. The National Address was a monthly governmental broadcast that covered The Rota, that is, a communication on how the country's scarce resources would be allocated across the fifty districts. It was usually mixed up with some bottom-of-the-barrel good news stories to sugar coat it as far as possible. But it was The Rota that people were interested in, as it set out how miserable their lives would be for the following four weeks. With dinner prepared, I went to join the others in the lounge. The room was just large enough for two double sofas placed at right-angles to each other. The curtains were drawn, and the room was dark, the only light coming from the eighteen-inch cathode ray television in the corner. It was old technology, practically an antique, but substantially more reliable than anything made after and thankfully still going strong. Cora and Grace cuddled up on one sofa, Zach was lying on the floor using his elbows as a bipod for his head, and Zoe was on the other sofa with a space next to her. I sat down in the empty seat, just in time to see Alvina take her place at the podium on the TV screen.

Alvina was the mononymous Prime Minister of Great Britain and leader of the British Democrat Party, formally known as the British Feminist Party, up until the point where the power balance had shifted sufficiently for the concept of feminism to be rendered absurd. Party rebranding came with a personal rebranding and her original name, Ava Lee, was changed to 'Alvina'. She saw herself, and was treated by many, as a demi-god, and someone of such immense importance had no need for something so trivial as a surname. She was dressed in a white trouser suit that matched the air of class and sophistication that followed her wherever she went. In her late seventies, she was tall and thin. Her features were shaped by an East Asian heritage, but her skin had been loosened by age and gravity pulled everything downwards. Her voice had a deep, croaky quality to it when she spoke. She had been in power for what seemed like forever. For many younger people, all their lives.

"Good evening," she began. *"Welcome to June's National Address. We begin this evening's broadcast with some news on the fantastic progress Professor Zoe Wilson and her talented team of women at the Department of Genetic Medicine at Kent University have made on the latest attempt to cure The Gaea."* I gave Zoe a nudge with my elbow. Zoe rolled her eyes. *"Professor Wilson has been working with a team in The United States and tests performed up until now have been promising. The results from the human clinical trials are expected this week. Let's hear from Professor Wilson herself on more of the detail."*

The screen cut to a video clip of Zoe in a white lab coat and safety glasses, walking and talking in her laboratory. She was explaining the design of the clinical studies, what animal tests had been performed, and the purpose of the numerous pieces of equipment.

"Wow Mum, super cool!" Cora shouted. "You're famous!"

We all stared at Zoe, bursting with pride. Even Zach cracked a little smile. Zoe ignored the excitement and Alvina's face reappeared on the TV.

"Please join me in wishing Professor Wilson and her team the best of luck for the week ahead."

A small round of applause from what sounded like an audience of ten came through the TV speaker.

"Next, I would like to provide clarification on rumours that have been circulating in certain foreign media channels about the British family that escaped to France in 2057. Nicholas and Patricia Atkins, along with their daughter, Emily, have been hidden by a relative in a remote part of the French countryside. This relative was allegedly part of the team from the University of Paris with which we collaborated in a previous attempt to treat

The Gaea. The reports claim that the mother and daughter have been cured of the genetic defect and that Emily Atkins is pregnant with her third baby boy. These reports have been proven to be unfounded. French authorities have confirmed that Emily Atkins is indeed pregnant with her third healthy son, but she has not been cured of The Gaea and the occurrence is merely a statistical anomaly. In line with foreign protocol, the Atkins family are being deported back to Britain to prevent wider contagion of The Gaea."

"I didn't hear about that," I said.

"It was on the news a few days ago," Zoe replied. "What a lucky girl."

"Lucky would be staying in France."

"On to The Rota for the next month," Alvina continued. A long pause. Her manner had shifted from authoritarian to nervous hesitancy. She appeared deep in contemplation. She took a deep breath. *"I'm not going to stand here and pretend that I'm happy about what I'm going to say. I took this job knowing that it would be difficult, and I admit that I underestimated the scale of the task."* The lady standing next to Alvina, presumably an advisor or assistant, glanced at her sideways, alarmed, like she was going off script. *"Despite the challenges we face today, I stand by the decision we took to adapt our economic model, but the continual decline in the able workforce means that it is not operating as efficiently as it needs to. This chart shows that only five of our fifty districts are meeting output targets and they are those focussed on energy production and are benefitting from this prolonged period of intense sunlight. Therefore, this month brings with it a further tightening of allocations. But remember this, there is not a single person in this country without a roof over their head and food in their belly, unless it's of their own choosing. That is not something that can be said by any government that presided under the patriarchal capitalist system that came before. I stand firmly behind the universal provision of basic services, and essential food, healthcare, energy, housing, clothing, and education will always remain free for everyone."*

"You heard it from her," I said. "You should be grateful for your daily penne pasta."

"I don't see you doing much to help the situation," Zoe replied.

"In line with previous months, petrol and diesel will be restricted to districts with limited electrical charging capability. That's D1 to D10, and D25 to D31."

"Great," I muttered to nobody.

"Due to the continued lack of rain, crop yields are steadily declining and are approaching record lows. We are therefore going to have to temporarily halt rotational rationing and implement national level restrictions on certain products until further notice. This will be managed at a district level depending on existing stocks. The hot weather is also causing problems with refuse and it's becoming a major health and safety hazard across all districts. We are therefore reprioritising duties to ensure rubbish is cleared as soon as possible. All Category C men with surnames ending in J to Z will report to their district office on Monday morning for this special assignment."

"She makes it sound like some sort of covert spy operation," I said. "Poor guys. Glad I'm not going through that maggot-ridden heap out there."

"As alluded to, one positive aspect of the hot weather is that hydrogen production is exceeding target to the point that storage has become an issue. Energy rationing will therefore be halted for the month of June to use up surplus inventory."

"Finally, some good news," I said. "Wheel out that old aircon unit. I'm going to be as cool as a cucumber in this house."

Even Zoe smiled at that development.

"Finally, some of you will be aware of the explosion at the hydrogen plant in D22 this morning."

"Hey, that's us," Cora said.

"Emergency Response are going through the wreckage, but

it's expected that at least fifty of the ninety men that worked there have died. As did, tragically, a substantial proportion of the management team."

"Oh my god that's horrible," I said.

"We therefore face the task of clearing the existing site and reinstalling the solar array that was severely damaged. Category B & C men in D22 with surnames ending A – H will be reassigned to the clear up operation. To minimise any disruption to essential services, we are conscripting all Category A men that are not currently employed by the government to assist the surviving workforce in repairing the facility. You will report to the district office on Monday for further instruction."

I sat wide mouthed and speechless, perfectly aware of the four pairs of eyes all staring at me.

A grin began to spread across Cora's face and I wondered whether it was ever going to stop. "Cool as a cucumber, eh Dad?"

Sure enough, thirty minutes after the broadcast had finished, one of the drawers in the kitchen began vibrating and beeping. I slid it open and took out the pager that was hidden amongst the clutter.

Report to D22 District office, 08:00 Monday 4th June.

"I'm not doing it. I can't," I said. "It's going to be forty-five degrees plus, and I don't know the first thing about building."

"Serves you right for being a Cat A smarty pants," Zoe replied. "I'm sure they'll find a job for you. You are good at making tea."

"It's not funny! Seriously, I can't do it. If anyone says anything I'll plead ignorance."

"That's why they page you," Zoe said.

"I'm surprised the battery works on that thing. It's the first time it's beeped since I had to work in the hospital during that bad flu season. That was what, two years ago? Or three?

I'll say I knew nothing about it."

"You know what happened to David across the road. He was put in confinement for a month. They'll have a list of names to check off. Who is going to look after the kids if you're in jail? Besides, getting out of the house and having something to occupy yourself is just what you need. You might enjoy it. You need to go. End of story."

She used that tone that meant 'end of story' without needing to verbalise the words, but obviously decided to make sure the message was doubly clear.

CHAPTER 3

Sunday 3rd June 2063

I woke up with my heart racing in a sense of euphoria, but not in a good way. My brain was in flight-mode, flooded with cortisol, anxious about what was happening the following day. I couldn't consolidate my thoughts so spent the morning lying in bed with the curtains drawn. Zoe seemed to understand and was happy to leave me there.

I resented being sucked in to clear up a mess that was not of my making. It wasn't the hours spent in sweltering heat that bothered me. It was having to deal with all those other people. The outside world was cruel and my sheltered existence in my own little bubble suited me fine. I didn't need to speak with any strangers beyond a courteous "please" and "thank you" to whoever was serving me in the shop. What was I supposed to say to all those people working on the building site? I didn't do socialising.

Gone were the days of male social banter, slapping each other on the back, chatting about sport, elbowing the guy sat next to you in the pub to check out the blonde standing at the bar. That would land you with a month in confinement and the girl wouldn't even need proof. It happened a lot, which was part of the reason why men avoided contact with other humans where possible. It was safer to keep your head down and get on with your own business. But it didn't stop there. 'A month in confinement' was the standard outcome to a long list of wrongdoings; offensive conduct towards women (where the definition of 'offensive' was entirely at the woman's discretion), not following official orders to attend an assignment, not attending a place of work due to sickness on more than one occasion in a rolling twelve-month period, social disturbance, gambling, consuming alcohol, plus a whole host of other things. The worst offence that applied to men, though, was collusion. That is, two or more men conspiring against the system. That would land you a ten-year stretch and the evidence didn't need to be that compelling. I once heard of a case where a group of five men were secretly betting on the outcome of the women's football, which was just called football. They were caught whispering, covertly handing small bits of paper around, and generally acting shifty. They didn't admit to gambling as that would get them a month in jail. So, because their behaviour had no other explanation, they were charged with collusion and before they knew what was going on, it was too late to back track. They couldn't prove that they weren't conspiring and that's all that was required to lock them all up for ten long years. It was all designed to make sure men stayed inline and maintain the status quo. To prevent them from building any camaraderie or confidence or getting drunk and having a fantastic idea to rise up and start a revolution. It got me thinking, why were the government supporting attempts to cure the condition that caused a situation that they evidently didn't want to change? It didn't make sense.

But lying there in bed, I wanted to know the answer.

My stomach was beginning to rumble so I dragged myself downstairs for some lunch. Zoe was at the kitchen table with her head buried in a pile of notebooks and was tapping furiously at a calculator with the end of her pen. She usually worked in her office but with the air-conditioning blasting out cool air, the kitchen was a much more comfortable temperature. I crept up, pulled out a chair and sat down next to her.

"Zoe?" I said.

"Oh, you're up," she replied.

"Yes. Can I ask you a question?"

"You can. But make it quick."

"If you had the choice of keeping things as they are, or going back to a fifty-fifty split, which would you choose?"

"That's a stupid question. Do we have to do this now?"

"Is it stupid, though? I'm interested to know your opinion."

"Jack, I dedicate my life to ridding the country of this wretched disease. Try using your brain and take a mental leap as to what my opinion might be."

"Yes, I suppose. But what about other women? And the government? I don't see how going back would be in their favour. Women have it pretty good as it is." That got her attention. Her head snapped in my direction and her eyes locked on to me with an intense glare. I instantly regretted my choice of words.

"Oh, I'm so glad to hear that women have it *pretty good*. I'll be sure to clarify that for our daughter when it turns out that she, like thousands of other women, has to go through the mental and physical trauma of having *another* abortion because a man couldn't control his penis. And the hundreds of thousands of women dealing with the anguish of denying their bodies the natural process of childbirth because they can't afford the IVF treatment. Women bear the sole responsibility for keeping this crap-hole of a country from collapsing entirely. How does that compare to your life, Jack? All you do is shop, cook and masturbate. I'd say *you* have it pretty good. Now please go away and do something useful instead of distracting me from trying to save the country."

I was somewhat taken aback by the outburst. Much of what she said was true, but to suggest that women didn't have the better end of the deal was disingenuous. They had preferential treatment in almost every aspect of life, social freedoms, career prospects, rule of law. The entire education system was designed to ensure girls prospered while boys were conditioned for a life of servitude. You only had to see how Zach was turning out to know that. I decided it best to keep that thought to myself, but her response was unsatisfactory. "I guess I'll leave you to it then," I said as I stood up.

I made some toast and took it back upstairs. As I passed Zach's bedroom, I saw him sitting at his desk, resting his head on his hand, doodling idly on a piece of paper. He looked bored. "What are you up to?" I said through the open door.

"Nothing. Just doing some drawing," he replied. "Did you want to do something together?" He perked up with a brightness in his face.

It was a beautiful Sunday afternoon, perfect for a kick-about in the park, or a hike through the fields, or a bike ride down by the river. A board game, even. The sorts of things that a father should be doing with his kids at the weekend when there was nothing else to do. Nice, wholesome, family time. I couldn't bring myself to consider it. It required something that I was missing. I wanted to, more than anything. But it was impossible. All I could think about was climbing back into my comfortable hole of self-pity.

"I can't," I said.

"Oh, ok then," he replied, the brightness fading to disappointment.

Back in my own bedroom, I threw the plate of toast across the room and got into bed. I buried my face in the pillow and screamed. I had never hated myself as much as that moment.

CHAPTER 4

06:10, Monday 4th June 2063

I had set my alarm for 06:45 but a restless night of anticipation meant that, again, I had barely slept. Zoe's side of the bed was empty and cold. Goodness knows what time she had left, but it meant that I must have had at least some sleep as I didn't notice her go. I heard a loud yelp come from downstairs. I jumped out of bed and ran down into the kitchen to find Cora sat at the table, eating dry cereal with a spoon, and watching TV through the open lounge door. Zach was sat opposite her, head hung low, with a huge red mark across his cheek.

"What's going on down here?" I said with my eyes darting between the two of them.

Silence.

"Zach?"

Silence.

"Cora!?"

"Huh, yeah?" she replied after managing to deflect her attention from the TV.

"I said, what is going on? What's happened to Zach's face?"

"I suggest you speak to him about that," she replied in a matter-of-fact tone that sounded like her mother.

"I am asking you, young lady."

"It's his own fault. I told him I wanted porridge, and he

got me the boring wheat flakes."

"And what?"

"Obviously I hit him with my belt."

"Across the face?" I said, gobsmacked. "Not that it matters where. You can't go around hitting people because they didn't do what you wanted."

"I know that! But Zach isn't people. He's just Zach. And he's an idiot and he deserved it." Cora turned to glare at Zach. "Didn't you?"

Zach nodded.

"No, he didn't," I said. "Zach, you didn't. Cora, go and get ready for school. I never want to see you doing something like that again. Clear?"

Cora placed her spoon down on the table and walked off with a slow, arrogant swagger. I sat down next to Zach and tried to get him to look me in the face. The rectangular mark on his cheek was swollen and looked incredibly painful. I could see three white dots in a row where the belt holes must have been.

"Zach, you mustn't let her treat you like that. If you do, she will do it more and more. I know it's not easy, but you need to find a way of sticking up for yourself."

"But… that's not what we are supposed to do," Zach replied in a timid voice.

"What do you mean?"

"My teacher said that we… I mean boys… must respect girls."

"Oh my goodness, Zach. Of course, you should respect girls. You should respect everyone, but only if they deserve it. Respect is earned. It doesn't mean doing as you are told, and it doesn't mean taking physical abuse. It's nice to do things for people but it needs to be a two-way deal and the person asking should be polite. Next time Cora tells you to do something, you at least make sure she says please. And it's ok for you to ask her for something every now and again."

Zach appeared to be in deep in thought. "You do things for mum all the time and she is never polite to you," he eventually said.

I was momentarily lost for words. Then I managed, "Your mother and I respect each other very much. She works hard and is often tired when she gets home, that's all. You go get ready for school and try to remember what I said."

I left the house at 07:25 to begin the two-and-a-bit mile walk to the District Office. The house had reached a comfortable temperature with the air-conditioning running so the barrage of warm, foul-smelling air that hit me as I opened the front door was a nasty shock. I walked down the uneven garden path and paused as I passed the silver 2029 BMW M3 sitting on the drive, covered in a thick layer of orange dust. It was a beautiful machine, what was left of it. One of the last petrol models to be made. At over thirty-years-old the body work had seen better days, but it ran smoothly when I was able to get fuel for it. There was nothing more thrilling than taking it out for a spin in the countryside. It reignited a deep primeval feeling in my stomach. The exhilaration of breaking the rules, taking risks, knowing that I was beyond the boundaries of what was acceptable. It gave me a sense of power and control that had long been lost. It made me feel alive. Sadly, these joy rides were an infrequent occurrence ever since petrol had become a scarce commodity. Pootling along Zoe's silent, electric hatchback to the shop and back didn't deliver the same sensation.

I began walking down the street and was dazzled by the morning sun that hung low in the clear blue sky. I wasn't typically out and about at that time of day and noticed how the air had a tranquil peacefulness to it. I could see a handful of other solitary men walking in the same direction, absorbed in their own internal universes, which were undoubtedly more pleasant than the neglected, dilapidated hellhole we were occupying. Those moments of solitude were probably the best part of their day. My mind, however, was fixed on what Zach had said to me at breakfast.

You do things for mum all the time and she is never polite to you.

It wasn't until then that the gravity of what he had said fully hit me. Firstly, I had never considered that the kids were taking notes and it struck me that I was Zach's only male role model and should be setting the example of how men should conduct themselves. Secondly, and more worryingly, he was right! Being a fulltime homemaker was never high up my list of ambitions, but fate led me there and I did the job as best I could manage on any given day. But there was no appreciation for what I did. I knew the way society operated was different, but I still deserved some respect.

The image of Zach's swollen face dominated my thoughts.

It needed addressing, for Zach's sake if not my own. A wave of anxiety crashed over me even thinking about it. My heart raced as I pictured myself standing toe-to-toe with Zoe. But a tiny spark of courage had ignited deep inside, and I wasn't going to let it go out. I was going to put my foot down. After the day's work was over, I was going to do what I hadn't been able to for a long time. I was going to use what little petrol I had left, and I was taking the BMW out. Zach was going to come with me, and I wasn't going to ask for permission.

CHAPTER 5

I arrived at the District Office a fraction before 08:00 to find several queues of at least fifty men each, heading toward different entrances. D22 must have had the most spectacular district office in the country. The district incorporated what used to be known as the city of Canterbury and the local government took possession of Canterbury Cathedral following the breakdown of mainstream Christianity in the UK during the early 2050s. The number of people attending church had been on a steady decline for decades. However, the horror brought by The Gaea was enough to test the faith of many moderate Christians and it ended up being the straw that broke the camel's back. A population largely disinterested in religion, along with the associated collapse in funding, meant the church's position in society became untenable. Of course, The Gaea was seen by some as a punishment sent by God and there still existed an underground cult of devout Christians that tried to spread The Lord's word and warn against further retribution. But this was from street corners rather than from inside a church.

I joined the queue that was headed towards the building's main entrance as it was moving fastest. I shuffled, half step by half step, toward the great stone archway that led inside and gazed up to see the colossal gothic towers that pierced the sky above. Nobody made eye-contact. Nobody spoke. The eerie silence was intensified by the medieval surroundings, creating an unnerving, solemn ambience like we were queuing up for The Last Judgement. I passed through the doorway and the temperature dropped by ten degrees as the shaded stone structure sucked the energy from the air. The impossibly high vaulted ceiling was supported by two rows of broad stone columns that ran the length of the building. The original pews had been removed and were replaced with a vast grid of office-style desks, each occupied by a female in local government uniform and a computer monitor. The queue split in to six smaller queues which each led toward a separate desk. I eventually reached a desk to find a woman in her standard blue shirt and tie uniform, who I knew was called Pippa because of her name badge. Pippa looked in her mid-twenties and had brown, shoulder-length hair. She had a round face, wore thick-rimmed glasses and couldn't look more bored if she tried.

"ID," she said.

"Pardon?" I replied.

"ID. I need your government ID."

I searched my pockets.

Shit.

I had left it in my other trousers.

"I don't have it. I must have left it at home. I'm here for the hydrogen plant assignment," I said.

"It's compulsory for men to carry ID at all times."

"Yes, I know, and I do, usually."

Pippa let out a dramatic sigh. "If I can't verify your identity, I have to mark you as not attending."

"But that means I'll have to go to jail for a month!"

"Probably, yes. Well actually two, one for not carrying your ID and one for not attending a mandatory assignment. Nothing I can do I'm afraid. Please leave the queue, Mr...?" Pippa said without the slightest hint of emotion.

"Wilson," I said as I fumbled in my pockets, hoping I might find something that would satisfy the self-important little madam. I pulled out my wallet and presented a selection of random cards. "Here you go. I have my driving licence which has my photo and current address."

"Driving licences don't have the biometric data or confirm your category."

"Really? Come on," I said, failing to disguise my frustration. "I'm trying to turn up for work and you're not letting me. It hardly seems fair. Why would a random guy come here and volunteer to work in this heat?"

Pippa snatched the driving licence from my hand and looked at it, and then back at me from over the top of her glasses. "OK. On this occasion I'm going to issue you with a caution. You must bring your government ID tomorrow, or the caution will be replaced with an offense."

A surge of relief hit me. "Thank you," I said, grateful for her mercy.

Pippa turned back to her computer screen, tapped a few keys on the keyboard and then spoke without looking at me. "You are on construction duty at the new site. Site management will give you more information when you arrive. Coach twelve. You better hurry as it's leaving in three minutes. Be earlier tomorrow. Next."

I walked as fast as I could without running to avoid drawing any unnecessary attention and exited through the same stone archway that I had entered, into the blazing morning sun. I squinted as my eyes adjusted to the blinding light. Once I was able to see, I spotted coach twelve fifty metres ahead of me in the car park. Another young female in official uniform had just closed the side luggage compartment and was getting on the coach herself. This time I didn't hesitate to sprint as fast as I could. I reached the coach as the doors were closing and had to bang on the window with my palm to get the driver's attention. The doors hissed open to reveal a militant female with short blonde hair pulled back in a tight ponytail and slits where her eyes should have been. She was holding a clipboard and was glaring down at me with a face of pure disdain.

"Can I help you?" she said.

"Yes… sorry," I managed underneath deep panting. "I had a few issues at registration but I'm ready."

She scanned down the piece of paper attached to her clipboard. "Mr Wilson, I presume."

"Yes, that's right. I really am sorry, it's the first time I've had to —"

"Does it look like I'm interested in your excuses?" she said.

"Well —"

"It was a rhetorical question. I'm not. You are late and so I'm issuing you with a caution. Don't let it happen tomorrow."

"Of course," I said, this time not quite so grateful. Two cautions in the space of five minutes was not good. They stayed on record for twelve months and having three at any one time resulted in… a month in jail. I needed to be on best behaviour from that point on.

I took my seat in the only available space and tried to put the worry out of my mind. It was the first time I had needed to do that sort of thing in a long while. The next day would be better. I distracted myself by thinking about Zoe and the work she was doing. If it all worked out, we could be rid of this dreadful affliction and things could get back to the way they used to be. It would take time, longer than I had left on the planet, but there was hope for Zach. It made me feel a bit better.

The coach pulled off and I stared out of the window, letting myself drift into absentmindedness. Derelict buildings and abandoned cars zoomed past. The rhythmic passing of the redundant streetlamps became hypnotic and my eyelids grew heavy. As I was about to fall asleep, I was pulled back to reality by the sound of someone crying. The guy sitting next to me, a thin man in his late forties, was weeping into his hands like a child. His body heaved and twitched as he sobbed uncontrollably. None of the other men made the slightest acknowledgement. No kind gestures or efforts to comfort him. Everyone remained in their own little world with eyes fixed on the back of the headrest in front; silent and sombre.

My modicum of positivity was overwhelmed by a dark feeling of doubt.

Would anything ever change?

CHAPTER 6

After forty minutes of driving, the coach came to a stop beside a large expanse of land next to the destroyed hydrogen farm. It must have been one hell of an explosion. All buildings within a fifty-metre radius of the site were severely damaged. On the site itself, columns of thick, black smoke rose from piles of smouldering rubble and drifted off with the wind. It even smelled of disaster as a combination of dust, smoke and fuel filled the air.

The original buildings on the plot of land were levelled and the final remnants of debris were being pushed to one side by a fleet of archaic bulldozers. In their place stood the beginnings of a large metal frame, which must have been eighty-by-eighty metres, presumably intended as the internal structure of the new hydrogen farm building. In the middle of the plot sat several clusters of industrial equipment wrapped in blue cling-film. Over to the right was a huge pile of metal beams and a rusty yellow crane. Around it all buzzed a busy swarm of women in grubby hi-vis jackets, dust masks, and dirty, white hard hats, interspersed with a less enthusiastic herd of men with no personal protective equipment whatsoever. Bearing in mind how slowly things usually happened, if they happened at all, it was an impressive sight given the explosion was two days before.

The blonde girl from the coach stood up at the front and spoke into a megaphone.

"Listen in coach twelve, today you are on solar panel inspection duty. Your job will be to unpack the solar panels and check that they work. There is three thousand of them and nobody is going home until they are all done. It should be an easy task for the fifty of you. Any questions?"

I wanted to know about the break schedule, so I raised my hand.

"No? Good. Follow me to your station where you will receive further training. And do watch your step, scraping up men squashed by steel girders slows things down."

We snaked single-file across the building site. The noise was incredible; drilling, banging, the siren of a reversing forklift truck, and female voices amplified by megaphones filling what space in the air was left. I had to admit, it was all rather exciting and a stark contrast from my normal dull routine. If it wasn't for the relentless and inescapable heat, I would say I was happy to be there. If nothing else, it was a change of scenery. We arrived at the location where we would be spending the day. A ten-by-ten-by-three cuboid of wooden crates cast a long morning shadow that everyone instinctively moved towards. The blonde lady spoke briefly to a young redhead in standard issue hi-vis jacket and white hard-hat, before making her way back the way we came. Redhead lifted a megaphone and spoke with unconvincing authority. I guessed she was new to this.

"Ahem, excuse me. My name is Matilda, and I will be your supervisor for the day."

A few men exchanged glances, probably wondering how we ended up being bossed about by a secondary school child.

"As you can see, we have three hundred crates of solar panels that need unpacking and testing. Ten panels in each crate. They are from the original batch of solar hydrogen generation equipment that was air-dropped by the US once they had moved on to fission. Previous experience suggests approximately twenty percent of the panels will be damaged and unusable. Your job is to unpack them, perform a visual inspection for signs of obvious damage and use one of these meters to check it's working." Matilda held a grey plastic box with two dangling wires above her head. "Any broken panels should be placed over there." She pointed to a pile of rubbish a few metres away. "Any that are good are to be returned to the crate and will be collected for transport to installation. Any questions?"

I didn't have an answer to my question on the plan for breaks so put my hand up and didn't wait to be asked to speak. "Yes, hi. Will we be getting a break at any point? I'm already thirsty in this heat."

"Lunch break will be at midday for thirty minutes. We have plenty of water for you to drink over at the drink station, but don't spend too long hanging around there or you will be issued with a warning." Matilda gestured with an open palm towards a row or four open-topped barrels brimming with water. "And don't drink too much. Our lavatories are back toward the canteen truck so you will need to wait until lunchtime for any toilet visits. Any other questions?"

A guy in his mid-twenties with scruffy black hair and a smug face flashed a sarcastic smile and put his hand up. You came across these types every so often, always of a certain age; old enough to have not been through the current style of 'education', but young enough not to have had the cockiness knocked out of them. But it would happen.

"Yes, how do these 'meters' work?" He used two fingers on each hand to put quotation marks around the word meters for some bizarre reason. "I mean, what do they do and how do we know if the panel is working?" He looked around arrogantly as if to say "gotcha", obviously trying to catch Matilda out and show up her lack of technical knowledge.

"The meters measure the completeness of the circuitry within the solar panel by applying an electrical current," Matilda replied. "For it to be viable, the panel needs enough functional photo-voltaic cells to produce a minimum power output of two-hundred watts. But we have marked a little blue line on the gauge to make it easy for you. Just press the button and make sure the needle reaches the blue line, ok?"

"Thanks," the scruffy haired man replied, disappearing into himself.

He'll learn, I thought.

"Let's get to work then. Come and collect your meter and work in pairs to carry the crates into enough space to work. The forklifts will be moving back and forth so don't get run over."

I found myself standing next to the man that had broken down on the coach and offered to partner up with him. It transpired that misery was a relative concept as next to him I felt on top of the world. I thought he could do with a chat and helping him might help me, in a way. It was surely a safe enough environment to talk freely. They had summoned me there after all, so it's not like I had arranged to meet him.

"Hey, do you want to work together on this?" I said, nodding towards the stack of crates.

"Ok," the man replied.

"Great, I'm Jack."

"Pete," he replied, staring at the floor between the two of us. Evidently not the talkative type.

Introductions between men had become awkward. A firm handshake had always been an effective way of breaking the ice and making a connection with whomever you were meeting. But two men making bodily contact of any kind had become a bad idea in case it was mistaken as passing secret messages. Instead, you just sort of stood there, perhaps offering a little wave because you didn't know what else to do with your hands. In the case of Pete, I was glad I didn't have to shake his hand as there was a reasonable chance I would have caught something from it.

Pete was under-weight, to the point of sickness. He had concave cheeks and sunken eyes that were dark and soulless, like the flame of life had been extinguished for some time. He had longish but thinning, greasy brown hair and a good five days of stubble growth. He wore a tatty, red t-shirt that was overdue a wash. He looked tired and broken. I decided not to force the chat and hoped he'd warm up after a period of working together.

We walked over to the first crate that had been placed down by the forklift truck, grabbed hold of the rope handles, and heaved the crate off the floor. It was heavy, about eighty kilos, but was manageable with the two of us. Pete was a strong guy, despite his slight physique. We moved across the space with instinctive and wordless cooperation. It was a skill that seemed particular to men, a practical connectedness of knowing what the other person was thinking, where to go and what needed to be done. We put the crate down in a long, thin strip of shadow that was cast by a beam overhead. The lid of the crate was hinged along the longest edge and fastened by two rusty metal catches that took a bit of persuasion to click open. Pete flipped the lid to reveal the solar panels. They looked like pieces of black glass separated by grassy-straw packing material. I lifted the first panel and heard Pete utter the first unprompted word of the day.

"Broken," he mumbled.

"Pardon me?" I said, not having caught what he had said.

"It's broken. There is a big crack." He pointed with a bony finger to the side of the panel facing away from me. I checked and sure enough a long crack arced diagonally from corner to corner.

"That's an easy start," I said with a grin as I tossed the panel on to the dusty ground. The edges of Pete's mouth curled upwards slightly, like he was remembering how to smile.

We worked this way, in near silence, for three hours until Matilda's megaphone voice interrupted us. "Finish the crate you are doing and then gather over here. Lunchtime."

I nodded towards the stack of completed crates. We must have gotten through at least ten of the three hundred. "Not a bad morning's work," I said as I wiped the sweat from my brow with the back of my hand. Pete nodded which I took as a sign of agreement.

"Follow me, this way," Matilda shouted and pointed toward the way we came in the morning.

Lunch was a bread roll and a chunk of plasticky cheese slapped on a plate by a sweaty, bald man in the back of the canteen truck. Pete and I joined the meandering queue, made it to the front, grabbed our food and found a shady spot against a giant sack of sand to sit down. The process had taken seventeen minutes of our half an hour lunch break. In the thirteen minutes that remained I was determined to get something out of Pete. I wanted to know his story. It took some persistence, but he opened up. The similarity in our backgrounds was frightening. There were just a few minor variations that had led us to vastly different outcomes.

Peter Harris. Forty-eight-years old. Originally an army PT instructor, but like me and all those others serving, was forced into retirement when the UK's armed forces were disbanded.

The year 2049 was a rough one for military troops. Britain had been living with The Gaia for twenty-six years, and although the quality of life in general was better then than it had become, the structural changes in society had begun and the tilt of power towards women was significant enough to allow what happened to occur. The main reason for the breakup of the armed forces was that they had become a redundant and expensive boy scout group. For the first twenty years after Britain was placed under quarantine by our foreign neighbours, small units of elite British soldiers were often called upon to support in global conflict. It was the only exception to goods and personnel crossing the border and was strictly controlled: males only, electronically tagged, and counted out and in, dead or alive. It was one way of us repaying the nations that collaborated on cure projects and was responsible for one hundred percent of my active duty.

However, the horror of what was happening in Britain caused a shockwave that rippled through the major global organisations, UN, G20, WEF, WHO, which over time pulled together in to ever increasing unity. The endpoint was the signature of a global cooperation agreement covering all aspects of security, environmental research, energy, and food production. Humanity had finally realised that working together was for the greater good of the planet and everything that lived on it. So back in Britain, there was no need for a national defence force as there were no aggressors, bar a handful of insignificant rogue states that were kept in check by the Global Alliance and had no interest in invading a disease-ridden quarantine zone with no useful natural resources. There was only so much training and military exercise that could go on within our own borders before even the staunchest of deniers began to question the value. In economic terms, the decision to disband made sense, but there were strong opinions held by many that the maintenance of a scaled back military force was essential in any democracy to keep the government in check. The problem there was that Britain hadn't been a properly functioning democracy for a decade.

In 2049 the split was around 60:40 and the disparity had been great enough for a number of years to entrench a feminist-led party in government. There was no viable opposition and our democracy had already become a dictatorship, led by Alvina the Great. Early noises of a military coup were quashed by paying off the top brass. They weren't stupid and knew the irreversible trajectory we were on.

What happened to those serving largely depended on where they ranked in the organisation. Senior officers were given government roles as reward for toeing the line, but they didn't last there for long. Mid ranking soldiers, like me and Pete, who had wives and kids and were able to support themselves, either did what I did and stayed at home, or found jobs in the fire service, police or as teachers for example, again, temporarily. The younger and lower ranking infantry soldiers felt the hardest impact. For the most part, they had no partners to support them and so were conscripted in to working for the government in whatever manual labour was the priority at any given time.

To begin with it, wasn't dissimilar to being in the army, but over time deteriorated into borderline slavery, with horrific working conditions and even worse living conditions. The country became reliant on these men to function, but they didn't live long. Mental burnout. Industrial accidents. Suicide. Dwindling numbers became a problem for the government. It was at that point the education system was repurposed from teaching boys to conditioning them, to ensure a constant stream of workforce replenishment. That's your Category B & C men: B for semi-skilled, C for non-skilled. For those in the minority bright enough for Category A, they were placed into roles that required a bit more trust but were always closely monitored.

After leaving the army, Pete moved in to teaching P.E. at secondary school. It was a perfect transition for a man of his physical capability. He was married to a successful lawyer and had a good life until he was sacked during the shake-up of the education system. Boys no longer did P.E., and it wasn't considered appropriate for a man to be teaching girls. From there, he struggled to find further employment that he found interesting, and his wife got fed up supporting him. After six months of unemployment, she kicked him out, and her new girlfriend moved in. Ever since then, the poor guy had been living in district dormitories and had been on permanent, six day-a-week duty. That's six days of graft per week for twelve, long years, without any break whatsoever. It's what was deemed reasonable in exchange for food and board for those men without anywhere else to go. So that explained Pete's breakdown on the bus. And his general demeanour. He was exhausted and was undoubtedly suffering from severe depression. He was a man in a terrible place with no means of escape.

We finished our lunch and began the reverse trek back to our station. I wanted to help Pete. The knowledge that I could have ended up like him shook me to the core. Next to him I felt fortunate, and I wanted to share that fortune. Helping him would be a risky move. But in the Special Forces, we never left a man behind.

"Hey, listen," I said as we walked. "Why don't you come to mine for dinner tonight? We'll have a proper chat about what your options might be". So long as we made the journey separately, Zoe's presence should reduce the likelihood of any accusations of collusion.

Pete didn't respond.

"Come on," I pressed. "I know it's been a while since you've done anything like that, but I want to help. If you carry on like this for much longer, it's not going to end well for you."

Pete looked like he wanted to say something.

I stopped walking, spun Pete around to face me and stared him in the eyes, waiting for him to fill the silence. But it didn't happen.

"Please give it some thought," I said. "If not tonight, then maybe another night. Or the weekend, lunch or dinner, your choice."

I noticed a tiny glint in his empty eyes. He was about to cry.

"Thank you," he said with a nod. It was a barely perceptible nod, but I sensed that it signalled something, a small hint of optimism, or determination, or hope. It was a start.

We walked the rest of the way in silence. Once back at our station we continued with the back and forth, carrying and unpacking the crates, gradually moving with our sheltering shadow that traced across the floor as the sun moved through the sky. It was a tough job, but we hit a good rhythm and were the most productive pair by a long margin. By 17:00 we had gotten through twenty crates, far more than the twelve that was our equal share of the task.

There were a handful of crates left, so Pete and I went for one last crate with an agreement we would stretch it out until the rest were finished. We grabbed hold the handles and noticed that the markings on the crate were different from the others. We tried to lift it and struggled to get it off the ground. Pete and I exchanged a puzzled glance. Since it was one of the last crates, we had some space and opened it where it stood. The lid swung open to reveal the same dry grassy packing material as the others, but as I moved the top layer aside it wasn't solar panels that I discovered.

CHAPTER 7

DESERT EAGLE. MADE IN USA, embossed on brushed steel.

Guns.

Lots of guns.

But the Desert Eagle wasn't just any gun, it was one of the most powerful handguns in the world. It fired bullets that were half an inch in diameter and could take down an elephant with one shot.

Time stood still as we both stared into the crate in disbelief. It was one of those surreal, out-of-body experiences where you're not sure whether it's happening. Pete reached out and in one swift movement, picked up a pistol, released the magazine to check if it was loaded, which it was, reinserted it and stuck the gun down the back of his trousers. Before I knew what was happening, my hand did the same. The movement was involuntary, again, some deeply ingrained instinct, and I instantly regretted it. It was an idiotic thing to do. I was about to put the gun back when Pete slammed the lid closed and fastened the catch. My mouth turned into a sandpit, so I headed over to the water station. The cold steel pressed against my hip as I walked, reminding me of my terrible judgment. I sank a filthy cup into the tepid water, downed it in one and then took another. My eyes were closed as I gulped, trying to clear my head. After a third cup I had collected my thoughts and decided that I was going to give the gun back. I'd hand the gun to Matilda and inform her about the anomalous crate. Then it would be her problem to deal with. I had no use for a gun and getting caught with one didn't bear thinking about. I was much happier having regained my sanity and turned to walk back to the crate and action my plan. I needed to convince Pete to hand his in also. He didn't strike me as the sort of person who should be carrying weapons around.

It turned out I was right.

As our workstation came in to view, I saw Pete pull the gun from his trousers and aim it, arms out straight, into the crowd of people working on the solar panels.

Out-of-body experience number two. It all happened in slow motion, even the sound of my voice as I shouted.

"Pete! Noooo!"

But my words were drowned out by a thundering, explosive bang, as a flash of orange light blasted out of the weapon in Pete's hand. I ducked and covered my ears, as did everyone in the area he was pointing it at.

Everyone except Matilda.

Matilda's head vanished in a cloud of red mist. Her legs gave way and her body collapsed on to the ground with a heavy thud. Blood spread from her neck making a viscous, black lake on the ground. Everyone gawped at Matilda's body, then at Pete, who was still pointing the gun. His eyes darted from person-to-person as he surveyed his audience and weighed up his next move. The air was filled with an electric buzz. I could sense the collective energy of the fifty brains working in overdrive, all doing the same subconscious, primal calculation; run or fight. Until a decision was made, it was paralysis that endured.

Bang.

A petite brunette took a round to the shoulder that sent her spinning as gravity pulled her to the dusty ground.

A scream rang out over to the left. "Oh shit!"

I turned to see the young, scruffy-haired, smug-faced

man with his hands in the air. He didn't look so smug.

Bang. Bang.

Two rounds to the chest that made an exit wound in his back the size of a basketball.

People were screaming and running in all directions. I stood still, trying to recall how many bullets the magazine held.

More than four apparently.

Bang.

An older lady shot in the back as she tried to flee.

Bang.

Another shot rang out followed by a metallic twang as it ricocheted of a piece of machinery.

That made six.

By that point everyone had decided that running was the best option and had scattered to safety, hiding behind whatever they could find, leaving Pete and myself.

Pete aimed the gun at me.

Out-of-body experience number three.

But this time it was different. When people say that your life flashes before your eyes in those moments, it sounds like a cliché, but it was true. All the people that I cared about —Zoe, the kids, my parents. I couldn't see them, I could feel them. Like they were standing right there with me, waving me off on my journey to the afterlife. The odd thing was, I felt at peace. There was no fear. In fact, there was a part of me that wanted him to pull the trigger.

I stared Pete in the eyes. He stared right back. He seemed different. He wasn't the broken man of thirty-minutes before. The piece of metal that Pete held in his hand had transformed him into a god. He had the power to decide who lived and who died. He was in control. His once empty eyes were ablaze. I waited. There was no thought process of what I should do as I had no choice. My life was in Pete's hands and whatever happened next was entirely his decision. He bent his elbows and placed the muzzle of the gun under his chin. His expressionless face morphed into a beaming smile that revealed a mouthful of decaying brown teeth. The Desert Eagle's seventh and final round turned Pete's body into a fountain, spraying blood into the air, before slumping into the dirt.

CHAPTER 8

Within ten minutes, the building site had been evacuated and the swarm of hi-vis, hard-hat wearing females was replaced with a much more intimidating swarm of body-armoured, machine-gun carrying females that scoured the area to make sure it was clear of further danger. We were bundled back on to the coach which pulled off down the crater-stricken track, rocking from side-to-side. I winced in pain with every bump and lurch, as hard metal jabbed me in the abdomen. I still had the gun. I wanted more than anything to throw it away, but it was covered with my fingerprints, and I couldn't have any connection between myself and what had happened that day. It would make me an easy scapegoat for the hysterical masses that would be demanding justice. I needed to clean it and dispose of it properly. Unfortunately, that meant taking it home.

The journey to the district office and my subsequent walk back home passed in an instant. My mind was numb, with no capacity for conscious perception of the outside world. I opened the back door that led into the kitchen and found Zoe sitting at the dining table. She immediately stood up and, for what I realised was the first time in many years, had a look of genuine concern on her face.

"Oh my god I was so worried," she said. "Are you ok? It's been all over the news."

"I'm not hurt," I replied. "But I don't think I can stretch to ok. It turns out having a gun pointed at your head with no means of defence takes something out of you."

"Come and sit down. Let me get you a drink. A coffee or something stronger?"

"I'm not allowed anything stronger. You know that," I said.

"I won't tell anyone if you won't. I think we can let it slide this one time, considering the circumstances."

I found her fussing odd. It was so out of character as to be comical. Maybe she did care about me after all, and it took something like that to remind her of the fact. Or was it the relief of the home-help not having had his head blown off. Either way, what happened that day did seem to have an effect.

"Here you go," she said as she placed a glass with an inch of colourless, drinking spirit in front of me. She seemed not to notice the bottle was a fair bit emptier than it should have been.

"Thanks." I took a long gulp. It burned its way down my oesophagus, but I instantly felt better as the alcohol hit my bloodstream.

"What I don't understand is how an obvious psychopath was able to get hold of a gun," Zoe said in her trademark matter-of-fact tone.

It irritated me immensely.

"Pete wasn't a psychopath," I replied. "He was a man that had been pushed over the edge by a horrible set of circumstances."

"Pete? What, was he a chum of yours or something? I can't believe you would begin to defend what happened today. Three women were brutally executed!"

"Three women and one man, Zoe. And a young man at that. Did the news omit that fact?"

"No, I didn't hear that bit but…"

"Precisely," I said. A long-suppressed rage was building

in the pit of my stomach. Fourteen years of bitterness and resentment bubbling up, expanding and at risk of catastrophic explosion. I needed to vent. Before I knew it, I was on my feet, pointing at Zoe with my index finger. "Pete was robbed of his career, his wife, and his home. He spent the last twelve years of his life working himself to the bone without being paid a penny. Not one penny, Zoe. He got a dirty mattress and his daily gruel. That's it. For six days a week and no holiday. You wouldn't treat a dog so badly."

Zoe looked like she wanted to say something but couldn't get any words out.

I, on the other hand, was on a roll.

"It's no wonder the poor guy snapped. He saw a way out and he took it. And he took some revenge at the same time. I don't condone it, but you know what? I don't blame him either. And there are thousands more like him. Thousands!" She was clearly speechless at my outburst as she didn't try to interject. "So next time I ask you why you are trying to cure The Gaia, don't feed me the bullshit about men having it better than women. This world is shit if you're a man and I don't know whether I want to be in it anymore." I necked the rest of the alcohol, slammed the glass on the table and stormed up the stairs.

"Oh, that old chestnut again," I heard Zoe shout after me. "Make sure you do it properly this time."

I went into the bathroom and stood at the sink, examining myself in the mirror. Feral eyes with dilated pupils stared back. My hands were shaking as I turned the tap and splashed cold water on to my face. My mind was rushing with a million thoughts and the high-pitched buzz in my ears caused my vision to vibrate. I wasn't in my own body, but above it, watching down, hanging over the precipice, clinging on by the tips of my fingers. I couldn't fight it any longer. My grip was weakening and I didn't have the strength to hold on. I wanted to succumb to it. Let myself fall and allow the darkness to consume me. Relinquish my mind. Absolve myself of all responsibility. Let whatever will be, just be.

Make sure you do it properly this time.

That was a good idea. Perhaps I would do just that.

I whipped out the gun from the back of my trousers and rammed the barrel into the roof of my mouth. Cold metal clunked against my teeth as I bit down hard. I breathed heavily through my nose sending a stream of mucus flowing over my top lip. I took one final look at myself, appalled at how far I had fallen. The Jack of ten years prior wouldn't have even considered it. He would have given me a slap and told me to not be such a coward. "Tomorrow could be different. Tomorrow is what you make it," he would say. But that Jack had not lived through what I had. That Jack didn't know we would reach the point of no return. There was no way back. There was no brighter tomorrow. Cowardice meant nothing in the face of oblivion. At that moment, as I closed my eyes for the last time, it all made perfect sense.

The bathroom door opened. Zach stood in the doorway. It must have taken him a moment to register what was happening as he was frozen to the spot. I lowered the gun. Then he dived at my waist with the full weight of his shoulder, knocking me off my feet and sending us both clattering into a pile on the floor. The gun fell, spinning across the tiles and smashing into the wall.

He was hyperventilating as he pushed himself up on to his knees, his eyes protruding from their sockets. "Dad... what ... what are you doing?" He stepped over and locked the bathroom door. "Dad... please... Dad?"

I had no words for him. Only shame. I had hit rock bottom at terminal velocity. I thought I had been there before, but this time, I was sure, looking at Zach's bruised face filled with hurt and confusion. He was more of a man than I was. He took whatever was dealt to him without a word of complaint. Then he'd get up the next day and do it all over again. He shouldn't have to, but he did, and there was me, taking the easy way out, leaving him behind to fend for himself. A single tear rolled down my cheek and all I could say was. "I'm sorry."

"It's... ok, Dad... I'll... look after you," he said, hugging his arms around my neck. The rising and falling of his chest slowed as his breathing returned to normal.

"Thank you," I said. "But you shouldn't have to do that. I should be the one looking after you."

"We can look after each other," he said.

That did it. The damn burst and tears flooded out as I wept into Zach's shoulder. He sat holding me as I heaved and sobbed until all those years of pain had been purged from my body. It was the best possible therapy. The good thing about hitting rock bottom is that there is only one way to go. I wiped my nose and eyes with my sleeve and took hold of Zach's face in my hands.

"I'm going to do better," I said with a sniff.

"I know," he replied.

"Can we keep this as our little secret?"

"Uhuh." He nodded.

I reached across the floor and picked up the gun. "And this too?"

"Yes."

I released the magazine from the gun and pulled back the rail to eject the round from the chamber. It hit the hard floor with a clink and rolled in a circle.

"Do you want to go for a drive in my car?" I asked.

"What, now?"

"Yes."

He cracked a wide smile. "Okay!"

"Give me ten minutes. I'll get cleaned up and we'll head out."

I closed the door behind Zach as he left and re-locked it.

Standing on the edge of the bath, I pushed open the hatch in the ceiling that led to the loft a few inches. I slid the gun up on to the floor of the loft and let the hatch back down. I needed to devise a way of disposing of it properly, but it would be safe enough for a few days until I came up with a more permanent solution. Nobody ever went up there. I ran the bath as hot as I could stand it. The room filled with steam as I undressed and dropped my sweaty clothes in a heap on the floor. I braced as I stepped into the scorching water and slid down on to my back, allowing my body to be submerged, inch by inch. I needed to wash away the wretched filth that day had covered me with. I was contaminated. Tainted. Purification by fire was the only way. I closed my eyes and tried to relax as the water reached the back of my neck and ears.

With each moment that passed the disturbing images that intruded behind my eyelids faded away. Blood, death, Pete's manic smile, all of it melted leaving a sense of calm. I found myself pleased that Zach had walked in on me. It was undoubtedly traumatic for him, and I needed to make damn sure there would be no lasting damage, but thanks to Zach, for the first time in many years, I was tilting towards an upward trajectory. I may have been lower than where I began that day in absolute terms, but it was the direction of travel that mattered as that gave hope and with hope comes motivation. A virtuous circle of positivity that I was not going to let go of. The storm clouds began to recede to reveal clear blue skies and I found myself with the capacity of optimistic thought. It was the most glorious feeling of clarity.

It was then that it hit me slap bang in the face. Out of Zoe and me, who was it that had changed the most? Zoe's behaviour toward me over the recent years wasn't a result of her environment. It was because she was falling out of love with a hopeless loser who had no self-respect. Who could blame her? I could have done more with my life after leaving the army. I could have gotten another job. Volunteered somewhere. I could have done what I was doing, but with more passion and vigour. A proper father who proactively guided his children and a proper husband that supported a successful wife. Instead, I chose to drift along with the current, descending ever deeper into 'woe is me' despair. I didn't like myself so how could I expect Zoe to love or respect me? I needed a reason to live, whatever that might be. The essence of man, I realised, is purpose.

I leapt out of the bath like a modern-day Archimedes, but instead of yelling 'Eureka!' I shouted to Zach. "Come on, let's go." I got dressed into some clean clothes and ran downstairs. Zoe was sitting at the table with tear tracks streaking her face. She turned to face me, like she wanted to say something.

"Look," she said. "I'm sorry. I didn't mean what I said."

"Don't be sorry," I said. "It's me that should be apologising." I walked up to her, took hold of her head, and planted a forceful kiss square on her lips. I released her and gazed deep into her big brown eyes. "*I'm* sorry."

She looked flabbergasted. "Ok then... that's great."

"Hurry up, Zach, or it's going to be too late," I shouted as I picked up the keys to the M3.

"I'm coming," he shouted back.

"Where are you two going?" Zoe asked.

"Out," I replied.

"Yes, I can see that," she said. "But where?"

"That, Zoe dear, is none of your concern," I said with a little smile, just as Zach bounded into the kitchen.

We left the house through the front door and stepped out on to the drive. I opened the passenger side door of the M3 for Zach to get in, then got in the driver's side and sat down in the bucket seat. I started the ignition and the three litre, twin turbo engine growled to life. I had missed it badly. I sat, gripping the steering wheel, feeling vibrations, and absorbing the sounds. I looked across at Zach and revved the engine which responded with an aggressive roar that rose in pitch before settling back down.

"Woah!" Zach said. "That is cool!"

The fuel gauge was on the inside edge of the red and the mileage indicator told me that I had a forty-mile range. It was enough.

"Buckle up," I said. "Things are about to get hairy."

The front door of the house opened, and Zoe's face peered through the gap.

"Ready?" I said.

"Yeah!" Zach shouted.

I slammed the car in to reverse, skidded off the drive and wheel-spun off into the distance, leaving Zoe wafting away a cloud of smoke and dust.

CHAPTER 9

A police car tailed us for the final mile of our drive home, so I dropped my speed to the limit. My anxiety increased with every corner we took. They refused to remove themselves from my rear-view mirror. Zach was having the time of his life and wasn't best pleased with this new lawful approach to driving.

"Come on Dad, go faster!"

"Fun is over. We're almost home," I tried not to let on that I was worried.

When they followed us into the cul-de-sac, my heart sank. If they had caught me speeding, they would have pulled me over. I couldn't see why they would follow me all the way home. I hoped it was nothing to do with me at all, but that hope was dashed when they parked up outside my house, blocking in the M3 that I had pulled on to the driveway.

"Ok buddy," I said to Zach. "You go on inside. I'm going to see what the police officers want." Zach seemed reluctant to leave me, eyeing the two females in police uniform suspiciously as they got out of their car. "Go on. Off you go," I said, shoeing him off. "Evening officers. Is there something I can help you with?" I said in my most confident voice.

"We're looking for a Jack Wilson," one of them said, a stocky, middle-aged lady with tight, curly hair.

"That's me," I said. "What is it about?"

"We'd like you to come with us to the station. We believe you might have some information that is relevant to the shooting that happened today."

"That was nothing to do with me," I said.

"Then you have nothing to fear."

"Am I under arrest?"

"No, but it could be arranged if you don't wish to cooperate."

I looked into the black night sky and let out a long exhale. "Fine. Let me tell my wife where I'm going."

"I'd prefer it if you got into our car." The preference wasn't coming across as optional.

It was a fifteen-minute drive sat in awkward silence. It suited me fine as I used the time to get my thoughts straight and attempt to work out what they wanted to speak to me about. I had met Pete for the first time that day and was nowhere near him when he started shooting, so there was no way I could have had anything to do with it. The one thing I could think of was the item I had stashed in the loft, but they couldn't know about that, and they would have searched the house if there was the slightest suspicion. I was none the wiser as we pulled up to the police station. The stocky lady opened the door for me, and I stepped out into the warm evening air. The surrounding area, and police building itself, was the same as everywhere else in the district: in serious need of repair. The same potholes. The same weeds sprouting from cracks in the tarmac. The same mountains of rubbish, and the accompanying smell. The police station, or P LI E station, if you were to go by the malfunctioning illumined sign, was a single storey, block-built cuboid that was suffering from a major case subsidence, if the giant, step-like crack climbing up the mortar between the bricks was anything to go by.

The officers followed as I led the way, pushing a filthy pane of the revolving glass door and stepping into the lobby. It was surprisingly busy for the time of night, presumably because of the shooting. Women in navy blue uniforms were marching in every direction. Every chair in the lobby was occupied by police officers scrutinising bits of paper. I glanced around, overwhelmed.

"Please take a seat and someone will call you in shortly," the escorting officer said before walking up to the reception desk and speaking to the lady behind the counter.

I searched for a vacant chair, but there were none to be found, so I propped myself up against the wall next to the water cooler. The air was uncomfortably warm. Beads of sweat started to form on my forehead, so I poured myself a drink and stood waiting, watching the hustle and bustle of the broads-in-blue with fascination. After a few minutes, a lady with mousey-brown hair pulled back ponytail and dressed in a dark-grey suit entered the room and called out, "Jack Wilson?" as if it could be anyone other than the only male standing casually by the water machine. I raised my hand and was waved over by the lady who turned her back and began walking down the shadowy corridor from which she had appeared. I followed until she stopped, turned to face me, and offered a silent gesture indicating that I was to go through a door to the left. I found myself in an interview room that was no more than eight-foot square. Three of the walls were painted dirty white and the fourth covered by a huge mirror. The floor was covered with speckled grey, industrial vinyl. Harsh white light beamed down from two tubes in the ceiling. In the middle of the room was a basic table surrounded by four tubular-framed chairs. Sitting at one of the chairs was a woman, also wearing a dark-grey suit, but with an intense expression on her face.

Ponytail introduced us. "This is Detective Chief Inspector Steele." Ms Steele stood, reached out hand and offered the firmest handshake I had ever experienced. "DCI Steele is leading the investigation of the incident at the building site. I'm Detective Inspector Travis."

Another silent gesture told me to sit down opposite DCI Steele before Travis took the seat next to her. I sat up straight with my hands resting on my closed knees. Out of the three humans in the room, I felt the least masculine by far.

DCI Steele hadn't stopped watching me since I had entered the room. She studied me with an intense mix of suspicion and curiosity. Her emerald-green eyes were glistening behind a penetrating scowl. Under different circumstances I would have described her as attractive. At that moment, however, the only appropriate descriptor was formidably intimidating. She wore an interesting pin badge on her lapel, the female symbol ♀ surrounded in a triangle with the horizontal line forming an A. She clocked my eyes aimed at her chest and my heart leapt into my mouth. She let it slide, pressing a red button on a tape recorder while holding my gaze.

"For the benefit of the recording please can you confirm your name?" she said.

"Jack Wilson," I said, suddenly feeling under pressure. I just needed to remember I had nothing to hide, except the gun in my loft. Under no circumstances could I be placed near the crate of guns or let them know I had taken one.

"Thanks for coming in to see us, Jack. Could we start by you giving us your account of what happened today at the construction site, in your own words?"

"Where should I start?"

"At the beginning."

"Okay... I was working with Pete, the man that did the shooting, unpacking the crates of solar panels. We had come to the end of the day and were about to start on our last crate, but I needed a drink. It was seriously hot out there today, so I headed over to the drink station. Then, whilst I was there, I heard a commotion. People started shouting. Followed by gunshots. Then people were running all over the place." The words were falling out of my mouth without me thinking about what I was saying. I had assumed that my lack of involvement would be obvious. However, the ambiance wasn't one of a friendly chit-chat and it dawned on me that I needed to be much more intentional about my choice of words. *Come on, Jack! You're trained for this!*

DCI Steele seemed dissatisfied. "I know all of that. I said to start at the beginning."

"I'm not sure what you mean," I replied, confused.

"Mr Harris's gunning down of innocent civilians is the end of the story. I want to know how the story began so I might understand why and, more importantly, how he did it."

"I'm afraid I can't help you with that," I said. "Today was the first time I had met Pete." Steele and Travis sat staring at me, saying nothing, their eyes boring deep into my soul. A drip of sweat ran down the side of my face. The silence persisted for a beat too long and I was compelled to fill it. "I'm not sure what you want me to say. I don't know the guy."

"We only want the truth, Sergeant Wilson," DCI Steele said.

The words hit me between the eyes like a lightning bolt. I hadn't been called that for fourteen years. The deep recesses of my brain ruptured flooding my mind with long forgotten memories. A swell of emotion grew inside. I was choked. But that wasn't who I was any longer. I didn't see what relevance it had.

Steele continued. "Your background checks show you to be an impressive man, Jack. Heavy Weapons Specialist. Senior Sniper Rifle Instructor in the Special Weapons School. Highly decorated for your services overseas. Says here one of the finest marksmen the forces have ever produced."

"That was a long time ago."

DI Travis cut in. "So, if your assertion that you don't know Peter Harris well is the truth, today has seen a remarkable set of coincidences, hasn't it?" This time I let Travis fill the silence. "One, a pair of ex-military servicemen sit next to each other on the coach during the journey this morning. Two, you were partnered with him for the work that was required. Three, you lunched together and were seen to be in deep conversation for the entire duration of the lunch break. Then lastly, and most oddly, a man that had gunned down four people at random had the weapon he was holding aimed directly at you, but for some reason decided to spare your life. How do you explain that, Jack?"

Admittedly, the way she described it made it seem suspicious and I wasn't sure where to begin explaining myself. I opened my mouth to try, but Steele cut back in. "How did an ex-army soldier get hold of a Desert Eagle handgun?"

"I don't know. I'm sorry."

"Do you expect me to believe that it is merely another coincidence that he, of all the people there on site today, was the one that accidentally stumbled across a crate full of guns and ammunition? Out of the many hundreds of people at the building site, there were two people with the expert knowledge and skill to handle firearms, Mr Harris, and yourself. You were partnered up by chance and spent most of the day together, but Mr Harris found a crate of handguns during the few minutes you were apart, then decided to start shooting people at random? Just like that?"

"I guess so. Like I said, I was at the drink station when he started shooting." I had a horrible sense that things were about to unravel.

"So you say. But we have already spoken to several people this afternoon and have had multiple confirmations that you were with Mr Harris at the point when the crate containing the guns was opened. So, I would respectfully suggest that you know as well as I do where Peter got the gun. Why are you hiding this fact, Jack?"

That was it. Checkmate. The bottom fell out the floor and my stomach went with it. My mind went blank, and the blood drained from my face. The lies that needed to be told to get myself out of the stupid mistake of taking the gun had made it seem like I was covering up something much worse. I sat, speechless, ready to offer my wrists up for cuffing. Collusion was ten-years. Accomplice to murder would be life, or death, or even worse, a life like Pete's. I was about to spill my guts and come clean about the gun when there was a knock at the door and a uniformed officer entered the room without being invited. She passed a piece of paper to DCI Steele who studied it before dismissing the officer and returning her attention to me.

"I'm sorry Mr Wilson, there has been a misunderstanding," she said, her expression softening. "You are, of course, free to go. We will make arrangements for you to be excused from any duties for the rest of the assignment. Today must have been quite the ordeal. Do you have a way to make it home or can I have one of the officers drive you?"

"What?!" I said in astonishment.

"I said you are free to go."

"I heard you, but why?" I found myself in the obscure situation of demanding to know why I wasn't being charged with something I didn't do.

"Your family check has identified you as the spouse of Zoe Wilson. Professor Wilson's work is an inspiration to every woman in the country. Considering this information, there is no doubt of your lack of involvement in Mr Harris's offence."

"Wait a minute. I have more that I want to say," I said, instilled with some kind of death wish, but I wanted them to know that I was innocent.

"Jack, please, leave the building, now." Her expression had re-hardened.

I stood up in a burst of anger and sent the chair flying with the back of my knees as they straightened. I stormed out of the station and stomped down the street. I knew I was being ridiculous. I should have been ecstatic. But I wanted to be found innocent of wrongdoing because I was innocent. Not because my wife was a little bit famous. Besides, I knew she was well respected amongst the academic community, but for her to be a get out of jail card for any acts of criminality was absurd. It had been a long day and I was mentally and physically exhausted, but I couldn't shake the feeling that there was something more ominous behind the bizarre situation.

CHAPTER 10

Tuesday 5th June 2063

I'm lying prone in the dusty, orange dirt that covered the rooftop. The sun's prickly heat is on the back of my neck. A warm breeze gusts, blowing sand into my mouth and sticking it against the moist skin on my face and bare arms. A drip of sweat runs past my ear and under my jaw. I hear my breathing, controlled and calm. I sense my heartbeat, slow and relaxed.

A low voice to my right, a man with binoculars.

"Three klicks out."

I have one eye closed. The black SUV appears over the horizon, shimmering in the haze. Crosshairs trace the vehicle's journey through the desert towards the village.

That voice again.

"Wind, five miles per hour, left to right."

I adjust the sight on my rifle, three notches.

"Two klicks. Ready up."

I rest my gloved index finger on the trigger-guard.

The SUV is heading towards us on a dead straight road that is lined by rickety, wooden shacks where the locals sell their wares. The crosshairs are trained over the silhouette in the driver's seat. Nothing exists in the periphery. The vehicle is the universe.

"One point five klicks, take the shot."

I half fill my lungs and hold it. I have twenty seconds before my vision begins to deteriorate. I am one with my heart's rhythm. At this distance, one misplaced beat means missing the target by twenty feet.

Crosswind, moving target, air rising from the hot tarmac. So many variables.

But I've done my calculations. I am ready.

A gentle squeeze on the trigger looses a fifty calibre round that follows a parabola towards the target at two-thousand feet per second.

One...two...three...

The round punctures through the windscreen, which shatters white then flashes dark red. The SUV swerves off the road and crashes into a stall, sending fruit and vegetables scattering and flattening its owner, a young woman carrying a baby.

I woke up with a start and stared at the ceiling, my vivid dream a sign of a deep sleep. They say you remember the face of every man you kill. I didn't always see their face, but I still remembered. Being a sniper wasn't like fighting in the infantry. The adrenaline of active combat speeds things up. The mental scars are there, but because things happen more quickly, details can be sketchy. For me, the relaxed concentration slowed things down. I needed to analyse the minutest details of the environment: wind, temperature, humidity, location of every civilian and every hostile. Each battle scenario is logged in crystal clarity, ultra-high-definition, ready to be replayed when I slept. The most haunting part is that ninety-nine percent of them didn't know it was coming. Expelled from existence without knowing why.

I was alone in bed. Zoe had been asleep when I arrived home the night before and left that morning without me realising. The house was filled with a suspicious silence. I strained my ears, listening hard for any sign of life. But there was nothing, no sound at all. I reached across to the bedside table to check my watch.

09:15

I had overslept, massively.

I leapt out of bed and went downstairs to find a hand scrawled note on the dining table.

I'm driving the kids to school on the way to meet Grace at the hospital. She's having the scan this morning. See you later. xxx

Leaving me to sleep and writing xxx on letters was new behaviour. Well, perhaps not new, but not something that had happened for as long as I could remember. It made me think I needed to force kisses on my wife more often. It was handy as it meant that I had the morning to myself which presented a good opportunity to deal with the gun. Zoe had taken the car and the BMW was running on fumes after the drive the night before, so I wouldn't be able to dispose of it far enough from the house, but I could get it cleaned and packaged up ready to go.

Still in my underwear, I took my washing up gloves from under the kitchen sink. Then I went up to the bathroom, retrieved the gun from the loft and placed it on the edge of the bathroom sink with a solid, metallic clunk. I began digging around in the basket of miscellaneous toiletries that never got used until I found what I was searching for, Zoe's old nail polish remover, which I figured would be good at removing any traces of greasy fingerprints.

I squirted some of the liquid on to the corner of a towel and began rubbing the metal surface. I passed the gun between my gloved hands, flipping it over to make sure I cleaned every square-millimetre. I had handled countless handguns in Weapons School, but never a Desert Eagle. The weight of the thing was unbelievable, and I found it incredible that anyone could hold and aim it with any degree of accuracy. I held it in my right palm with my fingers curled around the handle and ran my left index finger over the diagonal ridges that slanted their way down the barrel. I was filled with a strong feeling of familiarity. Competence and confidence. It was what I knew. It was what I did. It was me, in my truest form.

I brought my hands together, straightened my arms, and with my left eye closed, aimed the gun at myself in the bathroom mirror. I delicately rested my finger on the trigger. I recalled what it felt like to aim a gun at another person, what it took to pull the trigger and extinguish another life. The power a simple lump of metal bestowed on a person was absolute. It was both beautiful and horrific. My philosophising was interrupted by the sudden realisation of what a ridiculous sight it must have been to have a man in boxer shorts and bright yellow rubber gloves aiming a gun at himself in the mirror. With the gun wiped clean I wrapped it in clingfilm and stashed it back in the loft.

I headed downstairs to make a coffee and noticed that Zoe had left her bag on the kitchen work surface. I picked it up to move it out of the way and as I did so, caught a glimpse of an A4 cardboard folder with the words STRICTLY CONFIDENTIAL written in large red letters across the front. Zoe had always been cagey about her work. I knew the basics of what she was working on but nothing in detail and she kept all her paperwork locked away in her office. Leaving something like that laying around was a major slip in her standards. It was inevitable that I would see it in the kitchen, so she wouldn't have left it there on purpose. I knew the right thing to do was to leave it alone, but *Strictly Confidential* got me irresistibly curious. I opened the folder and flicked through the loose sheets of paper contained within. It was mostly tables of numerical data that didn't mean anything to me. I found a sheet titled "Summary and Conclusions" that was coloured in with yellow highlighter pen. I skim read.

Summary of Efficacy

The data show that when administered intravenously, the retrovirus was successful in replacing defective genes in human subjects....... the effect of substantial repair of genome seen in pre-clinical mammalian studies at 8 weeks is also observed in humans......protein profile in blood samples taken from females in early pregnancy considered normal.

<u>*Summary of Safety*</u>

Significant numbers of adverse reactions recorded.

Greater than 1 in 10 subjects: Skin rash/dermatitis, diarrhoea, dizziness, drowsiness, headache, insomnia, nausea.

Greater than 1 in 100 subjects: Abnormal heart rhythms, internal bleeding, heart inflammation, renal failure.

Greater than 1 in 1000 subjects: Seizures, deterioration of the optic nerve.

Greater than 1 in 10000 subjects: Death

On the next page an email, a single line from a peculiar email address...

From: os@altior.org. To: z.wilson@ku.ac.uk

Suboptimal dataset. Cleanse for final draft.

I wasn't sure what to make of it. On the one hand it sounded like whatever Zoe was developing was working. But it also sounded like an awful lot of negative effects. Cleansing of datasets also sounded unethical. *Altior?* Zoe had never mentioned anything about an Altior. It must have been a company of some kind.

Now, reading something that had been openly left in plain sight was one thing, but what happened next, I'm not proud of. In fact, it was an enormous breach of marital trust. A niggling nugget of suspicion made it feel justified though, at least that what I told myself. I rooted through Zoe's bag and pulled out a shiny, chrome key which I took to Zoe's office door. It fitted, so I turned it, and the door swung open. It was the one room of the house I had rarely set foot, just once in fact when I helped move her furniture in there. The term office makes it sound grander than it was, which in reality was barely more than a windowless under-stair cupboard. There was a small desk with a lamp, a shredder on the floor and a filing cabinet. The desk was covered with more loose paper which detailed recent email correspondence. The address os@altior.org, I determined, belonged to someone named Olivia.

From: os@altior.org. To: z.wilson@ku.ac.uk

I assume we are on track for the end of the week?

From: z.wilson@ku.ac.uk, To: os@altior.org.

Olivia,

We can achieve it by scaling back safety measures. We do not have the capacity to process this number of subjects.

ZW

From: os@altior.org. To: z.wilson@ku.ac.uk

Whatever it takes. Alvina wants it done; therefore, it shall be done.

It seemed like Zoe was being put under a lot of pressure which explained the long working hours over the previous weeks. But achieving deadlines by cutting corners did not sound like Zoe at all. She had always been a woman of strict integrity. But I had to admit, there was a huge part of her life I knew nothing about.

The front door opened and slammed shut.

Zoe.

Paralysis kicked in as I froze to the spot in my boxer shorts.

CHAPTER 11

"What are you doing in my office?" Zoe said with a mix of surprise and annoyance.

"Nothing. I noticed that you had been working in the kitchen a lot recently, so thought I'd open the door and let the cooler air in. Make it more comfortable for you in there." It was the first and only thing that came to mind. It was plausible, I thought.

"Have you been going through my bag?"

"I wasn't snooping, I just…"

"Why aren't you at your assignment?" she cut me off.

"They said I didn't have to go back after what happened yesterday."

"Who's they?"

"The police. I got picked up last night for questioning. It's why I was back so late."

The inquisition paused as she processed the evidence. I could see the cogs turning. She must have found it satisfactory.

"We need to talk," she said.

Talk about what?

I wondered if Zach had spilled his guts about the day before. I didn't want to talk about that. I was much more of a 'bottle it up and move on pretending it didn't happen' kind of person. Admittedly it hadn't worked well for me in the past, but I wasn't going to just start wearing my heart on my sleeve.

"What's up?" I said, gearing up defence mode.

"Come and sit down," she said. We sat down next to each other at the table. "I went to the hospital with Grace for the scan. It's a boy. It's not good news."

I didn't have anything to say to that. As any parent knows, you would give up your own life to save that of your child, and I would rather Pete had gunned me down ten times over than hear those words spoken by Zoe. An affected boy means one thing, an abortion. Another abortion.

When she was growing up, Grace had a promising future ahead of her. She was pretty and popular, in a likeable, down-to-earth kind of way. I like to think of that as my genetic contribution. Zoe's contribution, the brains, shone through just as clearly and Grace excelled in every subject. However, things started to go awry once she started college. She was studying Chemistry, Physics and Biology and wanted to go on to study Medicine at University. Over the course of the first year, she took a shine to a young guy who worked as a lab technician in her Chemistry class. Nathan, his name was. A pleasant Category A man, a couple of years older than Grace. They would hang out together at weekends and have a laugh. It didn't seem to be anything serious, just good friends. But during the summer holidays between first and second year, on the weekend after her 17th birthday, Grace and Nathan took their friendship to the next level.

Zoe and I had let Grace use the house for a party to celebrate her birthday, a smallish gathering of ten of her best friends, Nathan included. Zoe and I knew nothing of what went on that night until two months after when Grace came to us with the news that she was pregnant. It was a huge shock and neither of us were exactly over the moon, but it was difficult not to be proud of how maturely Grace handled it. She recognised the impact it would have on her education and career ambitions in the short term, but had it all planned out with how she would get back on track once the baby had arrived.

She wasn't fazed by her new alternative future and seemed genuinely happy. So as the days passed, after succumbing to Grace's radiant positivity, we had largely come to terms with the prospect of grandparenthood, even if we were younger for it than we would have liked. The outward feelings of anger and disappointment were gradually replaced with acceptance, and even a bit of excitement. The internal feelings, however, remained dark; horrible trepidation for the inevitable dice roll that would determine whether we eventually got our grandchild, or not. It was weighted in our favour, just. Fifty-six percent chance of happiness, forty-four percent chance of despair. Grace had convinced herself that she was having a girl and was content in her state of denial. I was happy to leave her there because for me, the three-week period between being told of the pregnancy and the first trimester scan, was a sleepless nightmare of fear and dread.

The day arrived and Zoe and I escorted Grace to the hospital. We met the sonographer and were ushered to a small, curtained off booth with a bed and some medical equipment. Grace lay back on the bed with a beaming smile. She pulled up her t-shirt to reveal her bulging little belly, on which the sonographer squirted some clear gel, before moving a handheld wand back and forth, pressing, what seemed to me to be far too hard, into Grace's swollen abdomen. We all watched the grainy image on the small screen in front of us. Circular blobs moving in and out of focus. It meant nothing to me, but Zoe had spotted something, judging by the sharp intake of breath and her hands moving to cover her mouth. Even then I couldn't work out if it was good news or bad, excitement or shock. It wasn't until Zoe's hands moved from her mouth to her eyes, and her head bowed forward that I realised it wasn't good.

The smile on Grace's face dissolved as she picked up on her mother's reaction.

"Mum?" she said, in a desperate tone that said so much more than what that single word meant. *Tell me it's not true.*

Do something to help me. It must be a mistake.

To this day, the sterile smell of hospital disinfectant takes me back to that moment and makes me want to vomit. Being so helpless while my daughter's heart was smashed to pieces was the most horrendous feeling I had ever experienced.

"I'm sorry," was all the sonographer could manage. Clinical and detached. No doubt she had been there a thousand times before. To her, Grace was just another young woman. Our grandson another deformed foetus destined for termination. What happened next was just as emotionless. Grace was given a tablet there and then, and was told to come back in two days' time for a second one, after which the baby would pass in hospital.

That night at home we sat on the sofa and cuddled, her head buried into my chest, like when she was small and had fallen and hurt her knee. She was still my little girl and I wished there was something I could do to take the pain away. She hadn't done anything to deserve what she was going through. I had no plans for the following day and wanted to do something to distract Grace from the downward spiral of turmoil that she was getting herself in to. I persuaded her to join me for a walk to get some fresh air. We walked into town in silence, hand-in-hand. We didn't say a word but there was no awkwardness. There was an unspoken, mutual understanding that we were both grieving; Grace for her never-to-be-born child, me for my own child walking next to me, dying from the inside out. At least I stood a chance of getting mine back.

We went into the supermarket to pick up some essentials. I left Grace in the freezer aisle on a futile hunt for ice cream, while I went to find some milk. They had run out of semi-skimmed again. It annoyed me immensely that there was always loads of all the other types, but semi-skimmed always empty. I understood that food was scarce but surely they employed some woman smart enough to analyse product purchase rates and adjust their manufacturing levels accordingly...

"Daaad!" my huffing was interrupted by a brain-piercing shrill.

I dropped my shopping basket on the floor and sprinted back to where I left Grace. As I turned in to the freezer aisle the sight before me was like something out of a horror movie. Grace was kneeing on the floor in a pool of bloody fluid, clawing at her face with her nails. Her screams were being broadcast from the depths of hell, like no sound I had ever heard. My instinct was to cover my ears. It was so surreal. Then the magnitude of what was happening smacked me in the face. I ran to her and wrapped my arms around her like a vice, shielding her from the small crowd of people that was beginning to form.

"Don't just stand there! Call an ambulance!" I yelled at the onlookers.

All I could do was hold her as she shook and rocked back and forth. I had no idea how long we were there for. Could have been minutes. Could have been hours. The entire experience was devoid of time and space. In that moment, nothing, or nobody, mattered, or even existed. Just me and my little girl in our personal world.

At some point an ambulance arrived and Grace was put on to a stretcher. She was taken to hospital to be checked over. As was obvious, the baby has passed earlier than it should have. They offered no concrete explanation. Could have been a reaction to the first set of medication. Could have been stress. Could have just been a horribly timed coincidence. Not that it mattered why. What mattered was the emotional impact of my child being saturated in bloody amniotic fluid and seeing her dead baby on the floor of a supermarket, and that took months to unfold.

For the next two weeks, Grace was in some kind of... 'wakeful coma', is the only way I can describe it. Completely unresponsive to input from the outside world. She didn't speak or acknowledge being spoken to. She just sat on her bed curled up in a ball, hugging her knees into her chest. Day-after-day, plates of food were left untouched, and I could see her beginning to vanish before my eyes. She wasn't exactly big to begin with.

A few days in to the third week, Zoe and I were in the kitchen eating a late breakfast. As we were chatting, a noise of what sounded like a piano being thrown down the stairs made us leap out of our chairs and dart across the room to investigate. At the bottom of the stairs, we found Grace in an awkward pile with arms and legs pointed in impossible directions. She had evidently attempted to come downstairs but either dizziness or weakness meant it was a task beyond her physical means. A full body x-ray revealed a broken leg and a fractured collar bone, plus her shoulder was dislocated. In a perverse kind of way, it was the best thing that could have happened. She was kept in hospital for three weeks and fed through a canula on the back of her hand. We also discussed her mental condition with the doctor, and she was prescribed some antidepressants.

As the weeks passed, the hollows in her cheeks filled out and her sunken eyes regained some of their spark. She was far from the fun-loving Grace that existed before, partly due to the anti-depressants which left her permanently immersed in a dense fog, but she was stable and my fears of something terminally awful happening were somewhat allayed.

Things never returned to normal. Despite several attempts to come off the medication, each saw a relapse and Grace had become dependent on it. The doctors had managed to get her down to the lowest effective dose but was still enough to take the edge off her sharpness and she never regained the confidence to return to college. Our main aim was to ensure she stayed occupied and happy, which she managed to do working in the local library. She worked with young schoolgirls and got genuine fulfilment from being part of their education.

"Jack? Are you listening?" said Zoe.

"Yes, but I'm not sure what to say. How is she?"

"Not great. She is refusing to take the pill and they won't discharge her until she has."

"You can hardly blame her after what happened last time."

"I don't. But the longer she leaves it the worse the experience is going to be."

Again, I didn't have anything to say.

"The timing of this is bloody awful," Zoe continued. "I need to get to the lab this afternoon. Data for the phase III trials is in and we need to decide on whether we are recommending proceeding with roll-out."

"Jesus Zoe, can't that wait a day?"

"It kills me to say it, but this is bigger than all of us, Jack."

It was regrettable, but I knew she was right. "Alright. I'll go and see her this evening and have a chat once the other two are home from school. You do what you need to do."

CHAPTER 12

I skulked about the kitchen, trying to distract myself from the terrible news Zoe had shared by organising the cupboards. A shiver ran down my spine and for the first time in months I realised I was cold. I turned off the air-con and enjoyed the new level of silence that filled the room. I stood a chance of being able to hear the news on the TV so turned up the volume. I watched, peering over my shoulder, as I lined up mugs in to colour coordinated rows. The news presenter was talking about the Atkins family, the ones who had managed to escape Britain and reach France.

"The family, Mr and Mrs Atkins, along with their pregnant daughter and two grandsons, were found dead in a car wreck within a mile of where they had been hiding. No other cars were involved, and their death appears to be a tragic accident."

"Jesus," I said to myself. The entire family gone at once, just like that.

"The accident comes a matter days after Miss Atkins publicly revealed herself as having escaped Britain and allegedly being cured of The Gaia. A claim understood by UK officials to have been proven false. In other news, US officials have placed the city of Chicago under quarantine after two separate cases of holoprosencephaly were detected at a single hospital this week. It is not yet clear whether it is coincidental."

"Zach!" Cora's voice came screeching through the open window. "I said, get back here!" The front door burst open, and Zach came through covered in blood coming from a gash over his left eye. He sped straight past me without acknowledgement and went upstairs. Cora followed closely behind. "Zach!"

I grabbed Cora's arm as she marched past.

"What the hell is going on?" I demanded.

"Get your hands off me!" She spat the words like a hissing cat.

"Excuse me young lady, who do you think you are talking to?"

"You know who I'm talking to… Dad," she said in a way that made 'Dad' sound like a derogatory insult.

"What's happened to Zach? Why is he bleeding?"

"I told him to carry my bag home from school, and do you know what he said?"

"What did he say?"

"He said… say please!"

"And what? You hit him again?"

"No, Ashley did. She was as shocked by his rudeness as I was. It was lucky she had her hockey stick."

"Lucky she… Cora… for God's sake!" I was so furious I couldn't get my words out. "We have already been through this. You can't go round hitting people just because they don't do as you ask. Zach is your brother, your family, you should be looking out for each other."

"Yes, we have been through this, Dad," again with the 'Dad', "and I already told you Zach is not people. It is just Zach. Brother means nothing. Brother is an embarrassment. Brother is another male waste of food and oxygen."

"That is a horrible thing to say about anyone, but especially your family. I don't know what you have been hearing to make you talk like that, but I want you to stop. This is way past acceptable. Consider yourself grounded."

She laughed in my face. "You need to get with the times.

You don't get to talk to me like that. Boys are only good for doing the things that girls don't want to do, and they are not even very good at that. This country is run by women, for women, and you need to fall in line." Cora rolled up her sleeve and thrust her forearm in my face, her intense glare not wavering. I looked down to see the female symbol ♀ tattooed in thick, black marker, surrounded by a triangle. "Altior!" she said, without taking her eyes off mine.

She removed her school backpack and dropped it at my feet. Then turned her back and walked up to her bedroom. I followed, but I wasn't interested in dealing with Cora at that moment. I was more concerned by Zach's injuries. I opened Zach's bedroom door and found him sat on his bed hugging his knees. I sat next to him and examined the cut above his eye. The area around his eye-socket was deep purple and swollen, like he had a plum stuck to his face. The cut was a gaping wound that would need stitches but had stopped bleeding.

"Zach? Will you let me clean that up a bit? I think we'll need to get you to the hospital."

"Please just leave me," he said.

"Zach, come on, let me help you."

"That's just it." He looked up, his eyes were ablaze. "You don't help. You make things worse. I did what you said. I asked Cora to say please when she asked me to carry her bag and she got angry. Now look what's happened. Just let me do things my own way."

"The things that have been happening to you are not ok. You can't give in to this because of violence. That needs to stop. And I'll make it stop. But you must keep believing in yourself."

"It's just the way things are. Maybe it was different when you were younger, but not anymore. They are in charge now. Just get out and leave me alone!" He shoved me off the bed on to the floor.

He was right, things had changed. Not for the better and, as I was coming to realise, in a way that was beyond my control. I knew that school was not the same for them as it was for me, and Zach's experience was different to that of Cora, as it had a different intended outcome. But I had always thought, so long as I kept things on the straight and narrow at home, treated them the same and had the same expectations of them both, that they would grow up level-headed, well balanced and kind children.

It turned out I was wrong.

I was powerless against the overwhelming force of society, peer influence, the education system. For many years I had known the direction of travel. I had seen the imbalances grow greater, the chasm separating the treatment, fairness and wellbeing of men and women widen. But so long as I kept myself to myself and got on with life without making a fuss, I had never feared for my safety. Sitting there, trying to comfort my wounded, blood-drenched son, for the first time in my life, I was scared.

CHAPTER 13

They are in charge now.

I couldn't get the altercation with Cora out of my mind. I had lost any sense of authority over her. It was like she genuinely believed she had moral superiority.

And Altior again!

This word had never entered my ears but then twice in a matter of hours. It sounded like an organisation of some sort. I couldn't fathom what organisation would link Zoe and her work with an apparent cult that Cora had gotten mixed up in, but there was a chance Zach knew something. I needed to get him to the hospital so I could ask him on the way.

I would have happily taken the sixty-minute walk but couldn't expect Zach to in his condition. So, I picked up the handset of the landline and called a cab. Then I shouted up the stairs to Cora.

"We're heading off in ten minutes and will be gone a few hours. You have a choice. You can either come with us to see Grace or you can stay here by yourself. Up to you."

"I'll stay."

"Fine. You will have to make yourself something to eat. There's stuff in the fridge. Not sure what time mum will be back."

"Whatever."

The taxi arrived in a plume of black smoke — a rattly blue hatchback held together with duct tape. The driver was a man of Indian descent, with a bushy moustache, a face mottled by liver spots and the belly of a person who spends all day sitting down. The interior of the car was filthy and had an offensive smell that mixed smoke with damp. The broken springs of the chair dug into my back like I was sitting on a sack of rocks. Zach sat in silence, staring out the window, watching the world go by deep in thought. It felt like a suitable time to find out what he knew.

"Cora had something drawn her arm. Have you seen it? Like a triangle."

"Yes, lot of girls do it," he replied without shifting his gaze. "The mean ones especially."

"What does it mean?"

"It's their club."

"What sort of club?"

"The club that hates boys. Lots of girls just ignore us. But some hate us. The ones that hate us draw that picture."

"What kind of thing do they do?"

He turned to face me, looking perplexed. I saw the cut above his eye.

"Ok silly question," I said. "Does the club have a name? Cora said something beginning with A. Altior or something."

The taxi driver glared at me in the rear-view mirror.

"Yes, that's it," Zach replied.

"Hmm."

It didn't make much sense to me. Kids had gangs. I got that much. But I couldn't make connection with Zoe. I left it there and we rode the rest of the way in silence. My mind was working overtime trying to join dots that kept moving or vanishing altogether.

We pulled up outside the hospital and got out of the car. I handed the driver some cash through the open window. He snatched it with a scowl, his dark brown eyes filled with judgement.

"I'd watch what questions you ask in public if I were you," he said before pulling off without another word.

The main hospital in D22 was a decaying, grey building dating back to the 1990s: four storeys of cracked and chipped concrete with exposed, rusty rebars, and rows of tiny windows. More what you'd expect from a high-security prison, minus the razor wire and guards with guns. The automatic doors struggled to slide open, and I was hit with that smell, flooding me with memories and flipping my stomach.

Zach and I followed the signs for A&E through the labyrinth of corridors, until we reached the reception and waiting room area. It was full of people, mostly men, using dirty rags to apply pressure to various body parts to stem the bleeding from wherever it was leaking. Cut heads. Mangled arms. A guy with a metal spike sticking out of the front of his shoulder. A thoroughly gruesome sight. Fortunately, emergency healthcare was the one public service where there was no priority for females. Men were the most loyal customers by far, mostly arising from workplace accidents, but they were also in short supply and so it was important to keep the ones we had alive.

I checked Zach in at reception and prepared myself for the typical eight-hour wait. As I scanned the area, searching amongst the array of wounded people for somewhere to sit, I saw a man waving frantically, trying to get my attention. It took a moment but then I recognised him. It was a guy from the supermarket, the one that stacks shelves. Leeroy his name was. I knew that because he was the most friendly, positive, and animated man ever to have existed and would accost anyone doing their shopping for a good old chin wag without any fear of repercussions to himself or others. But I felt safe talking to him. He was so loud that the detail of the conversation was audible to everyone and there would be no suspicion of anything underhand going on.

Leeroy was from a Caribbean family and inherited a

strong Jamaican accent. Every sentence ended in *mon*, and he found everything hilariously funny, regularly releasing a belly-laugh like you've never heard. He had dark skin, and his hair was twisted into small tufts that covered his head. His fatness suited his jolliness. It was the first time I'd seen him out of uniform. He was wearing a red, yellow, and green striped t-shirt that stretched over his large belly.

"Jack, mon! Nice to see a familiar face!" followed by that laugh, albeit more downbeat than usual.

"Likewise," I replied. "Shame it's not under better circumstances. What are you doing here?"

Leeroy sucked his teeth. "My boy is not in a good way, mon. He's all mashed up."

"Your son, you mean?"

"Yeah, mon. He was working on a job, building something big, he said. Like a dormitory or something. He fell off the roof, banged his head and snapped his back."

"Oh wow. That sounds awful. Sorry to hear that. Do they think he'll be ok?"

"No idea, mon. Been here for five hours already while they do their thing. Waiting for some news. What you doing here?"

I gestured with my thumb, pointing at Zach. "I'm here with my son too. He's bumped his head and needs a few stitches."

Leeroy looked over and sucked his teeth again. "That's nasty, mon. You're gonna have a bad-boy scar there."

Zach stared at his feet.

"Talk to me, mon," Leeroy continued. "I'm bored stiff sitting here, you know. What's new?"

I wasn't sure where to begin. The idiotic stealing of a gun? Witnessing mass murder? Almost being shot dead? Being hauled in front of the police only to be miraculously let free? I decided to keep it simple and let Leeroy do the talking. "Oh, not much. This and that. Same old, same old. What was it your son was working on? A dormitory you said?"

"Yeah, mon. He got pulled into this job a few months back. Been on it the whole time since. Like a living-quarters, but big. Real big. Like big enough for five thousand people. Across in D21"

"Wow, what's it for?"

"No idea, mon, but nothing good is my guess."

He was right. What use could they have for a dormitory for five-thousand people? It could have been a new form of social housing, but some areas had entire streets of homes lying vacant. Why build new housing from scratch? "Government job, is it?"

"Odd one. He said it's a government job but it's being run by this other company. Called Altior."

They say bad omens come in threes.

"Never heard of them," I bluffed "What do they do?"

"No idea, mon. But didn't you pay attention in your Latin classes?" Leeroy let out one of his laughs. "It mean 'eyer," he said.

"'eyer?" I was confused.

"*Higher*," Leeroy repeated in a fake posh English accent.

The taxi driver's parting words rang in my ears.

I'd watch what questions you ask in public if I were you.

I was suddenly filled with a horrible sense of paranoia, like the room was closing in and everyone was staring at us. I glanced around the ceiling, checking for security cameras.

Altior.

Academic institution. School girl cult. Building contractor.

It made no sense, but I felt inexplicably, and

increasingly, uncomfortable. My desire for idle chitchat evaporated.

"Leeroy, could I ask you a massive favour?"

"Yeah, mon."

"My daughter is over in the maternity wing, and I am supposed to be visiting her as well. It would be helpful if I could get that done while we wait for Zach to get seen. Would you mind keeping an eye on him for an hour while I go over and see my daughter? I'll be back before he gets called in."

"Sure thing, mon. I'll be here for hours yet. You go do what you need. Me and the boy will have a nice chat."

Good luck with that, I thought. But if anyone could get a word out of Zach, it would be Leeroy.

"Amazing, thanks so much," I said. "Zach, sit and relax here, I won't be long." Zach didn't look up and continued biting his fingernails.

CHAPTER 14

The maternity department was on the other side of the hospital. Luckily, there was a navy-blue line painted on the wall that guided me through the maze. Roaming the hospital corridors brought back memories of being here with Zoe during her pregnancies, with Cora, Zach, and with Grace, so many years before. It was frightening how quickly those twenty-two years had passed. I could picture it as if it were the day before. Zoe was wearing a pink flowery dress, waddling along, supporting the underside of her big round belly with one hand, while the other gripped my hand like a vice to the point where the circulation to my fingers had stopped. I hadn't known she was capable of such strength. Grace was two weeks early and by the time I got the call at the barracks and made my way home, Zoe's labour had progressed to the final stages, and I was worried that Grace would be delivered into the passenger footwell of our car on the journey to the hospital.

Zoe managed to hold her in just long enough. Long enough for Zoe to make it on to a bed at least, but not long enough for her to get changed out of her own clothes before Grace forced her way out of her warm, protective cocoon and into the harsh reality of life on the outside. I had this vivid recollection of the midwife asking if I wanted to cut the umbilical cord. I don't know why she thought the arrival of my first-born child would be an appropriate time for me, someone with zero medical training, to try their hand at being a surgeon. So, I politely declined and left it to the professionals. The midwife wrapped Grace in a white towel and passed her to Zoe. The ambiance in the room immediately switched from the frantic stress and panic of labour to an infectious love and joy like I'd never experienced. Zoe's maternal love for her new baby, and toward me for giving it to her. My love for Zoe for being so amazing and producing a perfect little human being, and a different adoration toward my new baby daughter; protectiveness, gratitude, pride. We were the perfect family unit and I missed those days desperately.

My eyes welled and I swallowed the cricket-ball size lump that had risen into the back of my throat.

I reached the end of the navy-blue line and pushed open the door to the maternity wing, taking a moment to compose myself before speaking to the nurse at reception, who directed me to the ward where Grace was staying. It was a cramped room with eight beds and seven other women, five of whom were cradling new-born babies while the other two sat alone. Grace's bed was enclosed by a drawn green curtain. It felt hugely insensitive to put grieving mothers in the same room as women cooing over their new babies. A surge of annoyance bubbled up, but I stifled it as best I could. It wasn't what Grace needed.

I poked my head through the curtain that shrouded Grace's bed and was faced with something I had not anticipated. I had expected to find an inconsolable wreck — crying, screaming, stubbornly refusing to cooperate. But the vision in front of me was what I could only describe as an exhausted angel, radiating an aura of tranquil purity. Her pale white skin was indistinguishable from her flowing white gown. Her long auburn hair fell straight down either side of her face, and her tired, sunken eyes were encircled in dark grey. The strange part was the smile on her face. A gentle, accepting smile of someone who had found inner peace.

"Hey sweetheart," I said, softly. "How are you?" I sat on the flimsy plastic chair that was next to Grace's bed.

"I'm ok. Thanks for coming to see me."

"Don't be silly. How could I not? Mum said you were having a rough time. But you're looking better than I expected."

"It was a shock to begin with, of course, but I have had time to think about it all. I... I think it's probably for the best."

"I'm glad you are feeling better about it, but you know what comes next. We're here for you, but don't underestimate what it takes."

"It's fine Dad, I know, and I've already taken the tablets."

"Oh right, that's... good, I suppose." My words were awkward, but I wasn't sure what an appropriate response should be.

"Yes, they want me to stay here after what happened last time, until, you know..."

"Yes. Yes of course," I said. "I'm pleased you are taking it so well. What has made you feel this way?"

"I don't want a baby right now. I thought that in a few years, if things kept going well with Logan, then, who knows, maybe we could have given it a shot. But not yet. Plus, now I know what he's like, going behind my back like that and making life-changing decisions without asking me, how can I stay with him? If I had the baby I'd be on my own and it would be a disaster."

"You know for sure he did that?"

"Yes, he told me. He's been making holes in the condoms. He said he did it because he loves me and wants us to be together as a family. But I can't look at him."

"Okay..." I said through gritted teeth. *Keep a lid on it Jack!* "I'm... I'm proud of how you're dealing with this, Gracie. You're a good girl and you deserve the best." Logan could wait. But he'd get what was due.

"Thanks Dad, and with the good news that mum shared earlier, when I'm ready, I might even get a healthy boy. I really want a baby boy, one day." A look of genuine excitement spread across her face.

"What news is that?"

"About the cure. She said I mustn't tell anyone, but she must have told you?"

"I haven't seen much of her over the past few days. We've both been busy. What did she say?"

"That it's worked! It's all going to be over soon. A fresh start for all of us."

I thought back to what I read in the documents from Zoe's handbag. "That's brilliant news. Just brilliant."

I didn't know how convincing I was.

CHAPTER 15

"Four across, one-humped camel, nine letters, ends in Y," I read out loud as Grace and I spent the rest of the hour doing the crossword in a newspaper.

"Dromedary," Grace replied instantly.

"How on earth do you know that?"

"Not sure," she said.

We both fell about laughing, like there wasn't a care in the world.

Crosswords used to be our thing, before she moved out. We both had a good brain for random facts and often surprised ourselves with the nuggets of useless information we were able to dredge up. We were a good crossword team. I insisted that she move back home for a while, due to the Logan situation, so I made a mental note to dig out the old puzzle books when I got home. I kissed her on the head, and we said our goodbyes. I told her I'd be back to pick her up the following day, once it was all over.

"Oh, before you go," Grace said. "Mum mentioned that Cora has been playing up a bit."

"Yeah, I guess you could say that." Understatement of the century. "She's been getting violent towards Zach. I didn't want to bother you with it, but he's here at the hospital, in A&E with a cut above his eye."

"Honestly, that girl." Grace screwed up her face and turned her head away. "The problem is, it's not entirely her fault. They get all sorts drummed into them at school, then they get all worked up amongst their friend groups. You know what peer pressure can be like."

"Zach mentioned a club that they are all in. Altior. Have you heard of it?"

"Yes, I hear the teachers talking about it at the library. Sounds like an external company has been brought in to overhaul the curriculum. The teachers aren't happy as it's getting a bit extreme."

"I see."

"It's going to be more important than ever that you are strict with her, Dad. You can't allow her to be brainwashed."

"I think it might be too late."

"Don't give up on her."

"Ok, Sweetie. I'll see you later." Other than tying Cora permanently to a chair, I was running short of ideas.

The navy-blue line led me back to the A&E waiting room and I arrived to find Zach sat next to Leeroy, bandaged up and smiling like I'd never seen. Leeroy slapped him on the back and they both doubled over with laughter. I stood back and watched with a mixture of delight and heartbreak. It made me so happy to see him like that, laughing like a child should, but at the same time full of sorrow that I, his own father, hadn't given that to him.

That was going to change.

After a few minutes of spectating, I interrupted. "Hospital isn't meant to be fun you know."

"Oh, hi Dad," Zach said, looking me in the eyes.

"He's a funny boy, this one. You must be proud," Leeroy said.

"I am Leeroy, I certainly am."

It turned out that head injuries were being prioritised, and Zach was seen within twenty minutes. He would have a nasty scar as Leeroy suggested but the injury was superficial and would heal in a few weeks with the stitches he had received. Leeroy did me a huge favour and escorted him to the treatment room.

"I owe you one for today, Leeroy, in fact, I owe you two," I said.

"Don't mention it. It's been a pleasure," Leeroy replied.

"I hope your son makes a full recovery. Let me know if there is anything I can do to help. I mean it."

I left the hospital feeling warm and fuzzy. The trip was meant to be disaster management, but instead I was reminded of how lucky I was to have such wonderful children, and of the potential kindness of fellow human-beings. It was reassuring to know that there were good people in the world, capable of such selfless acts, of taking on the burden of someone else's rubbish day and turning it around, despite their own troubles. I didn't want the feeling to end, so, even though it was late, Zach and I walked home. Bathed in the glow of the orange streetlamps, we took slow step after slow step, and had the first proper conversation in years. Genuine father and son stuff. Although for once, Zach did most of the talking.

"Leeroy said that in Jamaica there are swordfish as long as a minibus."

"Wow, that's big," I said.

"Yeah, and you have to catch them using a steel rope because they are so heavy. And the boat needs four engines otherwise the swordfish will pull the boat along!"

"Incredible."

"And there is this other one, called a sailfish. It looks like a swordfish, but it has a big fin on its back, like a sail. It's a bit smaller than a swordfish but is the fastest fish in the sea and goes as fast as a car on the motorway."

"You're kidding."

"I'm not. It's true." Zach paused for breath for a moment

and appeared to be deep in thought. "Could we go fishing one day, Dad? I think I might like to be a fisherman when I grow up."

"You know what Zach, I would love that. And I think being a fisherman would be a fine job…" The statement was true, but I would need to give it some thought. Could we, two males, get away with sitting alone in the wilderness? Perhaps Zoe could come with us. Or even Cora. Spending time together like that could be what we needed to help us all bond. I would do what I could to make it work.

Never once had Zach shown any signs of having an idea of what lay ahead of him. No plans. No dreams or aspirations. Just a desperate need to get from one day to the next without abuse or injury. Survival in its most basic form. But the twinkle in his eye was unmistakable. It was excitement. More, it was hope. If what Grace had said about Zoe's progress with the cure was true, then that hope was well placed. We could be on the road to recovery within weeks. Nothing would change in the short term, but being on the journey would make a difference. It would prove that we all wanted the same thing. That we, us men, could be part of the team again, not second-class citizens, at best.

But what I had read in the file from Zoe's handbag kept niggling at me, like an irritating itch. I could have misunderstood. Zoe was a woman of honour and would never put anyone in danger. Or so I thought. But I didn't know what to believe. The one thing I did know was that I needed some questions answered, and fast, before I turned full conspiracy theorist.

Zach and I continued on our way, making grand plans of fishing trips we would take. He would learn on the river, then take a small boat in the sea locally. We would go big-game fishing in the UK, and then when he was eighteen, we would catch a swordfish in the Caribbean. Most of it would never happen of course, but I would say anything to keep his spirits up.

ASHKADE

We turned on to the cul-de-sac a few minutes past ten o'clock. In the darkness up ahead, a car was parked outside our house. A car I didn't recognise. A large black Jaguar with no number plate. It looked brand new. There couldn't have been more than a handful of such cars in the entire country. It could only mean one thing. But surely not. Not at my house.

CHAPTER 16

"Good evening, Mr Wilson. I hope you have come to join us in our celebrations. You are married to an incredible woman."

Alvina, the Prime Minister of Great Britain, was standing in my kitchen, holding a bottle of champagne.

"I..." My eyes darted between Zoe and Alvina. "I wasn't expecting..."

Alvina let out a laugh. "You don't need to look so surprised. Honestly, I'm nothing next to this woman," she said, rubbing Zoe's shoulder. "Let me pour you a glass." She obviously sensed my hesitation, as she added, "Don't worry, it'll be our little secret. I insist."

I whispered to Zach to take himself upstairs and he did as instructed.

"In that case I suppose it would be rude of me to refuse," I replied. Zoe still hadn't said a word, even ignoring Zach's bandaged head. I could tell she wasn't comfortable. "So, I assume there is some good news?" I looked at Zoe, trying to get her to say something.

"It worked," Zoe said. "We've done it." She gave a small smile.

"Just brilliant," Alvina said as she passed me a glass of champagne.

"Oh wow," I said. "So, the cure works, and is... safe, is it?"

"Yes, perfectly safe," Alvina said, answering my question to Zoe.

"That's amazing news then, I guess." I awkwardly raised my glass looking at Zoe, who in turn was looking everywhere except at me.

"Allow me to propose a toast," Alvina jumped in. "To Professor Zoe Wilson, pioneer, genius, saviour." We all bumped glasses and sipped the champagne. It immediately went to my head. "I've had a challenging run in this job," Alvina continued. "You know, a large part of political leadership is learning from past mistakes to avoid making them in the future. It's important to know your history as there aren't many things that haven't been tried before. But The Gaia and what it inflicted upon us is unprecedented. No experience in the records of time could help steer our path. Leadership in the absence of experience is a difficult thing." I didn't know where she was going with her monologue. "You were a military man, weren't you Jack? What does successful leadership mean to you?"

"I suppose for me it was about inspiring people, instilling confidence, and delivery of commitments."

"Precisely! Couldn't agree more. Tell me, do you find me inspiring?"

What sort of loaded question is that?!

"Umm…" I looked at Zoe for support, who stared back with an expression of absolute dread. A long sip of champagne provided time while my brain searched for an acceptable response.

"Come on, be honest," Alvina said. "Leadership is also about listening to feedback. I want to know what you think."

"I've never given it much thought but, if I'm being honest, it's difficult to be inspired by anything when the world is so bleak, and you can't see a way out." The alcohol had loosened my tongue, but I was happy with my response.

"Exactly. As you said, successful leadership is about inspiring people and delivery of results. You can't have one without the other. I haven't been a successful leader, I know that, and I don't have many years left to fix it, but thanks to Zoe here, I will succeed in the slightest bit of redemption before I go. This country will be left in a better place than where I found it. Not in terms of where we are at the moment, but in its journey ahead, and for that I am eternally grateful. We finally have a future that inspires hope." She took a deep breath, like she was taken aback by her own profundity.

Her beaming optimism was admirable, but none of it matched with anything she had said or done over her forty-year reign, or with what I saw with my own eyeballs when I looked out the window.

I was starting to feel tipsy. Even before my imposed abstinence I was never a big drinker and always had issues with anything fizzy. But I liked it. I was relaxed and confident.

Perhaps too confident.

"So, Jack, Zoe tells me you've had a tough few days. Sounds horrendous, I must say. I offer my sincere and heartfelt apologies about it all. Considering your supportive role for Zoe here, and the importance of her work, you should never have been called in for that assignment. I'll make sure we get the records updated."

"Yes, it's certainly been... interesting," I said. "But I've discovered a lot about myself."

"Oh, how so?" Alvina replied.

Zoe gave a barely perceptible shake of the head, but there was movement, willing me to stop talking. But it struck me as the perfect opportunity to get some answers to my questions.

"I have an active imagination," I continued. "Like, when you feel as though you're the lead character in a weird, messed-up movie, your brain starts to embellish the plot. You would not believe some of the thoughts going around inside my head. There is this one thing... in fact, you may be able to help me with this... who or what is Altior?"

"Ok Jack," Zoe interrupted. "Perhaps you should go and tuck Zach in. It's been a long day."

"One moment Professor," Alvina said calmly. "I think we should do Jack the courtesy of answering his question. I know there are some rumours circulating about this organisation and it's about time we did some more positive PR around it." She turned to face me. "Altior is a privately funded, quasi-autonomous organisation with a certain interest in, let's say, matters of national concern. They have been instrumental in the funding and building of numerous infrastructure projects, as well as significant input to directing Zoe's own work, even more so in the next phase as we scale up given their large footprint in pharmaceuticals. I can understand that some people might not like the idea of a private company being so heavily involved in government matters, but I can assure you no decisions are made without going through appropriate parliamentary process."

"And what do they get out of it?" I said.

"I'm sure you can appreciate there needs to be a bit of give and take in certain areas. It wouldn't be appropriate for me to give any details, but I can say that we, the public, get the better end of the deal. That's certain."

I found her response irritating. It was obvious that she was hiding something with her evasive vagueness. And I didn't like the way she kept talking over Zoe. Something inside me snapped. I was going to go in for the jugular. I'd never get the opportunity again, and I owed it to Zach. "That's funny," I said. "My son didn't feel like he had the better end of the deal when he got clocked around the head with a hockey stick because of some ideologically driven education, if you can call it that."

"Jack!" Zoe shouted this time.

"It's alright, Zoe," Alvina said. "We're just adults having a conversation. Jack should be able to speak his mind. I am familiar with the concern you raise, but you are mistaken.

Indeed, Altior are involved in funding and design of specific parts of the school curriculum, aimed at stretching the brighter children to reach their full capability. However, some of our younger and more impressionable minds have 'embellished the plot' as you like to say and believe Altior are leading some sort of female-supremacy, anti-male agenda, which is clearly absurd."

"It should be absurd," I said. "But it's what I'm seeing. It makes me wonder why you are so happy about a successful cure. Do you really want things back the way they were?"

"I never said that," she replied. "Remember what I said. You need to learn from history. It was never the case that an equal number of men and women led to equality among the two. Women have been disadvantaged since the dawn of time. We need to do more than merely hope that things would be better next time."

"I don't remember the young girls being attacked on the streets by mobs of vicious boys when I was growing up. At least not ones that had been emboldened by the state."

"Perhaps not, but fortunately you and I are too young to remember the days where women were not allowed to vote, or sit on a jury, or have their own bank account and take out a loan without the permission of their husband or father. Women had to fight hard for these things over decades. Hell, it wasn't until 1994 that it was a criminal offense for a husband to rape his wife for goodness sake. I have no intention of going back to how things were before." Her previous calmness and dignity slipped, then she regained her composure. "We will need to find a way that works better for everyone. Anyway, this is all getting a bit intense," she said with a smile. "This is a moment for celebration, and I would like to invite you both to a more formal event to celebrate appropriately. Tomorrow evening, we will hold a press conference to share the news, and afterwards, you will come to my living quarters at Downing Street with the other team members.

Zoe glared at me sideways and transmitted her

thoughts directly into my head. *Do not say another word!* "That would be lovely, thank you," Zoe said.

"It's been lovely meeting you, Jack. I have enjoyed our debate. And again, huge congratulations, Professor."

Alvina left with a courteous nod.

"What a load of bollocks," I said.

"Don't talk to me. I've never been so embarrassed." Zoe's response was sharp.

"What have I done?"

"You are plastered after a glass and a half of champagne! You called the Prime Minister uninspiring and made yourself out to be a complete crackpot. I need to work with these people, Jack. There is no way you are coming tomorrow. I have a professional reputation to uphold. I don't want everyone to think I'm married to a lunatic."

"*I'm* a lunatic? A lunatic is someone who spends forty years hammering men into the ground and then suddenly changes her story and makes out she's all for taking us back."

"I'd be interested to know which part of what she said you disagree with. Because it all sounded reasonable to me. She didn't talk about taking us back. It's about a different way forward."

"If you believe that then you are more of a fool than I thought. There is no way she is going to give up her power. And this Altior lot seem to be fully ingrained in everything we do." I wanted to mention what I had read on the document from her bag, but I wasn't ready for that admission.

"That's enough! You have no idea what you are talking about. I'm going to bed," she said, turning and heading upstairs.

Zoe placed a barrier of pillows down the centre of the bed, preventing bodily contact of any kind. I was in the doghouse, but I didn't care. For once, I was sure I was in the right. I agreed with most of what Alvina had said about women's history, but I didn't believe the way forward she described was what she truly wanted. And I didn't like the way Zoe was on her side. It wasn't like the situation was working for women either.

CHAPTER 17

10:30, Wednesday 6th June 2063

The train arrived at London St Pancras. I gazed up at the enormous, iron-scaffold, arched tunnel that covered the multitude of platforms at the terminal. Quite the feat of engineering. It must have been impressive when it was fully intact and properly maintained. But its scale only exaggerated the sense of neglect. Most of the glass panels were broken, rendering it useless in its function of protecting the station from the outside elements. Leaves and litter covered the platforms, and rows of units that were once shops housed scores of rough sleeping men in filthy clothes, lying under flattened cardboard boxes. It was a depressing sight, but even that could not suppress my excitement.

Zoe had calmed down from the night before and decided that it would be strange for her to turn up alone after the specific invitation to us both, and I had promised to be on my best behaviour, would stay in the background, and keep talking to a minimum. Besides, I wouldn't be drinking alcohol in public.

A day trip to London was a rare occurrence. The train journey took an hour and a half, but the service was infrequent and unreliable. Thankfully, that day, we made it without issue. Zoe had a busy day ahead, starting with a government meeting to discuss the roll out plan for the cure, followed by preparation for the press conference. I had a few hours to kill until Zoe would be finished around 16:00, to get ready for the broadcast at 18:00, but had planned to take a walk around the city and had brought a crossword book, which would keep me occupied for a while. Zoe was dressed up in a black skirt and blazer, so I thought it necessary to match her smartness as best I could. I wore an old pair of suit trousers and a blue collared shirt with the sleeves folded to the elbows. I thought we looked good together.

The stretched black car that had been sent to pick us up was waiting at the taxi rank. The driver, a smartly dressed but otherwise haggard man in his fifties, opened the rear door for us and we got in. My trousers squeaked on the shiny black leather as I sat back and placed my elbows on the arm rests. It was the most comfortable chair I had ever sat in, like a giant squishy sofa in the back of the car.

"Look," I said excitedly. "They have bottled water."

Zoe shot me one of those glances. I had already broken rule number one: keep talking to a minimum. The driver returned to his seat and pulled off with smooth professionalism. The government offices were in Whitehall. It was a part of the city that I wasn't familiar with, and I enjoyed the journey. We passed the British Museum with its pillared façade looking like it had been lifted straight out of ancient Greece. A long queue of school-aged girls snaked along the pavement. A sign out front informed that it was open on Wednesdays and Saturdays, no doubt the absence of foreign tourists limiting footfall. Next, we drove past Trafalgar Square, and its fifty-metre stone column topped by a statue of Emmeline Pankhurst. The four lion sculptures at the column's base representing the heroism of Britain's most famous Suffragette instead of the previous occupant, Lord Nelson, who was toppled for being considered a controversial figure, a symbol of the patriarchy with links to the slave trade.

We approached Whitehall and pulled up to a security checkpoint that cordoned off the area that contained the government offices. The buildings were striking, grey stone structures of grandiose Palladian architecture: an enthusiastic use of columns, pillars, floor-to-ceiling windows, and imposing doors. It was difficult not to be impressed. The driver showed his ID to a giant of a woman who was dressed in black SWAT gear and carried a small machine gun. She peered into the rear of the car, checking out Zoe and me sitting in the back, before waving us through. Our final stop was a four-storey office building with a large red door, black iron railings and a neat hedgerow. The driver opened the doors, indicating for us to get out. The streets within the cordoned area were immaculate.

The mansion-like, buildings were beautifully maintained. All window glass was intact. Garden areas manicured. The floor was free of weeds, litter, and debris. It was like arriving at a different country. The red door was heavy and required some force to push open into the vast reception foyer. We were hit by a waft of floral cleanliness. The white marble floor was polished to a mirror finish and the red runner carpet that led up the double staircase was plush and spotless. We were greeted by a lady dressed in a smart black suit. Her greying-brown hair was wrenched up in a bun, giving her a non-surgical facelift. She wore bright red lipstick.

"Professor and Mr Wilson? We've been expecting you. Please can I ask you to sign in and I'll issue your security passes."

Zoe scribbled some information on a sheet of paper and the lady handed us two passes on lanyards.

"Professor Wilson, your meeting is being held in the Brontë room, first floor on the left. Mr Wilson, we have arranged a room for you to wait in on the ground floor, over here on the right. You should find some light refreshments in there. If you would like some fresh air, then you may use the riverside gardens. I would advise that you do not leave the compound, but if you wish to, please leave your security pass with the guard at the gate."

"Thank you," Zoe said.

I nodded, indicating my acknowledgment and

gratitude.

Stay in the background. Keep talking to a minimum.

I turned to face Zoe. "I'm going to head straight out for a walk. Hope today goes well for you. Good luck," I said quietly.

"Thank you," she said, seeming genuinely grateful.

I left the building and started walking down the impeccably kept street. It was like being on a movie set. Fake and surreal. Like a simulation of an eerie alternate reality. I had this sense that I was being watched, my every step being monitored, and didn't feel at ease. So, despite the warning from the receptionist, I handed my pass to the giant SWAT lady and made my way out of the compound, down to the Thames by Embankment and set off in the direction of Waterloo Bridge.

Zoe's behaviour that morning had been odd. I mean, not what I would have expected after achieving the medical breakthrough of the century. Her every waking hour had been devoted to the cause for many years and I thought she would be ecstatic, and yet having succeeded, her mood was... flat. She seemed withdrawn and deep in thought. She hadn't said more than ten words for the entire train journey, just gazed out the window, biting her nails in contemplative silence. Perhaps the gravity of the situation hadn't fully hit her. Or was it because there was still so much work to do, and she didn't feel like she had finished? Maybe she was pondering on what came next.

This last point had been on my mind a lot.

What comes next?

My sincere hope was that Zoe would wind back the working hours. Surely there would be huge compensation for such an achievement. Early retirement with enhanced pension. I knew that she could never pull back fully, and neither should she. Her brilliant mind had a lot to offer the scientific community and I would never want to deprive her of what she loved. But perhaps a slight course correction on priorities. Spend more time at home with the kids. With me. Try to rekindle what we had lost and return to being the great team we once were. A proper partnership. Equals.

Some people believe in fate. Others have an appreciation of how apparently insignificant random events can have life changing consequences. Whatever your perspective, that was how Zoe and I got together. Statistically improbable but meant to be.

December of 2035, before Zoe and I had met, the country was in a period of readjustment to its new economic reality. Twelve years into The Gaia and standards of living had taken a hit from the quarantine, but the dynamics of society hadn't changed much. I had returned from a four-week counter terrorism mission in Somalia and was due five days R&R. My plan was to travel down to the south coast and spend the week in a tent, as far away from other humans as possible. Take in the sea air. Decompress. Come to terms with what I had done while on tour. Many soldiers wanted to spend time with their friends and family during R&R, but a period of solitude helped me process my experiences. However, before leaving for the coast, I had some paperwork to file at the sniper school in Pirbright, Surrey.

It turned out to be Day One for a new batch of special weapons recruits, so while there, I was asked to spot for the sniper instructor, Sergeant Mark Cairn, as a special treat for them. My reputation must have preceded me because as I approached, the line of disciplined soldiers all standing bolt upright and looking forward started elbowing each other and whispering the way you'd expect a group of school children to after seeing their favourite pop singer. I saluted, they saluted back, and order was resumed. Cairn was lying on the deck, demonstrating the basic operation of the L115A3 long range rifle. I lay next to him and picked up the spotting scope. Cairn asked for a round. I lifted the lid on a box of rounds, a ten-by-ten grid of bullets arranged tip down. One hundred to choose from. I plucked one at random and handed it to Cairn, who loaded it into the rifle. He talked through his every move.

"Once the bolt is firmly slid forward to the engaged position, reacquire your target through the scope. Breathe slowly, relax, and when you are ready to fire, apply gentle pressure to the trigger."

There was a thunderous bang, and a flash of bright light, but not from where it was supposed to come. The chamber of the rifle exploded, sending a cloud of white-hot chemical gas into the face of Cairn. Lucky for him, his safety specs saved his eyesight, but he suffered major facial burns and lost the hearing in his right ear. An overcharged round is one in a million, a manufacturing fault where too much propellant is used causing catastrophic damage to the weapon. I had never seen one before that day, or even knew of anyone who had seen one. But we had found one. It put Cairn in hospital and postponed my R&R while I was asked to cover for him until a full-time replacement instructor could be found. My moment of solitude would have to wait. But ironically, that faulty round that could have cost Cairn his life, possibly saved mine.

I was given the Saturday off and took the opportunity to escape. The area surrounding the base was covered in expansive forest and rolling heathland and it was possible to walk for hours without seeing another soul. I packed my hiking gear, a flask of tea and some sandwiches and set off early for a day in the wilderness. Around midday I was approaching a popular dog walking spot. It could be busy early in the morning but would quieten down as people headed home for lunch. It was bitterly cold with the temperature not having risen above zero all day. Frosted leaves crunched under my boots and plumes of white-water vapour escaped my nose and mouth. I could hear the yapping of a small dog in the distance, which grew louder as I continued along the path. I reached a long sweeping righthand bend and discovered the source of the noise, a little Yorkshire Terrier that looked up at me and yapped even more frantically than before. It turned around and ran off, watching behind like he wanted me to follow. Ten metres further around the bend I found a woman sitting on the floor, with her knees hugged into her chest. She was a similar age to me, with freckles across her nose and cheeks, and tufts of brown hair poking out the pulled-up hood of her red parka. She looked freezing, her lips and hands having turned an icy shade of blue.

"Is everything ok?" I said, crouching down next to her.

"Not really," she replied, teeth chattering. "I've twisted my ankle and can't put any weight on it. I've got no phone signal out here and can't make it back to my car."

"May I?" I said, as I gently lifted the bottom of her trouser leg, revealing a grapefruit sized ankle. "Yep, you've done it good and proper. That's a nasty sprain." She winced as I pulled her trouser leg back down. "How far away is your car?"

"It's over a mile away, in the carpark at the entrance to the common."

I rubbed my stubble as I considered the options.

"I could run and find someone, try to get you an ambulance, but you are going to freeze sitting here," I said, watching her shiver. "Will you let me carry you?"

She looked at me like I was crazy. "How could you do that?"

"I've carried people twice your size, twice as far. It'll be a cinch."

I took hold of her elbow, lifted her on to her good leg and hoisted her up in to a piggyback. The warmth of her breath on the back of my neck was oddly sensual and I'll never forget the floral scent of her perfume that cemented that moment in eternity. The little dog nipped at my ankles as we set off, not happy with me kidnapping its owner.

"He's an excitable one," I said. "What's his name?"

"Gravy. He's my parents' dog," she replied.

"That's a good name for a Yorkie," I said, chuckling. "And you?"

"I'm Zoe."

"Good to meet you, Zoe. I'm Jack."

I carried her for a mile and a half. We chatted like good friends that hadn't seen each other for a while, curious and interested, but oddly familiar. I'd never been one for idle chit-chat but felt so at ease talking to her.

We reached the car and I drove her home. It turned out that she was visiting her parents who lived in a little village called Worplesdon, a last-minute trip as her father was unwell and her mother needed some help looking after him and running errands. We pulled up to a quaint stone cottage with a thatched roof and I helped Zoe to the door, her arm over my shoulders as she hopped along. We reached the door set in a stone archway and she pushed it open.

"Would you like to come in?" she said. "I owe you a cup of tea at least."

"Thanks, but I should think about heading back to base. Perhaps some other time?"

"I would like that," she said, and we exchanged details.

"Make sure you get that ankle checked over ASAP, soldier," I said with comedic sternness.

"Roger that," she replied. "Don't want to get into my hero's bad books." She kissed me on the cheek and hopped off into the house.

I was her hero.

It had been a rough ten years, but it felt like we were on the brink of closing that chapter. It put a spring in my step as I strolled by the riverside.

The pages of my old pocket map were dog-eared and creased. I leafed through, trying to find my location. Once I had the right page, I gazed around to get my bearings. On my map the river Thames was a bright blue line roaming through the city. In the real world it was filthy brown, uninviting and possibly the source of the next national biohazard. From where I was standing, I could see several of London's famous landmarks and was able to orientate myself. The Big Ben tower peaking over the roofline behind me. The City of London straight ahead, its fantastically shaped and outrageously named buildings forming the unmistakeable skyline; The Cheese Grater, The Walkie-Talkie, The Gherkin. Across the river to the right, the rusty remains of The London Eye, and The Shard piercing the sky behind, once western Europe's tallest building. With London's falling from grace as the financial capital of the world, I wondered what all these buildings were used for. High-end real estate perhaps. Or vacant and accumulating cobwebs. The Tower of London was around two miles east along the river, and was a reasonable target for a stroll, before turning back for lunch.

But I didn't get that far.

Three hundred metres into my walk I approached Waterloo Bridge. Beneath it was a congregation of around thirty homeless men spanning various ages, all huddled together in smaller groups. One group had a bottle of clear liquid that was being swigged and passed around, another played a makeshift game using pebbles and twigs. One man had a battered old guitar and strummed a melancholy tune that fitted the ambiance perfectly, along with the strong smell of urine and the fits of unhealthy coughing. It was an intimidating sight, but they were minding their own business and not causing any trouble. Regardless, I thought I'd quicken my pace. The next moment, a younger man from one of the groups looked up. His arm drifted upward with an outstretched index finger pointing at me. He got to his feet. A chill ran down my spine. I stopped in my tracks as more men stood and glared in my direction. Then I noticed their faces, not hostile, but full of fear and panic.

"They're coming! Run!"

Pandemonium ensued as dishevelled men in ragged clothes darted in all directions, at the same time as three black riot vans sped past me and screeched to a halt under the bridge. A small army of police officers piled out of the vans, dressed fully in black, wearing gas masks and armed with non-lethal shotguns. *Pop, Pop, Pop,* sounds filled the air as rubber bullets flew towards their fleeing targets. Five of the youngest men had sprinted clear, but the older, slower ones were taking rounds to the back as they fled, crippling over in agony. The policewomen were immediately upon them, cable-tying their wrists behind their backs and dragging them in to the back of the vans. A tear gas grenade detonated among a group of ten that had remained where they were, either asleep, or too old, or drunk, to move. White smoke billowed out and engulfed the poor men who sat coughing up their lungs. It seemed entirely unnecessary. One of the men, an elderly gentleman with a bushy grey beard and bare feet, stood to move himself from the noxious cloud, hands raised above his head.

Pop!

A rubber bullet hit him square in the face. He fell backwards cracking his head on the corner of a stone step, splitting his skull and leaking red fluid over the floor.

"He was unarmed! He had surrendered!" It jumped out my mouth before I had time to think.

The firing officer spun on her heels and pointed her weapon at me, looking me up and down, sizing up the threat. She took one step toward me. "Scram." The sound was muffled through her gas mask, but the instruction was clear.

I retreated a few steps, knowing I was leaving casualties behind, but also knowing I had no choice. I turned and sprinted back to the cordoned area, screams and wails echoing out from under the bridge behind me. I slowed to a stop by the riverside, out of sight of security while my heart rate returned to normal. I had heard of that sort of thing happening, but never seen it with my own eyes. Homeless men being rounded up, kidnapped, ready to be put to work. I wondered what sort of work a bunch of ailing vagrants would be useful for. But then, perhaps I was better off not knowing. It made me realise, having the country return to normal was going to be like turning an oil tanker, so much momentum to overcome.

That's assuming the captain agreed with the new course heading.

CHAPTER 18

Three down, Infinitely Small, thirteen letters... Infinitesimal.

The riverside gardens weren't such a bad place to pass the time after all. I had managed to complete two crosswords, which I was chuffed about as there was usually at least one clue I didn't know the answer to. *Capital city of Suriname.* You either knew it or you didn't. There was no educated guessing. But with two finished I was feeling accomplished. I was also feeling incredibly lucky. On reflection, I could easily have gotten caught up in the events at Waterloo Bridge. Getting hauled away in a meat wagon would complicate Zoe's big day, and a rubber bullet to the face would be preferable to the wrath that would follow. So as strongly as I felt about the injustice of the situation, I decided I'd keep that little episode to myself.

16:00 hit so I made my way back to the office building. A fleet of black cars was lined up out front. Inside, a group of around twenty women stood around chatting. I only recognised Zoe, Alvina, and a woman who I assumed was Alvina's righthand-woman, Chief Advisor, or something similar, as I often saw them standing together on TV. Some of the women were shaking hands and kissing each other on the cheek. Zoe's team members and their partners of being introduced perhaps. Over to the side against the wall, two men sat on a bench, attempting to avoid eye contact with anyone. Also probably team member's partners. I joined the men and sat down with a nod and a smile. I caught Zoe's eye and gave her a wave. She didn't wave back. She was obviously not happy and not joining in the conversation. I had a moment of panic as my brain rushed to explore possibilities of what I could have done wrong. I had arrived after the others, but I was bang on the time I was told. There was no way that she could have found out about the incident at the bridge. Even if she had, I wasn't sure what I should have done differently.

"Listen up everyone." Alvina's advisor silenced the room with a loud clap. "I think that's everyone present. Vehicles are outside to take you to Downing Street. Refreshments will be served on arrival before moving through to the press conference auditorium. Please make your way out of the building."

We all shuffled towards the open door, and I weaved my way through the gathering to Zoe. I took a deep breath, "Everything ok?"

"No," was all I got from her. Then, "Not here."

We sat in silence for the duration of the ludicrously short drive, before pulling up to the famous black door of number 10 Downing Street. The manic clicks and flashes of photographer's cameras were disorientating as we moved from the car to inside. It took me by surprise, and I prayed I didn't make it on to the front pages of any newspapers looking like a deer in highlights. We were escorted through the hallways and corridors of the Prime Minister's residence, as ornate and palatial as you would imagine. Luxurious patterned carpets covered the floor, oil paintings in ornamental gold frames covered the wall, door mouldings and ceiling cornices were elaborately decorative. A combination of wealth and antiquity oozed from every corner. We were offered smoked salmon blinis and champagne. I stayed clear after the previous night, and I wasn't a smoked salmon fan, but wondered how they were able to source that kind of thing so easily when the rest of the country was eating pasta day in day out.

Only once we had made through to the press

conference room, with the buzz of scores of other people stood around talking, did Zoe speak. Her words gushed out like water from a drainpipe.

"These people do not know what the hell they are doing. Reckless, incompetent idiots. We have qualified medics comfortable with putting people's lives at risk. How can I put my name to this? It's... it's..."

"Whoa there. Slow down. Take a breath. What's going on? I thought we were all good with the cure," I said.

"We are. Sort of."

"What does 'sort of' mean?"

"It works, that much is clear, but the safety profile in humans was... inconclusive."

I knew it! But I played dumb. "Inconclusive?"

"Yes."

"Zoe, I'll be honest, you're going to have to spell this out for me simply."

"The cure is a form of gene therapy. It uses a type of programmed virus that enters cells and repairs the defective gene sequence."

"Ok..."

"In some cases, the body's immune system sees the virus as a foreign threat and attacks it. This can lead to inflammation of bodily organs, and worst case, complete organ failure."

"I see."

"In the last trial we had three thousand women enrolled. We saw two hundred and fifty-two cases of major organ related problems, heart inflammation, loss of kidney function. Six of them died. Some subjects had underlying health issues before they enrolled, plus you should randomly expect some new cases in that size of population. There may be no causal link between the treatment and what we are seeing, but..."

"But you can't be sure."

"Exactly. Which is why we have always said we would implement with a small pilot and then go district by district, building confidence as we go and ensure there is no causal link. But this lot from Altior have turned around today and want to go nationally from the outset. They are also suggesting we bury any noise of side effects and make treatment compulsory. Whatever happened to informed consent for god's sake! You can't inject an entire country with an experimental medicine that has unproven safety. They could be sentencing millions of women to death, and that's before we consider any other issues not picked up in the trial that might arise at national scale." She was flustered. "I shouldn't be telling you all this. Forget it, I'm sorry."

"No, I'm pleased you did," I said. "I want you to be able to talk to me about these things. You are the expert and if they are not listening to your concerns then that's a serious problem. What are you going to do?"

"It's going to take them at least six weeks to set up manufacturing, testing and distribution of the first batches of product, plus they need to set up the treatment centres. I'm going to have to work at convincing them to change their mind, even if they go ahead with the announcement today. I have some time."

A voice boomed over the audio system. "Please take your seats. Broadcast will begin in ten minutes."

We moved to our place in the front row, although Zoe would be spending most of the time on stage answering questions. The platform in front was raised two feet off the ground, with a large Union Jack forming the backdrop. A sound engineer fiddled with the microphones on a podium in the centre, flanked by podiums either side. Zoe left her bag on her chair and took up her place on the stage. I was nervous for her, knowing how she felt about the roll out plans. Her professional integrity was important to her and the thought of her having to lie on stage was unthinkable. But I was happy that she had confided in me. She had let her guard down, a rare moment of vulnerability, of not being in control. I knew she regretted it, but in those few moments she told me more about her work than she had ever done before. It meant something. It meant that despite all else, when the chips were down, she still trusted me.

The auditorium lights lowered. Behind me the persistent chatter fell to a whisper, and then to silence. The dimly lit but bright-eyed faces of a hundred audience members all looked forward in anticipation. The air was filled with an electric buzz, like everyone knew something historic was about to happen. Zoe was already standing behind the lefthand podium with another woman on the right. The name plate in front of the stranger said, Dr Olivia Sharp. *Olivia from Altior!* She had an upturned pointed nose the shape of a tortilla chip. Thin lips in dark lipstick drew an expressionless line across her face. Thick-lensed glasses magnified squinty eyes and her blonde hair was just long enough to be pulled back in a ponytail. Everything about her was cold and edgy, almost two dimensional. Her angular geometry was in stark contrast standing next to Zoe's rounded beauty. Her surname was apt. Alvina walked in from the right of the stage and took the centre position. She was dressed for the occasion. A pink blouse with a huge, ruffled collar and matching shoes. Next to Alvina, Zoe & Olivia, in their black suits, vanished into nothingness.

"Good evening," Alvina began. "The spot upon which I am standing is incredibly familiar to me. I stand here month after month, year after year, delivering news I'd rather not deliver. Over the course of my long service to this country, I have come to dread standing on this spot. However, tonight, that changes." A dramatic pause. "Last Saturday, I mentioned the work Professor Zoe Wilson has been conducting to rid us of The Gaia. I am pleased to welcome Professor Wilson here in person this evening. I am also announcing this evening a new strategic alliance with a specially selected outsourcing partner, named Altior, and we are lucky to be joined by the head of this organisation, Dr Olivia Sharp. Altior will be instrumental in the next phase of what I am about to tell you." A wave of excited whispering rose and fell. "I am going to cut to the chase. This week saw the reporting of the phase three clinical trial for the treatment that Professor Wilson has developed. I am pleased to tell you that the trial was a resounding success. There were zero cases of Cyclopia in the three thousand pregnant women that took part in the trial. Professor Zoe Wilson has done it!"

A rapturous applause filled the room as everyone rose to their feet. Whistles, cheers, tears. Some people hugged their neighbours. Some stood wide-mouthed in disbelief. It was Zoe's moment. The summit of her struggle. The finish line of her relentless slog. The final round in her battle against all the odds.

She wasn't enjoying it one bit.

"Thank you. Thank you, everyone," Alvina attempted to quieten the celebrations. "I don't want to take any more of the limelight, so I will open the floor to questions."

One hundred hands shot in the air, each stretching higher than the next trying to get attention, waving on tiptoes. A microphone was handed to a lady in the front row who snatched it eagerly.

"A question for Professor Wilson. Can you tell us more about what this treatment is, how it works, and why this one worked when others have failed?"

"We have developed a sophisticated gene editing retrovirus that is able to repair the genetic defect that causes The Gaia. Previous attempts have failed because the treatment effects were negated by further genetic mutations. With this latest approach, as well as repairing the defective gene, the retrovirus programs the host's cells to produce further copies of itself. This creates an ongoing reparative process long after the initial administration."

"So, you're saying that we would be permanently infected with a virus? That doesn't sound safe." A low murmur spread across the room.

"We expect the continued mutation process to reduce over time, and therefore the activity of the retrovirus should also reduce. Your body is full of dormant viruses already so it's nothing that should cause concern. Instead of thinking of it as a viral infection, consider it a boosted immune system," Zoe was calm and composed. The lady seemed satisfied and sat down. I beamed, bursting with pride, gazing around to gauge the mood in the room. She was doing brilliantly. So far so good. The microphone passed to the next lady.

"Professor Wilson, what can we expect after taking the cure? How will it be given and are there any side effects?"

"Unlike the virus that caused The Gaia, the treatment virus is not transmissible from human to human, so we will need to treat all women on an individual basis. This means a single injection in the upper arm." She paused; I could tell she was choosing her words carefully. Her fists clenched, pushing the blood from her knuckles. "There will be a brief period of recovery, around a week, while the treatment gets to work, perhaps a bit longer for some. Full effect should be achieved by three months." Another pause as her eyes momentarily flicked in Oliva's direction. "Most women in the trial saw no long-term complications."

I could tell how agonising that was for her. What she had said was factually correct but meaningless in the context of the question asked. Even I knew 'most' meant just more than half. It could mean forty-nine percent of them dropped dead. But the woman asking the question seemed happy with the response and Oliva gave a nod indicating her contentment.

The next question came. "How quickly will this be given and what if someone doesn't want the injection?"

"I'll take this one," Olivia jumped in, her tone potent and assertive. "I'm sure most people would agree that freeing ourselves from the clutches of The Gaia is the country's top priority, but we do recognise that there may be some pockets of reluctance. We will monitor take up and if necessary, look at ways in which people may need to be… incentivised." Her words were menacing, nothing like Zoe's informed reassurance. I saw Zoe fidget, shifting her weight from foot to foot and pulling at the sleeves of her blazer. "As for how quickly, having known Professor Wilson's great confidence in this project, we have been planning for success and have been manufacturing in anticipation of today's announcement. We already have significant stockpiles that are ready to be sent to distribution centres across the districts. We need a few more days to finalise the treatment centres but hope to be administering first doses as soon as this coming Monday. The first wave of women should start to see invitations coming through within the next few days."

Judging by the delayed expression on her face, it took a moment for Zoe to register what Olivia had said. Then it hit, her face dropping into astonished disbelief before morphing in to burning anger. The jaw muscles below her ears bulged to golf balls. The wild-eyed glare she gave Olivia should have killed her where she stood. It moved to Alvina, and back to Olivia, who returned a smug smile.

"Ok thank you everyone," Alvina said, obviously sensing the tension and bringing the questioning to a close. "I think we'll leave it there for this evening. Let's close by giving a huge round of applause to these fantastic ladies."

The clapping and whooping were deafening but the combatants on stage seemed oblivious and were immersed in trying to murder each other with angry scowls. Olivia relented first and turned to exit the stage and Zoe followed in her footsteps like a woman possessed. I chased after.

"What do you think you are doing?" Zoe yelled once off stage, grabbing Olivia by the shoulder, and spinning her around.

"Please take your hands off me," Olivia said as she pushed Zoe away. "I'm doing what has been agreed, nothing more." Her voice was calm and controlled.

"I did NOT agree to this."

"These decisions have moved above your paygrade," Olivia said with a sneer.

"How can you think this is a good idea? You are a doctor for heaven's sake. You swore an oath, remember? First, do no harm!" Specks of salvia flew from her mouth as she spat the words.

"Oh, don't be so naïve, Zoe," Olivia started to become frustrated. "That only works at an individual level. You cannot apply that principle to an entire country of millions of people. Statistics forbid it. Give everyone in the country a paracetamol and fifty thousand people will react badly. It's what happens at scale."

"You could kill millions of women! And you just stood on that stage and made it sound like I was ok with it. I cannot put my name to this. I will not."

"In that case it's lucky you are no longer part of this equation."

"Bitch!"

Olivia's glasses flew across the room as Zoe's open hand smacked across her cheek. I stepped forward and took hold of Zoe's shoulders to protect her, and restrain her.

Olivia spun around, clutching at her face. Her short ponytail had popped out from the impact, leaving a messy crop of scarecrow-like hair falling just below her jawline. She straightened her glasses as she picked them up. "You need to be more careful Zoe," she said as she swaggered off. "You have served your purpose."

CHAPTER 19

Trees flashed past causing a horizontal blur of streaked green, the *clickety-clack* of the homeward bound train providing enough background noise for Zoe to feel comfortable talking in a low whisper. She had stormed out of Downing Street after the altercation with Olivia Sharp, so we missed whatever celebrations Alvina had in store. I wasn't looking forward to that part anyway. We sat opposite each other in a bay of four seats, keeping an eye out in both directions. We had the carriage to ourselves, and it needed to stay that way. Once Zoe started talking it flooded out in torrents: Olivia's meddling in Zoe's project and the pressure she had been applying for Zoe to work faster. Corners being cut, clinical trials months shorter than they should have been. Minimal subject screening and no long-term safety follow-up.

"The whole study is a farce," she said. "We know it works on some level. I stand by that. But we know barely anything about the people we injected it into, what factors might impact treatment, and what's happening to the poor sods now. For all we know, every single one could have dropped down dead." She massaged her temples with a grimace.

I bit my lip, procrastinating over my words. "I'm a bit... surprised in what you are saying, Zoe. You have always been so... dedicated and... honest. How could you let this happen?"

Her head snapped up with a stunned expression which immediately softened. "They have leverage. You have no idea how deep this goes."

"What sort of leverage?"

"You. The kids. They said they would take you away from me if I didn't comply."

"They can't do that."

"They have people everywhere. The judiciary, the police. You know it doesn't take much to lock a man up for good. Jesus Christ, the schools are teaching children to spy on their parents. We need to be careful around Cora, you especially."

I thought back to the interview at the police station. How I was nailed to the wall, yet they let me go, despite all the evidence that was piling up against me. They had more than enough to convince themselves if that was what they wanted. That pin badge DCI Steele was wearing. *Altior*. It all fell into place. I *was* their leverage. The question was, was I still needed? Redundancy was not a good place to be in a world where the dead wood was piled up and burned.

You have served your purpose.

That feeling of helplessness began to creep back over me, like a cloak of weakness, deflecting the accountability, strengthening the apathy. There was nothing that I, a lonesome man, could do to fight back against an oppressive regime of government, police and this Altior, whoever they were. It was ridiculous to try, or even think it. I raised my eyes from the ground to look at Zoe, dejected, defeated. The pinnacle of her life's work in tatters. Her hard-built reputation about to be eviscerated.

"I feel so damn stupid!" Zoe shouted, stamping her foot, and punching the wall. I popped up like a meerkat, checking the carriage, but we were still alone.

"Shh," I said. "Don't talk like that. This is not your fault."

"Yes, it is," she said. "Something could have been done about it if I had raised concerns earlier. But I let it get too far, and now it's hopeless. I've played right into their hands and there is nothing we can do." She looked up with a sudden flash of urgency. "We need to take the kids and get away. Somewhere in the countryside where we can hide. Somewhere we won't be found."

I had never seen her that way, so defeatist, prepared to throw the towel in and run away from it all. She never accepted no as an answer to anything. She would debate until she was blue in the face, until her interlocutor bowed under the pressure and was forced into submission. That was who she was, and I loved her for that. I didn't like this new version of Zoe. She sounded so weak, so passive. She sounded like... me. I tore off the cloak, took hold of her hands and stared her in the eyes.

"No," I said. "You said we have time."

"Weren't you listening? They are starting on Monday."

"So, that's time. We will find a way through this."

She looked at me, analysing. "You've changed," she said.

"You could say I've had an epiphany. I'm here for you now."

"It's great to have you back," she said with a soft smile.

A full moon beamed a white glow that illuminated our treacherous journey down the cul-de-sac. I slipped into a pothole almost turning my ankle.

"Careful, clumsy, or *I'll* be needing to carry *you* home," Zoe said.

We both laughed.

We were almost at the house when bright lights shone from behind us, casting two long humanoid shadows on the road in front. We stepped to the side and let the police car move past, then stood rooted to the spot when we saw it pull up to our house. We weighed up the options. Going on the run and leaving two young children alone in bed wasn't a reasonable one. Should Zoe go alone? Or I go alone? No, we'd go and deal with whatever was thrown at us together. I led the way, up straight, shoulders back. Two police officers were waiting outside our front door.

"Can I help you?" I said.

"Mr Wilson?" said one of the officers.

"That's right."

"May we come in?"

I thought of the gun in the loft. *How quickly can I get to it if needed?*

"Mr Wilson?"

"Yes, sorry, sure," I said.

The threat evaluation instinct kicked into action as we entered the kitchen. *Two small females. No firearms. No body armour. Standard issue cuffs and baton.* I could take them both barehanded if it came to it, but judging by the equipment they were carrying, they weren't gunning for a fight. Regardless, I scanned the area searching for potential weapons, just in case. *Knife on the draining board. Scissors on the dresser.*

"May we sit down?"

"Of course," I said.

The four of us sat down at the kitchen table and the officers removed their black domed hats. Their expressions were blank, they weren't giving anything away.

"My name is Sergeant Watkins, and this is Constable Adebayo." Both were wearing standard bobby on the beat uniform, black shoes and trousers, white shirt, and a utility vest with its multitude of pockets and gadgets hanging off it. Adebayo had short, tightly curled black hair, long eyelashes, and a fit, athletic build. Watkins wore golden blonde hair up in a bun with long locks falling to frame her face, softening a heavy jawline. She was more rounded, in a mumsy kind of way, the sort of person you'd send to break unwelcome news. "We have something that's going to be difficult for you to hear," Watkins said.

I knew it. Time slowed as my mind went into overdrive, searching for what it could be. But I had no idea.

"It's about your daughter, Grace. I'm afraid she was found dead in hospital this evening. She has taken her own life."

I laughed. "I'm sorry but that's impossible. I saw Grace yesterday and she was the happiest I've seen her in years. She was talking all about what she wanted from her future, there is no way she would do that. There must have been a mistake."

"I know it's difficult, but the body matches Grace's description, and she was wearing her hospital ID tag around her wrist," Adebayo said.

"But... I don't understand... she seemed so happy." My brain was beginning to believe it was possible, but my heart was fighting back, refusing to accept that Grace would do that. I knew better than most what's possible when it feels like you have reached the end of the road, but Grace was not there, I was sure of it. I looked across to Zoe, who sat staring blankly ahead.

"It's not uncommon," Watkins said. "We often find that families of suicide victims are shocked because it comes unexpectedly. People who have taken their own life can come across perfectly happy moments before. It usually means they have been planning it. They have come to terms with what they are going to do and see it as a way of escaping whatever difficulties they are dealing with. It can mark the difference between someone who might react in a crisis, or someone that might do it as a cry for help." My cheeks flushed hot red. I saw Zoe's fingers curl into a tight ball.

"How did she do it?" Not that I wanted to know. I just wanted to be sure she didn't suffer.

"She was found in the shower with a severed femoral artery. She would have passed away within minutes. We are investigating how she got hold of the knife. It shouldn't have been allowed on the ward."

I wanted to vomit as a bottomless chasm of darkness cracked open beneath my chair. I tumbled down, spinning and turning, dizzy with all the emotions that were fighting for dominance. Denial, sadness, guilt, anger. Mostly anger. Angry at myself for letting her do it. I thought of my parting words. *I'll come back tomorrow.*

I left her. No, I abandoned her, when she was at her most vulnerable. What kind of father does that? I should have stayed with her. I looked across to Zoe for something, I don't know what, but she was good at fixing things, there must have been something she could do. She remained focused on a blank patch of wall, with unblinking eyes. I wasn't sure she had even heard anything that had been said.

"Zoe?" I said.

She turned to face me. "Make them go."

I didn't have to do anything. Watkins began speaking. "I know it must be a terrible shock. We will leave you in peace. When you are ready, the hospital has kept hold of Grace's belongings for you to collect." With that they stood up, replaced their hats and let themselves out, leaving Zoe and I sat hollow and wordless. Something had fractured inside Zoe. She had ceased to function.

"Zoe?" I said, trying to bring her back. "Zoe?"

"This is all my fault," she said.

"Don't be silly. It's more my fault than yours. I'm the one that left her alone in the hospital."

"You don't understand. It could have been over with, years ago."

"What could?"

"The Gaia. Grace didn't have to go through any of this."

"Zoe, what are you talking about?"

"You remember when I was assisting the group at Cambridge, working with the team from Paris University?"

"Yes. That was what, six years ago?"

"Seven. Alvina came to me with that offer I couldn't refuse. Lead the development of the new approach suggested by the team in Chicago, in return for a Professorship at Kent. An ambitious young researcher being approached by the Prime Minister with a promotion and an opportunity to be the one who saves the country."

"I don't think anyone would think badly of you for taking that."

"What about if I knew that the Cambridge project would be terminated as a result? We were so close. Maybe twelve months from success. Alvina sold the Chicago route as being cheaper. One that we had all the equipment for on campus. One that meant we wouldn't be forever indebted to the French. But I could tell there was something else behind it. They wanted the Cambridge project shut down. The academic community should have stuck together, our collective brainpower focused on the objective. But I put my career over the wellbeing of the country and probably set us back five years while we started from scratch."

"So, this could have all been over and done with five years ago?" I thought of all the pain and suffering the last five years of The Gaia had caused.

Zoe looked sad and ashamed. "Yes."

My head started to spin. "Anything else I should know?"

Zoe paused. "I'm beginning to doubt that it's the cure Altior has been stockpiling."

"Why?" I said.

"The treatment I developed has a two-week shelf-life and needs to be stored below minus twenty degrees. I can't see how it's possible to manufacture and store significant amounts for a prolonged period of time. It's another part of the reason we chose the phased approach. You make it and use it right away."

"So, what is it they have made?"

"I have no idea. But we need to find out before they start injecting it into people."

It was a question for another day. By the time we were in bed, the full gravity of Grace's untimely departure had hit, and all the mixed emotions made way for deepest sadness. I tried to remember all the joy and positivity she brought us. All the great lessons I had learned from a wonderful girl who was wise beyond her years. But all I could think about was what torment must have driven her to do such a thing. She must have been so unhappy, and it broke my heart that she didn't feel able to talk about it. I hoped that one day I could look back fondly and reminisce on our time together with a smile on my face, but that would take time. I held my wife in bed and let the grief overcome me.

CHAPTER 20

Thursday 7th June 2063

I had reached one hundred percent certainty that there was foul play at work. Who were the puppets and who were their masters was not clear, but somebody somewhere was pulling the strings. Best case was that they were exploiting The Gaia for their own twisted agenda. Worst case was something much more sinister. These people, whomever they might be, were responsible for unimaginable pain and suffering — for what Zach and other boys like him went through on a daily basis, for indoctrinating Cora and her peers into their cult. For putting Zoe under pressure, forcing her to compromise her professional integrity. And for the premature death of Grace, and nearly myself. There would be countless other families with similar stories. I was filled with an unrelenting intent to get even. Someone was going to pay.

Zach bounded down the stairs, full of the joys of life after his chat with Leeroy. He had removed his bandage and proudly displayed his stitched-up wound. The swelling around his eye had reduced, but the bruise had turned an even deeper purple. I didn't have the heart to bring him down from his lofty mood. Zoe and I had agreed not to tell the kids about Grace before school as they wouldn't be able to concentrate. We'd put our bravest faces on until the time was right.

Once they had left, Zoe suggested we go for a walk. We headed out of the cul-de-sac and down a narrow alley towards the river. At the end of the alley was a field of knee-high grass and we waded our way through, sending a kaleidoscope of butterflies fluttering into the cloudless blue sky. Electricity pylons towered overhead like giant steel robots, ivy creeping up and wrapping itself intrusively around their legs. Other than the low buzz of power cables, the gentle trickle of flowing water and the distant sound of birdsong, it was beautifully quiet. No other person within a quarter of a mile. A pair of ducks waddled off as we sat down by the river.

"We need a sample of whatever it is they have stockpiled. I can analyse it at the lab," Zoe said.

"Oh easy-peasy. I'll call up my new best friend Alvina and ask her," I replied.

"Don't be facetious. I'm being serious."

"I know. It's just you make it sound so straightforward. Where would they be storing it?"

"Their main pharmaceutical facility is in D20, near the old airport at Gatwick, so that would be a good place to start. How to get in, I have no idea."

"That's my area of expertise. I'm going to need some help, but I've got an idea. I know someone that won't be able to refuse."

"Who?"

"That's above your paygrade," I said in a voice, imitating Olivia Sharp.

"*You're* not too big for a slap you know?" Zoe said with a raised hand and a wry smile.

I leant away in faux fear. "I'll tell you, just not yet."

"We don't have much time."

"I know, I'll pay my contact a visit this afternoon and will drive over to D20 tonight. See if I can find a way in. What am I looking for?"

"It should be a small glass vial with a silver lid. About the same size as the pots you use for... you know."

"Yes, yes ok."

"It'll be kept in a freezer. But who knows what you might face when you get inside the compound."

We sat in silence for a moment, letting the sun warm our backs, basking in the tranquillity.

"Do you think Grace would have been in pain?" I asked.

"Not beyond the initial injury. Exsanguination should be a painless way to go, especially if quick."

"I wish she had said something. I hate the way she had to go through that alone."

"She was a strong-willed girl. I'm sure she thought she was doing the right thing, in her own head. As you said, she didn't go feeling sad."

Another moment of silence.

"You know I've killed people?" I said.

"Jack, I don't want to talk about that."

"It's important. It was my job. I've killed lots of people. Bad people, although admittedly that depends on your perspective."

"What's the point of this morbid conversation?"

"I killed lots of people, but never in anger. Each time I was in complete control. Composed and emotionless. It was never personal."

"And?"

"If I ever get close to the people responsible for Grace's death, that might change."

Zoe laughed. "If you're thinking of going on a Hollywood-style rampage of bloody vengeance then you can think again. We're talking about real people here and cold-blooded murder is not going to bring Grace back. And who are you talking about specifically? Olivia Sharp, Alvina, the whole Altior organisation, all of the government? There are countless people involved in countless decisions. Most of them are untouchable. And if you killed any one of them, you would be very dead very quickly."

I felt stupid. But the thought didn't go away. "Shall we get to it then?" I said.

"Yes. I'll sort the kids out this afternoon and start planning for the funeral. And I'll go to the lab this morning to use the computer and see what information I can get about the facility. You go *see your contact*."

"Don't make fun."

"I'm not. I'm pleased you're feeling better."

Any movements that followed needed to be untraceable. Cars were easy to identify so I stopped back at home to pick up my bike, and a few other items I would need for what came next. My old blue mountain bike hadn't been ridden in a while. The tyres were flat but held air when inflated. A drop of oil loosened up the rusty chain. I dusted off the saddle, slung my rucksack on to my back, and peddled off towards my destination.

The most direct route was a mile and a half along the main road, but I took a more convoluted route, around the park and down several residential streets, so it would be more difficult to place me at the location in case the afternoon didn't go as planned. After twenty-five minutes of steady peddling, I arrived at an apartment block, an L-shaped, three-storey building of dark brown brickwork and large single-glazed windows. Outside, wheelie bins overflowed to the point of being buried and a mattress with ominous brown and yellow stains was propped up against the wall. I chained my bike to a drainpipe that would come off the wall with a strong gust of wind but would provide an obstacle too cumbersome to be dragged along by a potential thief. I weaved my way across an expanse of dog mess, like I was avoiding landmines in a battlefield, until I reached the stairwell to the second and third storeys in the interior corner of the L. A high-pitched shrill of a baby crying echoed off the narrow walls, followed by the unmistakable shouting and banging of a domestic bust up behind one of the doors. On the third floor I reached the apartment I was looking for. Readying myself, I knocked on the cracked glass.

Nothing.

I knocked harder.

"Go away." A voice came from inside.

"Open the door before I kick it in," I said through the letterbox.

A long moment of rustling and banging before the sound of a chain sliding across the back of the door. It opened two inches and a dozy eye peered through the gap.

"Hello Logan," I said.

"J-J-Jack. What do you want? Grace isn't… isn't here. I thought she was… with you."

"It's you I want to speak to."

"Me? W-what for?"

"Open the door and you'll find out. It's rude to keep guests standing on the doorstep."

"S-s-sorry but I can't let you in. It's not a good time."

I reached into my rucksack, pulled out the Desert Eagle handgun and held it an inch away from the eye peering through the gap. "Open the fucking door."

CHAPTER 21

I hadn't had time to think through how I was going to play it. My rampage of bloody vengeance, as Zoe so eloquently put it, could begin at the door in front of me. Afterall, it was the direct actions of Logan that put Grace in hospital. But that would be counterproductive. There were more important things at stake and Logan could be useful. The problem was I didn't know him well enough to predict how he might respond to different persuasive tactics. Good Cop charm? Grieving Father guilt trip? A Violent Headcase rough-up worked on everyone, but a willing accomplice is always more effective than one recruited under duress. The slight complication was shoving a gun in his face had already narrowed my options. I decide to go with option three but begin a few notches down.

The door closed as the chain was released and opened again to reveal the man my daughter fell in love with. I couldn't for the life of me fathom why. Logan Duggen was asymmetrical in every respect. He had a mashed pudding face that had no discernible form, drooping eyes that were too far apart and half covered by his eyelids, a wonky dumpling nose, and gnarled ears, one higher than the other. A ridiculous hairstyle saw his lank black mop swept over to one side, and he couldn't even stand up straight, one shoulder higher than the other. He wore a baggy black t-shirt and dirty denim jeans. He stumbled backward as I approached, gun lowered but primed for action. I looked him up and down with disgust. "What did Grace ever see in you?"

"Did? Is... is she leaving me?" Logan reversed his

way down the hall into the lounge, both hands reaching for the walls to steady his backward steps. It was a disgraceful pigsty of a room that contained minimal furniture but with the empty space more than filled with junk of every kind. Natural light was blocked by a bed sheet nailed to the wall in place of curtains. Piles of filthy crockery were stacked up like precarious cairn rocks. A shadeless pendant lightbulb illuminated the room. I covered my nose with my sleeve to restrict the flow of the dank and musty air, cheesy, like athlete's foot.

"Sit," I said, pointing the gun at the armchair. The sofa was shiny with grime. I decided to stay standing. "How can you live like this?"

"Grace usually keeps it tidy, but she hasn't been home for days. Where is she?"

"Never mind that. I would like to know why you thought you could get her pregnant against her wishes."

"That's not what happened. We both want to have a baby. She told me." He fidgeted in the seat.

"That's your one chance of getting away with lying to me, Logan. Next time earns you a bullet." I pointed the gun at his knee.

"Ok, ok. Please, don't hurt me."

"Why did you get her pregnant against her wishes?" I repeated, this time more forcefully.

"She had been acting strangely and I was scared she was going to leave. If we had a baby together then it would give her a reason to stay."

"Look around, you imbecile. You're not capable of tying a shoelace, never mind raising a child. If Grace did end up having that baby, she would have been back home with us faster than you brush your rotten teeth." I was turning up the heat.

"We would —"

"Shut up."

"But Grace —"

"I said shut it. Grace is dead. She killed herself because of your idiotic selfishness. How does that make you feel? Because it makes me angry and I'm in the mood to take it out on someone. Stand up." Logan stood. I grabbed his shirt and slammed him against the wall. "You picked the wrong girl to manipulate into your sick little fantasy. Two things you should know about me, I hold a grudge forever and I always get even."

"Please... it's not like that... I loved Grace."

I hit maximum effort, screaming in his face, pressing the gun into his forehead. "Do not say that name with your filthy mouth!" A dark wet patch emerged in Logan's crotch and spread down the inside of his leg until a pool formed under his feet. "Turn around. I can't stand to look at your face. You disgust me." His face was squashed against the wall, gun pushed hard into the back of his skull. "Goodnight Logan."

"Please... please don't... kill me. I'll do anything. Please..." His words were punctuated by deep sobs.

"What use do I have for a blubbering little weasel like you?"

"I don't know. But I'll do anything you say. I promise."

I lowered the gun. "Sit back down." He was a snivelling wreck. It was harsh, but necessary. If you want to make someone do something by force, and mould them into something of use, you must first destroy them. Anything less and they will betray you at the first opportunity, or flee. Besides, I kind of enjoyed it.

Phase two was to reforge, to build the bond of trust so that they were on the right side. I made an obvious effort to assess him as he sat. "Do you work out?"

"No... not really. I mean, when I go to work, I have to lift some heavy stuff but..."

"I can tell. You have a good physique." I paused. "Can you run?"

"Yes sir, a bit."

"Excellent. I do have this one project that you might be able to help me with. I can't tell you much about it, for both of our safety, but essentially, I need to acquire something that might be heavily guarded."

"Steal something you mean?"

"It's not really stealing. And it's for a good cause. You'll just have to take my word for it."

"I don't know. It sounds dangerous."

"Have it your way." I leant forward to stand up.

"No, no, please. I'll do it."

"Good. But you should know, any funny business could get us both killed. So, I need to be sure you are on my team, and you need to bring your A game. Can you do that?"

"Yes sir."

"I believe you can too. Just to be clear, you and I will *never* be even. But do this for me and it will be enough to keep you alive."

"Yes sir."

"Good."

"Do you have a car?"

"My mum has a car, but… umm… she doesn't really use it. I borrow that sometimes."

"Can you get it tonight?"

"Yes sir."

"Pick me up from my place at ten o'clock. Wear dark clothes and a hat."

He repeated. "Ten o'clock. Your house. Dark clothes."

"And a hat."

"And a hat, got it."

"Don't be late. And not a word to anyone." With that, I left him to it. He had recovered surprisingly well from his prior ordeal to the point of enthusiasm. It's remarkable what showing a little faith and confidence in someone can do. Plus, now he had a purpose.

Back at the house I found Zoe sat at the kitchen table with print outs of satellite maps strewn all over.

"So, how did you get on?" she said.

"All good. I'm being picked up later this evening."

"Are you going to tell me who it is?"

I hesitated. "It's Logan."

"Jesus Christ Jack, you didn't hurt him, did you?"

"Not a cut or bruise on him, I swear." I omitted the potential for severe mental trauma.

"Are you sure it's a good idea? You never liked him and now, you know..."

"It's fine. Most important thing is having someone I can trust, and I'm one hundred percent confident he'll keep his mouth shut and do as he's told."

"Ok, if you are sure."

"I am. How are you getting on here?" I sat down next to Zoe.

"Nothing came up in the location when I searched for Altior, but they make most of the medicines we have under a company name of Altronia Pharmaceuticals, so that's what you are looking for. The map shows the site to have eight large buildings. It has a main road at the front, a foot path down the side and a train track to the rear that links it to the old airport about a mile away. It has its own station."

"Nice work. If the airport is abandoned, it might be best to head there and make the rest of the way on foot."

"If this is the right place and you manage to get hold of it, we're going to have to act fast. More than twelve hours out of cold storage and its likely to degrade and I might not be able to tell what it is. I'll take it to the lab as soon as you get back."

"Sounds good."

"I've been thinking," Zoe said, "I don't want to tell the kids that Grace committed suicide. They both looked up to her so much and I don't want them thinking that she would abandon them like that."

There was a secret message for me in there too, although she only knew about the first time. It hurt, but I held on to that pain because she was right. "That makes sense. What will we say is the cause?"

"We can say it was a complication with the pregnancy. They are too young to know any different."

"Good idea. Shall we tell them when they get back?"

"I think we need to."

Cora and Zach arrived home five minutes apart just after four o'clock. We sat around the table and broke the news. They took it as expected, with complete devastation. Grace meant so much to them both, in different ways. For Zach, she was the only positive female influence he had, before she moved out, more like a mother than a sister. Zoe spent so much time at the lab and when home would be locked in her office. When she was able to take a moment to step away, being a doting mum was often the last thing on her mind.

Grace had filled that motherly void. She would comfort Zach when he was upset, praise his little achievements to build his confidence, and guide him with gentle advice when he didn't get something right. He regarded her with such admiration, and I knew she would make a fantastic mother to her own children one day. *Could have made.* To Cora, she was a firm mentor. Like me, Grace could see the direction Cora was heading and did her best to counteract the effects of her education. Cora often seemed confused and conflicted by Grace's advice, as if she were fighting an internal battle, or trying to free herself from a supernatural possession. But she respected Grace far more than she respected me and would take on board some of what Grace had to say. Grace was the closest thing we had to authority over Cora, and without her I was fearful of what might happen.

CHAPTER 22

21:55

A piercing squeal of brakes followed by the rattly winding down of an old engine. Logan arrived in a clapped-out hatch back that could have come directly from a scrapyard. I don't know what I was expecting but it was about as stealthy as an HGV with a giant neon sign saying, 'Hey look at me!' It would have to do. I couldn't risk Zoe's car being seen anywhere in the area. It just meant that a remote on-foot entry wasn't *an* option, it was *the* option. At least Logan was early, that was a good sign.

He got out of the car wearing the same black t-shirt but had changed his wetted jeans for black denim. On his head was a bright yellow baseball cap.

"What is that thing on your head?" I said.

"You told me to bring a hat," he replied.

"Yes, and what did I say about the colour of your clothes?"

A long pause. "Ohhh... I thought you just meant..."

"Never mind, it might come in useful." A decoy needed to be visible after all.

"Shall I take it off?"

"For the time being. Fold the back seats down will you."

"What for?"

"Just do it." I rolled out my bike, took off the front

wheel and squeezed the frame in to the boot.

"What's that for?" Logan asked.

"Just in case."

"Just in case what?"

"Shush with the questions. Get in the passenger seat. I'll drive." I sat in the driver's seat and twisted around to deposit my rucksack in the boot. I saw Logan eye it nervously. "Yes, it's in there. But I don't intend on using it. It's an insurance policy. Don't worry." I started the engine.

"OK," he said. "By the way, the clutch on this…"

"I know how to drive a car." I pulled off and came to an immediate halt in a crunching stall.

"The bite point is very high. It's an old car you see," Logan said.

I gritted my teeth. "Thanks Logan."

The journey was sixty-five miles and took just over an hour. It was mostly spent in silence but as we drew closer, I ran over the basic premise of the plan. It was hardly sophisticated but needed to be simple given I was working with an amateur. I didn't want to use Logan unless necessary, so he would hold a position offsite and wait for a signal via the two-way radio. In the event of danger to myself, or me needing a distraction, I would send the signal and he would deploy. He appeared to grasp the concept.

We reached our junction on the motorway and peeled off down the dual carriageway that led towards the airport. A series of sizable buildings filled the horizon, aircraft hangars, warehouses, and the old terminal building. That part I had expected. What I hadn't expected was for it all to be lit up like a Christmas tree, shining an orange dome into the night sky. It was strange for a mothballed airport.

A few hundred metres further down the road we came to an abrupt stop as a row of large concrete blocks spread across the road and prevented any further progress, so we got out of the car and made the rest of the journey on foot. When we were close enough to get a proper view, it became evident that the entire airport complex was an active building site. Construction machinery and materials covered the area and industrial flood lights shone bright white light, illuminating the buildings, and causing intense contrast with angular shards of deep black shadow. It was deserted for the night, so we moved in for closer inspection, squeezing our way through a hole in the perimeter fence.

"What do you think they are building here?" Logan said.

"I have no idea, but it's an enormous project," I replied.

We edged our way along a corrugated steel building, backs to the wall and steeped in shadow, listening hard for any signs of activity. The end of the wall led to the front of the building which opened out into the main airfield. Discarded aircraft were scattered all over the runway having been stripped for parts, their original whiteness blighted by a coating of green mould. The front of the building was composed of a vast sliding double door, easily big enough for a plane to fit through. I peered around the corner of the open door into what was clearly an aircraft hangar, once used to store grounded aircraft, but under conversion to another use.

"What can you see?" Logan whispered, stood closely beside me.

"It looks like… a massive bathroom," I replied.

"What?"

"Follow me inside, nobody's here."

Inside, along the left interior wall, was a network of rudimentary plastic pipework with outlets at head height, every half metre, at least a hundred of them.

"Are they meant to be showers?" Logan asked.

"I think they might be."

"And that's a sink," Logan said. A twenty-metre metal

trough with more outlets at waist height. Along the opposite wall, a metre deep trench made a scar in the earth that ran the entire length of the building. Stacks of sewage waste pipes were placed intermittently. "And that's the crapper!"

"They're making another dormitory," I said in a moment of realisation. "A big one. I was speaking to someone yesterday who said their son was working on something similar in D20 and reckoned it was big enough for five thousand people. This one could be even bigger."

"Who is going to live here? The current dorms only house a couple of hundred men from each district."

"At the moment they do."

"This feels bad. This feels really bad. Is this anything to do with the reason you have brought me here?"

"I think it might be. Let's get a move on, we're wasting time."

"Roger."

"Don't do that."

"Sorry." He paused. "While we're here can I take a piss?"

"Jesus, Logan. Yes, but hurry up."

Zoe's map indicated that the train track leading to the factory was further west, so we headed in that direction, navigating our way around diggers, buildings, and piles of earth, keeping in the shadows wherever possible. We eventually found it, a single-track railway with parallel steel rails that ran off to a vanishing point on the horizon. It would have only been useful for a single train so was probably a shuttle connecting the factory to the airport. The ground on either side of the track fell off into a gully, so we began the mile long hike, side-by-side, straight down the middle of the track.

"Stop kicking the stones. Are you trying to give us away?" I said in a forceful whisper. "There could be security guards any point from here."

"Sorry, I was thinking."

"Don't. It's dangerous."

"Jack?" Logan said after a pause. "Don't be angry with me, but can I ask a question, about Grace?"

"What?"

"Was she pregnant when she died?"

"No. Well, yes, but she had already begun the procedure. It was a boy."

"Oh." He paused. "So that's why she did it."

"Partly. She had been there before and had a bad experience. Second time must have been too much for her."

"Sorry, I didn't know that."

"It's not something she liked to talk about. Better off forgotten."

"I see. It's not fair that someone like Grace should have to go through that. She didn't deserve it."

"Nothing about this is fair, Logan. Nothing at all. Now, no more talking. We're almost there."

CHAPTER 23

The factory perimeter was protected by a ten-foot fence with the top two feet angled outwards and laced with coils of razor wire. It was impossible to climb without specialist gear and I had nothing to cut through the chain-link mesh. Our only option was to go through the entrance at the train terminal, which was illuminated by floodlights, covered by security cameras, and overseen by a guard hut. The hut was a ten-foot square, single storey building with a large sliding window that overlooked the track. Logan and I crawled along and sat down on the floor underneath the window.

"This is as far as you go," I said in a low voice. "I want you to sit here, keep quiet and wait for the signal."

"What will the signal be?"

I handed him a two-way radio from my rucksack. "I'll send two sets of four clicks through this. One-two-three-four, pause, then one-two-three-four again."

"Then what do I do?"

"I'm getting to that." I took out a glass bottle filled with methylated spirit; the opening plugged with a rag. "You light this rag with these matches, let the flame take for a few seconds, and then jump over the security barrier and throw this at something. You then run away as fast as you can. Make sure your hat covers your face."

"Oh god. I'm not sure I can do this."

"Of course you can. But hopefully you won't need to. It's just a precaution."

"What should I throw it at?"

"You're going to have to make that judgement at the time. Just try not to hurt anyone. If things do go south, we don't want it more complicated than it needs to be."

"Ok."

"If anything strange happens out here I want you to let me know through the radio. But don't start blabbing away. Send a signal of three clicks, one-two-three, and if it's safe for me to talk I'll do the same back. It works both ways. Ok?"

"Yes."

"If I'm gone for more than an hour, get out of here."

"Right."

I peered over the windowsill and saw the back of the guard, sitting down reading at a desk. Chatter of a talk show came out of a radio speaker. Banging and clattering of machinery rang out in the distance. The beeping alarm of a reversing forklift. The factory was clearly operational. I pulled out the gun, stood, and carefully slid open the window.

"You said no killing!" Logan blurted.

"Shush you idiot! I won't."

"But why…"

"Shush!" I gave him a hard kick in the thigh.

"Ow!"

When the window was wide enough for me to fit through, I stepped one leg over and into the room, followed by the other. The guard was wearing a light blue shirt and a black cap. They had broad shoulders and hairy arms. It was, unexpectedly, a man. That changed things. He was probably just hired muscle, unlikely to be in on the bigger picture. There was a chance I could appeal to his better nature. If not, he was getting knocked out. I crouch-walked silently up to his chair and jabbed the gun under his ribcage from behind. He jumped but didn't make a sound.

"Listen buddy, I don't want to hurt you and I won't unless you make me. I need to fetch something, and then I'll be gone and out of your hair without a fuss." I said.

He paused in thought, like he was trying to work out if he was in danger. "This place is covered in cameras, you know."

"I can see that. Are there any other guards?"

"Two. At the front gate."

"Armed?"

"They're not carrying. But there are guns in the main security office." I could feel his body shaking against the gun.

"Like what?"

"Two shotguns and a rifle."

"Do you have a key?"

"Yes, but it will trigger an alarm as soon as it's opened."

"Give it to me." The guard fumbled to unclip a chain from his belt and pass it to me with a shaky hand. I needed to reassure him he was safe so that he didn't do anything rash. "What's your name?"

"Stuart."

"OK Stuart. My name is Jack. I'm telling you that because I want you to know that you can trust me, and I'm hoping I can trust you. This company you are working for is planning terrible things. I don't know what, but I do know that you and I are likely to be on the receiving end, if you know what I mean. I am trying to put a stop to it. All I need you to do is look the other way."

"Uh-huh."

"Is there a cold storage area here?"

"Yes, it's in the main factory building."

"Right Stuart. I'm going to go, and you are going to

carry on with whatever you were doing."

Stuart looked up with a sudden sense of urgency. "You can't get into the factory without a security pass. But there is access via the fire escape on the roof. If you were to wear this hi-vis, you could probably walk right up the ladder."

"Probably?"

"Better than lurking around in the dark with all those cameras." His smile suggested he was beginning to relax.

It wasn't the worst of ideas. I put on my black baseball cap and slipped the hi-vis jacket over my black t-shirt, then stood up and strode boldly out of the security hut and into the grounds of the facility. The main factory building was down a stretch of road straight ahead of me on the right. I could see a ladder running up the side of the building to the roof. I started off, doing my best to act casual. It's an odd thing how behaving normally is such a difficult thing to do. I tried to recall what I did when walking down the street. Did I look at people that passed in the face? Did I stare straight ahead and ignore them? What would make me seem least suspicious? I had no idea. I was used to working in the shadows. It was either cautious stealth or violent aggression, not walking around in plain sight. I felt exposed and vulnerable. Perhaps it wasn't such a good idea after all.

A forklift truck approached from down the road ahead. Something instinctive made me raise a hand in a wave. The driver looked at me and carried on driving. The building I was walking alongside was a laboratory with large windows. Scores of scientists were working at the bench facing me in their lab coats and safety goggles but were too busy mixing potions and squirting stuff in to test tubes to notice my presence. My heart was thumping. The ladder was thirty metres ahead. Something inside compelled me to run. I hit the corner of the lab building and collided into a woman who was coming around the corner from the other direction. She was carrying a file of papers that she dropped and scattered all over the floor.

"For god's sake what are you doing?" she said.

"I'm so sorry. I'm on an urgent call out. Someone has reported a leak in the factory." I crouched down and helped her pick up the paper.

"You shouldn't be running around corners like that. I'm going to have to report it as a safety incident. I could have been carrying something dangerous."

"I know. You're right. I'm sorry." I handed her a stack of haphazardly gathered notes.

"What's your name?"

"Andrew. Andrew Philips."

"Well Andrew. Given we're both in a rush we will have to deal with this later."

"Of course. Again, so sorry." I made my escape before she had a chance to probe any further. I made fifteen or twenty paces. I had gotten away with it, I thought.

"Hey, you, wait a minute!" I heard a call from behind me. I froze to the spot and closed my eyes. "You dropped this." The lady was holding out a dangling chain with a key.

"Ah, thank you," I said as I collected it. And then I exhaled.

I made it to the ladder without further encounter and shimmied to the top with ease. It turned out that Stuart had omitted an important piece of information: access to the roof was prevented by a cage that surrounded the top six feet of the ladder. The roof of the cage was a hatch that could swing open, but it was secured with a padlock. *Damn it.* The walls of the building were rendered smooth with no ledges or windows nearby to hold on to. There was no way to circumvent it. Well, there was one way, but it was life-endingly dangerous. Unfortunately, I had little choice.

Switching the direction of my feet on the rung, I turned so I was facing outward, away from the building. I leant forward and slipped my fingers through the holes in the mesh of the cage. I let my body swing forward. My legs dangled beneath me, fifty feet above solid tarmac. I switched my hands so that I was hanging on the outside of the cage and heaved myself up. My fingers burned as the metal mesh cut into my skin. I kicked forward with my legs, trying to get a foot on the ladder and relieve some of the pressure, but it was too far to reach. I continued to drag my way upward, agonising inch by agonising inch, until I managed to swing my leg over the top of the cage and pull myself up on to the roof. I sat in a moment of immense relief, panting heavily. Drops of sweat fell from the tip of my nose as I gazed down at my clawed hands, fingers red raw and unable to extend. I should have packed gloves. It was a massive error not to. A point of learning for the After-Action Report.

The flat roof was a large area surrounded by a barrier wall two feet high. Twenty-or-so pyramid shaped skylights were arranged in a systematic pattern across the roof area, glowing white with the illumination coming from within. Sadly, they were translucently opaque and offered no hint of what I might encounter inside the building. In the centre of the roof was a shed-sized brick structure that housed the fire escape roof access. I pulled the door open and stepped into a stairwell with six flights of galvanised steel stairs leading down into blackness. I descended, step-by-step; my hearing enhanced as my visual sense waned, but the only sound was the metallic twang of my boot soles on the steps.

The door at the bottom of the stairs led into a corridor running from left to right. The wall in front was made entirely of glass and looked out on to the factory floor. The machinery on the other side of the glass was the most impressive feat of engineering I had ever seen. A long chain of automated robotic equipment converted a steel vessel of liquid at one end into palletised containers of packaged medicine at the other. Small glass bottles were pushed, spun, filled, capped, shunted, labelled, wrapped, and collected at incredible speed, all without the input of a human, which I was pleased about. Above the door to the right of me was a sign reading: *Clean Room Access. Full PPE Mandatory.* The door to the left was signposted *Warehouse,* which sounded more like what I was after.

The warehouse was an enormous chamber reaching up to the flat roof and filled with long lines of ceiling height racking that contained all manner of materials, stacked on pallets, and shrink wrapped with cellophane. I made my way down the length of the warehouse, switching aisles and hiding amongst the shelving to avoid the forklift trucks that passed by with an electric whirr. I reached the refrigerated storage area with three, eight-foot square insulated doors built into the wall on the left-hand side of the warehouse. Each door had a red LED display panel above it. The first two showed 5.0 and the third one -25.0.

It'll be kept in a freezer.

Door number three.

It had a large lever handle that took some force to pull but released the door with a hiss as the frozen room on the other side sucked in the warmer air. Automatic lighting pinged to life, illuminating a surreal wintery scene of frosty, double-stacked pallets that glistened in the artificial lights. I pulled the door to, leaving a small gap, and wafted my way through the ethereal mist that filled the room. I searched through the pallets of medicines. From what I could tell there were two distinct types being stored; one was a small amber glass bottle with powder in the bottom, and the second was a transparent glass bottle containing liquid with a cap for a needle to be pushed through. I didn't know what I was looking at, so I grabbed one of each and dropped them into a thermos flask I retrieved from my rucksack. Mission accomplished. I just needed to ex-fil, which, if I was lucky, might just involve a lot of fast running. It had been easier than expected.

The room fell into darkness as the door's magnetic seal engaged and it pulled shut with a dreadful clunk.

CHAPTER 24

I was cast in a low green hue as the internal safety lighting switched on and the cooling fans kicked into action with a choppy whooshing sound. I made my way to the door and shoved. It was shut tight. I slammed my shoulder into it, one, two, three times, but it wouldn't budge. The hairs on my bare arms stood on end as the icy chill penetrated the top layers of my skin. Surviving in that temperature for more than an hour wearing a t-shirt was unlikely. Beside the door was an illuminated button that said *Emergency Alarm*. I weighed up my options. One, hit the alarm and deal with whatever I found on the other side when the door opened. Two, signal Logan using the radio and somehow get him to come and let me out. The probability of success for option number two was zero. Even if he made it to the ladder there was no way he could pull himself up on the outside of the cage. I put option one at seventy-thirty in my favour, on the assumption that security didn't access the firearms before coming to let me out. If they did it would be more of a coin flip, but it would certainly turn to a bloodbath and I didn't want that. There wasn't really a choice to be made. My hand hovered over the emergency button, I was about to push it, then I remembered.

Stuart.

Whether I could trust him was about to be put to the test.

Click-Click-Click.

I waited.

Click-Click-Click. Came back.

"Logan?"

"Yes?"

"We have a situation. I don't have time to explain but I'm trapped."

"Trapped where? You don't want me to come and get you, do you?"

"I'm in a freezer, and no, there is no chance of you getting here. Is the security guard still there?"

"Yes, I think so."

"Can you get his attention and then put him on. His name is Stuart."

"I don't like this. What if he arrests me?"

"Logan for Christ's sake. He can't arrest you and I will be dead within the hour if you don't. Do it now!"

A moment of silence.

"Hello?" a voice came through the radio.

"Stuart?"

"Yes."

"Listen, I need your help," I said.

"You're going to get me killed."

"It won't come to that, I promise. But I am trapped in the freezer in the warehouse. I got in, the door closed behind me, and I can't open it from the inside. I need you to come and let me out."

"Sorry, nothing I can do."

"My other option is to press the alarm and start shooting whoever opens the door. They are going to ask questions about how I made it this far. It would be unfortunate if your name came up in conversation wouldn't it, Stuart."

Silence.

"Argh! Give me five minutes," Stuart said.

Five minutes was more like fifteen and by the time the door opened I was curled up on the floor, knees hugged into my chest, and with my body shaking in heavy convulsions. Stuart came in and lifted me up, supporting me as I limped out into the warehouse. The ambient twenty degrees felt tropical. I rubbed my palms together and jumped up and down to get the blood circulating.

"Come on," Stuart said. "This way. We don't have much time."

"Before what?"

"It's break time in a few minutes and the place will be swarming with people going to the canteen."

Stuart led me to the end of the warehouse and through a door into another corridor. We turned left and crept another twenty metres, until we reached a doorway with a sign reading *Security Office*.

"Is that where the weapons are stored?" I asked.

Stuart was reluctant. "Yes. But we need to get out of here. Please, don't do this."

"You need to think bigger picture."

"What do you need them for?"

"I don't know yet. But things have the potential to get ugly and I'd rather be prepared."

"There is a guard in there. A female one. You are not going to be able to charm her into submission. You either kill her, or she will raise an alarm, and I will have to respond."

"Don't worry, I have a plan."

I told Stuart to stay where he was and to let me know when the guard inside left the room. He seemed confused but I told him it would be obvious. I went back to the warehouse and hid amongst the pallets on the racking.

One-two-three-four. Pause. *One-two-three-four*

I waited. It took less than two minutes. A blaring alarm sounded, punctuated by a robotic voice.

Fire has been detected. Please make your way to the nearest assembly point.

"I did it Jack. I did it!" Logan's excited voice crackled through the radio.

"Good job. Now get the hell out of here, as fast as you can."

Stuart burst through the door. "She's gone."

I sprinted towards the corridor and tried to open the door to the security office, but it was locked. I took a step back and gave it a heavy kick with my booted heel. The door frame splintered into fragments as the door smashed inward. The room inside was a dark office with two vacant swivel chairs which sat in front of a control console of blinking lights and a bank of monitors that displayed images of various parts of the facility's exterior. One of the monitors showed a waste storage area burning in an incredible blaze. Billows of thick black smoke rose into the air and a handful of uniformed security officers stood watching, helpless. Whatever was being stored there was seriously flammable. Logan had chosen well. On the wall at the back of the room was what I assumed was the weapons locker, a brushed steel cabinet that stood four-feet tall. Sure enough, Stuart's key fitted the lock. I was about to turn it when Stuart yelled out.

"Wait! When you open that it's going to trigger another alarm."

"I think everyone is occupied with that at the moment," I said, pointing at the inferno on the screen.

"Someone must respond. It's strict protocol."

"I see."

"I can call it in, but... I need you to shoot me."

"I'm not going to do that."

"I don't mean kill me. Shoot me in the leg."

I held up the Desert Eagle. "I've seen first-hand what this does to human flesh. It will take your leg off!"

"Alright, something else then. I need evidence that you overpowered me. I don't know… surprise me. But here, take my security pass. It'll get you out the building," Stuart said, unclipping his pass from his belt loop.

"I'd rather leave the guns."

"It's already too late for that. They'll be able to track my movements by which doors I've opened with my pass. I'm supposed to be manning the back entrance, not wandering around inside the factory."

It was regrettable, but he was right. I had a sudden pang of guilt for dragging him in to it. "I'm sorry," I said.

"Don't be. This is the most excitement I've had in years."

I stood, studying him, trying to work out if he meant it.

"Get on with in then!" he said.

As soon as I turned the key a different sound started coming out of the ceiling speakers, a piercing, high-pitched scream that sent shivers through me. Inside the cabinet was one shotgun, one rifle and one empty space, meaning one of the guards was armed. I picked up the rifle and slung the strap over my shoulder so that I was carrying it on my back.

"I guess this is it," Stuart said.

I aimed the handgun at the fleshiest part of Stuart's thigh. He closed his eyes and screwed up his face in anticipation of the pain that was about to come.

"Thank you. You're a brave man," I said, as I raised the gun above my head and brought the butt of the metal handle down hard into his temple. Stuart's knees buckled beneath him, and he slumped into a pile on the ground like a marionette whose strings had been cut. I was upset that I had to do it, but at least that way he wouldn't bleed to death and would still be able to walk.

I ran through the network of corridors, occasionally stopping to scan the security pass to allow passage through a locked door. The alarm was even more debilitating in the confines of the narrow walls as the sound bounced around before hitting my eardrums. Thanks to the fire evacuation the place was deserted, and I was grateful that for once a set of unintended consequences had gone in my favour. I pushed open a set of double doors that led into a reception area and heard a shout from behind.

"Hey!" It was a uniformed woman carrying a shotgun.

I bolted for the sliding glass door that led outside. A deafening boom rang out behind me, followed by the explosion of the wooden door as it was pelted with supersonic shot. I ducked and covered my head with my arms but kept moving quickly towards the exit, too quickly in fact, for the automated system to respond and open the doors. I leapt off the ground and charged into the glass door with my shoulder. Tiny cubes of broken safety glass sprayed over the pavement. I stumbled to the ground but steadied myself with my hands and scrambled to my feet.

The air was dense with acrid, black smoke. I coughed as it stung the back of my throat. I couldn't get my bearings. Another shot boomed out from behind and I heard lead shot whizz past, dangerously close to my ear. I figured Logan wouldn't have come far into the compound to start the fire so ran through the smoke towards the flame that was, by then, towering above the buildings. It was mayhem. Siren's blaring, the screaming and shouting of the workers, the roar of the fire, a sudden dramatic crash as the roof of the burning structure collapsed sending a shower of burning embers into the night sky like a spectacular firework display. Dogs barked in the distance. The smoke provided perfect cover and I made it to the security hut by the train tracks without much trouble. The barking got louder. I turned the corner on to the track and prepared for the home sprint.

I had done it.

But my elation was short-lived as I came face-to-face with something I did not want to see.

"Logan! What are you doing here? I told you to go!"

"I... I wanted to make sure you got out."

"Move it!" I said as I shoved him in the direction we needed to go.

We ran back down the centre of the track, large stones crunching under the impact of my boots. The rifle on my back was cumbersome, shaking from side-to-side under my ruck sack and slowing me down, but I was still faster than Logan. He was moving much too slowly.

"Come on, faster," I said as two German Shepherds skidded around the corner and chased us down the track. "Faster!"

He didn't have the speed in his legs. One of the dogs caught him within seconds, clamping its jaws around his calf and bringing him to a halt on his knees. "Help me," he screamed as the dog yanked its head from side-to-side, dragging Logan backwards as he fell on to his front.

I stopped in my tracks before the second dog sped past Logan and towards me. I turned and tried to outrun it, but it was too fast. I pulled the Desert Eagle out from the back of my trousers and fired behind me as I ran. I missed. The dog was six feet behind. It leapt up, snarling, mouth open wide, baring its sharp white teeth. I let off two more rounds. This time, I hit it in the chest. The dog yelped and fell to the floor, tumbling over several times, carried by its own momentum. I stopped and turned to go back for Logan. In the distance I could see him flailing around on the floor, thrashing his arms around and trying to scramble his way forward against the superior strength of the animal that heaved in the other direction. He managed to clamber on to his knees, and then up on to one leg, hopping along as the dog refused to release its prey. I thought he was about to get free when a phantom-like silhouette of a security guard materialised through the smoke that drifted on to the track, illuminated by powerful flood lights from behind. Then, with the dazzling flash of a shotgun muzzle, Logan's struggle was over, and his body hit the deck with a thud.

My lungs were on fire. The physical exertion of a mile long sprint and the burning from smoke inhalation meant I struggled to breathe. I reached the airport and found a secluded corner hidden in the shadows. The metallic taste of blood filled my mouth as I doubled over in fits of coughing. I turned my head in the direction I came from, my chest heaving up and down. The sky was lit up bright orange. I listened for signs of being followed but could only hear the distant sound of the fire alarm.

God damn it, Logan!

I was furious with him. Why hadn't he listened to me? He shouldn't have been there. He should have run for safety. His death was so... unnecessary. I don't know whether I would ever have forgiven him for what he did to Grace. But from the few hours we had spent together, I could tell he wasn't a bad kid. Misguided, and thick as two short planks, but his heart was in the right place. He didn't die with my forgiveness, but he died with my respect.

Once my breathing had returned close to normal, I jogged back to the car and jumped into the driver's seat. I drove away from the airport and back over the motorway. After two miles down a narrow lane I pulled into a layby, got out, and lifted my bike out of the boot. I took a second glass bottle from my rucksack, removed the rag plug, and emptied the volatile liquid contents into the interior of the car. With the flick of a match, the vehicle ignited with a whoosh. I stood watching the burning wreckage, making sure the fire did its thing, erasing the evidence as far as possible. I took my place on the saddle and pushed off the dusty ground with my foot. Sixty-five miles home. I hoped to make it before Zoe woke up.

CHAPTER 25

04:45 - Friday 8th June 2063

"Jack, where have you been? I thought something terrible had happened." I found Zoe downstairs, already awake. In fact, judging by the dark circles around her eyes, I wasn't sure she had slept. I had left the rifle in the garage. Zoe didn't need to know about that, for the time being.

"I thought I'd be back before you woke up," I said.

"How could I sleep? Are you ok? You stink of smoke. And sweat."

"Yes, I'm fine." It was partially true. I was fine in the sense that Zoe intended — not dead and mostly uninjured. I was, however, exhausted, dehydrated and ravenously hungry. The ride back had been much more challenging than I had expected. My mountain bike, with its chunky tyres and heavy frame, was not designed for that sort of distance, and there was a persistent headwind which made it feel like I was constantly cycling uphill. So, I was fine, but also utterly spent. I poured a large glass of water, downed it, and then poured another. I then rooted through the cupboards in search of something to satisfy the hunger cravings that dominated my consciousness.

"What about Logan?"

I hesitated. "I'll tell you all about it later. Let's deal with the matter at hand."

I needed to figure out how best to deal with Logan's death. Certain people needed to know, not least his mother.

But to do so immediately would be a distraction and I didn't want to derail what we were working on. Besides, what would be said about Logan's death, and its overall importance in the grand scheme of things, partially depended on the outcome of what Zoe was about to investigate. It's an easier message for a mother to hear that her son died courageously for a respectable cause, than being shot dead for committing arson for no reason other than vandalism. The other factor to consider was whether they could identify his body, in which case the situation would be taken out of my control. I hoped not as it would also lead them my way. He wasn't carrying any ID and torching the car should make tracing that more difficult if they made the connection between that and the events at the factory, but it was by no means guaranteed. It meant we needed to act even quicker. I stuffed a hunk of stale bread into my mouth and handed the flask that contained the retrieved items to Zoe. She tipped something out into her palm and then held the amber glass bottle up to the light, shaking the powdered contents which rattled inside.

"Damn. This isn't it. It's a lyophilised vaccine of some kind. Probably MMR." She obviously sensed my lack of understanding. "It means freeze dried. It increases the shelf life."

"There should be another one," I said with a deep sense of desperation.

Zoe shook the flask which clanged with the sound of the other container, and then inverted it, catching the clear, liquid-containing bottle. She studied the label and an excited grin spread across her face. "The label doesn't have a drug substance name, only a code. I don't recognise it, but it's experimental. This could be it. But once I get it to the lab I'll know for sure."

"Thank God," I said. Relief doesn't come close. Liberation from the most intense feeling of panic I had ever experienced. In my previous life I had undergone substantial training and conditioning in emotional control. Keeping a cool head on the battlefield was critical and I had made life or death decisions, impacting myself and others, under extreme stress. But never had I led a civilian to their death on a mission with sketchy intel and an unknown outcome. In retrospect, it was a reckless thing to do. Logan's death was tragic, but if it was also without purpose, then I'd have a hard time living with it. For the time being, there was hope.

"Shall we get going then?" I said.

"We? I can't take you to the lab. It's out of the question. The only man ever seen in the building is the cleaner. Your presence would be highly suspicious."

"I'm not comfortable with you being there alone. You heard what Olivia said at the press conference."

"Trust me, I'll be fine, especially at this time of day, there'll be hardly anyone about."

"So, let me come."

"No." That meant end of story.

As it happened, at that moment, I was overcome with a wave of fatigue that caused me to steady myself on the back of a chair. "Fine. I'll get a few hours of sleep. Don't spend any longer there than you need to and come straight home."

"I will. It won't take long to run the analysis. I should be back within a few hours."

The alarm wrenched me from a wondrous slumber. I prised opened my eyes, battling the weight of my eyelids. Just ten more minutes.

No!

I shook my head and sat up, forcing my eyes open and turning my gaze to the window, hoping the morning sunlight that poured through would be a reminder to my brain that it is daytime. The clock face showed 07:30. I had been dragged from the deepest depths of my sleep cycle. I was filled with this vague sense of urgency, something somewhere insisting that I had to wake myself up, but I couldn't remember why.

Zoe wasn't lying next to me, but that wasn't unusual. It took a few moments to work out what day of the week it was. Then the pieces of the puzzle all started falling in to place. As the gears started turning, I eventually remembered, there was so much to do.

While cycling home the night before I had a lot of time with my own thoughts. It was an effective way of directing my attention away from the burning in my quadriceps. My previous question to Zoe about why the government would want to cure the condition that tipped the balance of fortune in their favour had been answered, they probably didn't. Zoe's admission of winding the clock back five years added serious weight to that conclusion. At the very least it meant irradicating The Gaia wasn't as important to them as most people would think it ought to be.

Only the 'why now?' question was outstanding, even if their sudden willingness was all a big act. But that's not what was bothering me the most. It felt more than ever like there was something bigger at stake. I had always had this niggle in the back of my mind that there was an agenda at play, something deeper and more sinister than the simple poor treatment of males resulting from the effects of a virus of unknown origin. Alvina's government claimed to be victims of circumstance, doing their best in a tough situation. But there was evidence, at least circumstantial evidence, that this was not the case. You only had to look at the unfair way The Rota was run to see that.

The Gaia had already infected its way through the population before Alvina's party came to power, and she took the job in full knowledge of that. She capitalised on the social division and polarised intolerance that came to define the first part of the twenty-first century and was elected on a manifesto with grand promises of social harmony and a narrowing of the wealth divide. The Universal Provision of Basic Needs was sold as a liberation. The best bits of Capitalism and Communism combined. It would end poverty and transform the notion of paid work, freeing people to pursue careers they loved and not jobs they were forced to do out of need. But there can be no denying that it had been an unmitigated failure.

Poverty had been abolished, but only in the sense that everyone was equally poor. People pursuing careers they loved meant not enough people willing to do the basic work that needed to be done for a country to function, leading to the enslaving of the dwindling male population. Even if you were female, there weren't enough jobs to go around that provided the satisfaction and stimulation they had grown up being told they deserved and would achieve. And of course, many people were not motivated to work at all. But despite all of this, there had been no wavering from it. No admission of failure. No course correction. Nobody putting their hand up and saying, 'this is a bad idea'. Just a relentless slog, following a disastrous ideology into oblivion.

It was like it was intentional. Social cohesion, especially among women, was worse than ever. The notion of sisterhood abolished. Yet some of the policies, enacted by a supposed feminist party, were distinctly anti-female and only perpetuated the divide. Breast-feeding, the most natural and primeval function of a mother, was labelled as crude and dirty, deemed socially unacceptable and was banned in public spaces, and yet some women could not fight the maternal urge, leading to two polarised factions that clashed repeatedly. New mothers were given only two weeks paid leave following childbirth before being expected to return to work, leading to breakdown in family relationships. The breeders fought the abstainers that said bringing children into this world was immoral. Any woman below a certain age was labelled as filth if they considered partnering with a man. The list went on. The system was rigged towards women, but Zoe was right, it wasn't all fun and laughter for them either. So, my latest question was: what was it all about and where is the opposition? Not only in the formal sense of a shadow government, but anyone, anywhere, willing to stick their neck out and say, "This is not working for us!". My fear was that we had slipped too far into dictatorship territory for this ever to be allowed. Why did people not revolt against this woman who had her boot heal pressed firmly on their necks?

I sat opposite Zach as he was eating breakfast, already on my third coffee substitute of the day. His buoyant mood from the past couple of days had subsided. He sat staring at his porridge, pushing it around the bowl with his spoon. I thought he would be happy with the treat of having porridge. We didn't often have electricity to make it that early in the mornings.

"Are you not going to eat that?" I said.

"I'm not hungry," he replied.

"You're a growing lad and you need your energy. Get it down you," I said. "Anyway, I was thinking of trying to get hold of a couple of fishing rods from somewhere. We're going to be busy this weekend, but maybe we could give a try next week, down at the river. What do you think?"

"Oh, no. Don't worry, it's ok."

"I thought you'd be excited."

"I don't want to do that anymore."

"How come?"

"Cora said I was being stupid. That I can't choose what I do and stupid people like me get sent to work in the coal mines."

"Don't you listen to her. You are not stupid, and you can do whatever you want. It's important to have a dream. I know you will be a fisherman, if that's what you want to do. Besides, I was excited about going with you. I'll get some rods and we can give it a try. Even if you change your mind, it will be a fun thing for us to do, huh?"

"Yes ok." He brightened a little.

"Good lad." I gave him a friendly punch on the top of his

arm. "Listen, you have access to a library at school, right?"

"Not all of it, but boys have their own section."

"What sort of books are there in your section?"

"Mostly different ones that tell you how to behave properly. Some about famous people. Some about history."

"History? Like what? How far back do they go?" I was surprised by this fact but also puzzled.

"Really far back. Forty years maybe. Ones about how the virus came about and stuff like that."

"Wow, forty years," I said with faux astonishment. I guess it is a long time if you are fourteen. "Have you read any of those?"

"No, I haven't. I like the ones about famous people."

"That sounds interesting. Perhaps you could get hold of one about the virus and we could read it together?"

"Yes ok."

"Do they have any about Alvina in the famous people section?"

"I don't know, but they probably do."

"See if you can find one."

"Yes, I will. I better go or I will be late for school."

"Keep your chin up. Today will be a good day. Keep telling yourself that."

"Ok Dad, bye."

With that, he hoisted his bag on to his shoulder and plodded out the front door while staring at the ground. Moments later, Cora came thundering down the stairs, and ran through the kitchen.

"Hey," I said, which she ignored. "Hey!"

She stopped in the doorway and turned to face me. "What now?"

"I want you to be kind to Zach today. If you can't manage that then keep out of his way. Clear?"

Contempt flashed across her face. "When will you get it?" she said with a heavy sigh. "What you want doesn't matter to me. You have no say over what I do. I want *you* to get out my face and mind your own business."

"Your behaviour is my business, especially when it concerns Zach's wellbeing. As your parent I very much have a say over what you do and while you are living in this house you *will* do as I say."

Cora let out a huge laugh. "As my *father* what you have to say means nothing! I have been patient with you, but you are starting to piss me off. Fuck off and leave me alone!" She turned to stride through the door, bouncing off Zoe as she came through in the other direction.

"Woah there speedy. What's all the fuss about in here?" Zoe said.

"Sorry Mum. Gotta go. Bye."

I was so angered that my pulse was throbbing in my ears. My jaw was clenched, and I could have crushed a rock in my fist.

"You two are clashing again I see," Zoe said. "You know she's nearly a teenager. This hard-line approach of yours isn't going to work with her anymore. The more you push the harder she will push back, and you'll end up butting heads. I have been there myself don't forget. You need to find another way."

"Another way!? Jesus Zoe did you hear what she said to me? Never mind the swearing. This goes way beyond teenager stroppiness. She genuinely believes that *she* has authority over *me*! What are they teaching them at school?"

"You know what's it's like. We need to find a way of managing it, but shouting is only going to escalate things."

"Wow. Could you be any more condescending? It's

funny how you are suddenly mother of the year when all I can remember is Grace doing your job when you couldn't be bothered. How about I leave it all to you?" It was a horrible thing to say, and I could see the hurt in her eyes. I immediately regretted saying it. "I didn't mean that. I'm sorry. I'm just angry, and tired."

Zoe walked around behind me and put her arms around my neck as I sat. The softness of her cheek caressed against my own. Her natural smell was sweet and comforting. "It's ok. You are mostly right. I regret not being there more for you all and I want to change that. Things will be different going forward. Raising kids is difficult, especially troublesome ones. You do an excellent job."

"Thank you," I said. The pressure in my veins began to subside and the tension in my body started to melt away. I let out a deep, audible exhale. "Anyway, how did you get on at the lab? Any idea what we are dealing with?"

Zoe sat down next to me. "Yes, I ran the sample you got through the LCMS. The elution time on the chromatogram and the mass spectrum match with a compound on our database."

"Great, so do you know what it is?"

"I know exactly what it is. I developed it."

"And?"

"When I first started working at Cambridge there had already been several failed attempts at developing a cure. All the work conducted up until that point was aimed at reversing the virus's genetic effects, a full cure. I had an idea to see, if we couldn't completely cure it, could we at least shift the incidence rate so more baby boys would survive." She paused as if not wanting to continue.

"I assume it didn't work, otherwise you would have given it to people," I said.

"It did work, but not as we hoped. We couldn't decrease

the incidence, but we were able to increase it."

"Why would you want to do that?"

"Obviously we didn't, which is why the project was shelved. We created a whole series of compounds during screening and this..." she said holding up the small glass bottle, "...was one of them."

"So, what does it do?"

"It increases the rate of holoprosencephaly in male foetuses to one hundred percent."

CHAPTER 26

I remember when I was ten or eleven, before anyone had heard of Cyclopia, I used to enjoy watching old movies and always wished I was born in a different era. Life in 2023 was so unnecessarily negative. We had all the technology that was designed to make life easier, yet everyone was so stressed. People sat in gridlocked traffic jams or on late running trains on the commute to jobs that they despised. Spare time was spent fiercely debating with strangers on the internet about anything from dietary preferences to whether the earth was flat. Instead of bringing the world together, the internet created polarised groups of people that were considered enemies unless their thoughts and opinions were identical. My parents would reminisce nostalgically of their childhood growing up in the eighties. The simple life, they called it. Wholesome and uncomplicated. But at the same time, they never missed an opportunity to inform me how lucky I was. "We had four TV channels and children's programs were on for one hour a day after school," my dad would say. "None of this twenty-four-hour cartoons on demand." But I was fascinated by their stories of leaving the house after breakfast, spending the entire day playing by the river, climbing trees, making dens, and generally causing mischief. They said they could walk up to their friends' houses and knock on the door without arranging it first, and so long as they were home by the time the streetlights were on, they could do pretty much anything they wanted. It blew my mind. I wasn't allowed to go to the local park on my own for an hour in the middle of the day.

But it wasn't the eighties that appealed to me, and it wasn't only a different time that I wished I was born in to, but also a different country. For me, it was 1950s America. I loved the movies with the sleek cars, smart suits and rock'n'roll music. I wanted to go to a diner and order a huge milkshake with whipped cream and a cherry on top. I wanted to go bowling with a large group of friends and have a neighbourhood BBQ party, with my dad wearing an apron, standing over a huge chunk of chargrilled beef and holding a beer. Most of all I wanted the traditional family, with the stay-at-home mum baking cookies and the dad that gets back from the office at five-thirty with a "Hi Honey, I'm home!" slinging his briefcase on the floor, hanging his hat and coat on the stand, and ruffling my hair as he walked by. It was the antithesis of my life. Both of my parents were forced to work full time to maintain our modest three-bed semi and were often too tired to do anything in the evenings beyond putting a ready meal in the oven and slumping on the sofa with a glass of wine. I didn't blame them as that's what the financial situation demanded, but I couldn't understand how people worked much harder and yet were so much poorer.

The one thing that did excite me about living in the present day was that soon I'd be living in the future. I think that most people, when imagining the future, envisage something better than their present day. With the naïve optimism of childhood, the future I imagined was spectacular. Technology was moving at such an incredible pace, and I genuinely believed that something groundbreaking was just around the corner that would transform human existence. Maybe both of my parents wouldn't have to work any longer. Of course, that thing did come along, but it was not what I had imagined. It didn't make life better, it made it horribly worse.

But even then, despite trudging through a swamp of needless death and grief, never in my darkest nightmares did I imagine I would live to see the beginning of the complete extinction of men.

But there was one major flaw.

"If there are no boys born then how can the human race continue to exist?" I asked, in a bewildered state of shock.

"I know. It doesn't make sense," Zoe replied.

A thought occurred to me. "You know I was thinking the other day how strange it was that I had never been asked to stop taking my samples in. I should have only been allowed to do it for a year or two, but it's been more like eight. Maybe they have stock-piled enough to keep reproduction up using IVF."

"That thought occurred to me on the way home too, but it's not feasible. IVF accounts for around thirty percent of births currently and the system can't keep up. If we relied on IVF for every pregnancy, then the birth rate would plummet. We already have a population crisis."

"That could be part of their plan. Fewer people to feed means more food to go around."

"Yes, but also fewer people to produce it."

"Right, and I can't imagine women are queuing up for vegetable picking," I said. "There is something else. Last night, when we were at the old airport, I thought it was going to be derelict, but the place was full of construction machinery. They were converting the buildings into massive accommodation. I was speaking to someone I know from the supermarket, and he said his son was working on one in another district. I wonder if its linked."

"Could be, but who knows. We're missing pieces of the puzzle. Besides, it's all academic as it can't be allowed to happen. I checked my email at the university and Alvina has called an emergency meeting for this afternoon. I'll find out more then." She paused. "Speaking of last night, you never told me about it properly. I take it Logan is ok?"

Damn it.

Why did I bring up the previous night? Talk about

shooting myself in the foot. I tried to swallow but it was as if I had a huge rock in my throat. I rubbed my face vigorously with my hands, trying to find some words, but my brain was putting up a barrier. It wasn't ready to conjure those memories, but avoiding it was impossible. Zoe's interrogation technique was more effective than The Taliban's. The tone she used penetrated the soul and stirred up a feeling of dread that could not be matched by any other means.

"Jack. Tell me what's going on. Now." There it was.

A defeated sigh escaped my mouth. "It all went to shit. I got trapped and needed help to escape. Logan was waiting at the entrance, so I radioed him and asked him to put me on to Stuart."

"Who is Stuart?" Zoe interrupted.

"Stuart, the security guard. Anyway, never mind that. Stuart helped me escape. I had already managed to pick up what I went for, so I told Logan to make a run for it back to the car. But when I got back to the factory entrance, he was still sitting there like an absolute plum. They set dogs after us and he just wasn't fast enough. The dog caught him in seconds and took him down. Then he was shot by one of the armed security guards."

"And?" she stared at me, eyes wide. She was going to make me say the words out loud.

"Logan's dead."

"Bloody hell, Jack! And you left him there? How could you do that?"

"Please don't say that." My heart cracked as a pang of guilt hit me in the chest. "I had no choice. I had a vicious dog chasing me followed by a woman with a shotgun. Getting his body out would have meant risking my life or taking someone else's. I didn't want any more bloodshed."

"That poor boy. I can't believe you would drag him in to something like that. He was just a kid."

Another dagger. "I know. It was a horrible situation. He should have listened to me. He chose not to and put himself in danger. But in the end, his actions saved my life. I will be eternally thankful to him for that. And... you know... I ended up liking him."

Zoe slumped down into a chair. "You're going to have to tell his mother."

"Yes, I know, and I will. But I thought I'd give it a few days to see if we can get to the bottom of whatever is going on first. If she kicks off, then it's going to drop me in it. I can't be placed at that location. I may as well hand myself in now."

Zoe sighed. "You don't have to tell her the whole truth. But she needs to know her son has gone."

"Do I have to do it now? She's not going to realise anything is wrong for a few days. I don't even know where she lives."

"She is going to notice because she lives next door to him. Grace told me she is not well in some way. Logan moved in next door to keep an eye on her."

Just what I needed to hear. As if the burden of guilt I carried was not heavy enough, it transpired that Logan was a doting son to a sick mother. I had always believed in the reliability of first impressions and had needed to count on that many times to determine the intent of people I confronted in warzones. But on this occasion, I may have judged Logan too harshly. I put it down to being a protective father and in fairness to Logan, nobody would have been good enough for Grace in my eyes. It did mean, as usual, Zoe was right. Logan's mother needed to know immediately, and not just for her own sake. If she became concerned about Logan's absence, she might report him missing. The chances of the police being bothered by a missing young man were slim, but it was a variable better off eliminated. The way my luck had been going, the police would initiate a nationwide manhunt.

Getting back on the blasted bike was the last thing I

wanted or needed. My quads were beginning to ache, and I had acquired a wide-footed cowboy-like swagger on account of the unbearable chaffing down under. Zoe suggested she should drive me most of the way and I would walk the final five minutes. It should have been a five-minute walk, but it took more like twenty, not only due to the soreness between my legs but because I was giving myself time to think.

Lying to a mother about something of this nature did not sit well with me, in fact I hated the idea. But telling her the truth was not an option at that time. I swore to myself, when the time was right, I would go back and explain what had happened. She deserved to know the truth and only then could I move forward with letting it go. The cadence of my footsteps reduced even further as I struggled with what I was going to say. Putting together a feasible narrative was proving to be a challenge. There were too many threads that needed to be woven together and my exhausted brain couldn't decipher how it could be done in a way that was believable. What was the reason for death? Why hadn't I told the police? Where was the body? What the hell was he doing in D20? It wasn't possible to cover them all off fully so I would go with the best I could and hope the shock would stop her asking too many questions. The most convincing angle would be something linked to Grace's death, and the loss of my own child would hopefully stop her directing her anger at me, but it made me sick to use my daughter's passing in such a way. Unfortunately, I was short of options. Suicide driven by grief perhaps. A devastating car accident would also explain her missing vehicle. It was distasteful, but nothing about any of what was happening was particularly joyous.

Logan's front door, number twenty-eight, was the first in a row of five on the rear flank of the apartment block. He only had one next-door neighbour. I knocked on the door of number twenty-nine and moments later the net curtain that hung on the inside moved aside, and a distorted face-like shape appeared, pixelated behind the obscured glass. The door opened revealing a lady that was too old to be Logan's mother, or at least that was how it seemed. "Mrs Duggen?" I asked.

"Yes, that's right," she replied.

"My name is Jack. I am a friend of Logan's. I wonder if I might come in for a moment. There is something I'd like to talk to you about." As soon as I had said it, it occurred to me that I shouldn't have used my real name in case she decided to go to the police. Massive error.

"Ok then," she said, turning around. "I don't know anyone named Logan, but I'd be glad of some company. Watch your step as you come through, it's a bit of an obstacle course I'm afraid."

I crossed the threshold hesitantly. "But you are Mrs Duggen?"

"Last time I checked," she said. I would place her around mid-sixties. Her grey cardigan had a large hole at the elbow. She wore it over a white t-shirt with orange food stains down the front. A long black skirt covered her knees, leaving veiny calves on display. On her feet she had a pair of bright pink fluffy slippers tinged brown with years of dirt. Deep wrinkles formed crevices over her face and neck, as if she had double the amount of skin that she needed, and her thin grey hair partially covered an apple-sized dent in the side of her skull. She projected an air of cheeky playfulness that was at odds with her aged appearance, along with a large dose of eccentricity. "What's a handsome man like you going round knocking on stranger's doors for then?" she said as she shuffled down the hall with a slight hunch. I sensed a Westcountry twang.

Her flat was the mirror image of Logan's, and not just opposite in layout, but also in its state. Whereas Logan's place was sparse when it came to furnishing, Mrs Duggen's was packed from floor to ceiling. Several chests of drawers were placed around the living room, the drawers not able to close with the sheer volume of items bursting out of them. Stacks of boxes lined the walls, piled high with paperwork, books and vinyl records. A dark wooden dressing cabinet was crammed with mugs, pots, vases, ornaments, and photo frames, many containing pictures of Logan. A square coffee table housed around forty candles of various shapes and sizes that had been burnt down to stubs, and the shelf underneath was packed with old magazines and newspapers. Mrs Duggen was a hoarder. But despite the huge mass of clutter, it was sort of orderly and the flat was clean, with a sweet floral note hanging in the air. I walked to the dresser and picked up one of the photo frames, in which Logan posed next to the old lady by the seafront somewhere.

"Jeff, wasn't it?" she said. "Would you like a drink, Jeff?"

"Err... yes, that's right Mrs Duggen, it's Jeff. And no, I'm good, thanks."

"That's enough of all the Mrs Duggen stuff. You make me feel like the queen. Mauve will do. Have a seat." I sat down on a spongy beige sofa and Mauve on the adjacent matching armchair. "So, Jeff, how can I help?"

"As I mentioned before, I wanted to chat about Logan," I replied.

"I told you, I don't know any Logans."

I showed her the picture from the dresser. "This is a nice photo. Who's the lad?"

She took it from me and examined it, her dark grey eyes scrutinising the face that she didn't seem to recognise. "I can't remember to be honest with you. I gets a bit confused sometimes. Took a bang on the noggin a few years back," she tapped her dent. "Not so good with faces anymore."

"Do you live here alone, Mauve?"

"All by myself. Don't need no one else. Give me a crossword and a book and I'm as happy as Larry, thank you very much."

"I'm a fan of crosswords too."

"Keep the old grey matter ticking over, don't 'em."

"Yes, they do indeed," I said with a chuckle. "Does anyone come in to help you? Family or anything like that?"

"Don't have no family and don't need no help. I can get me self to the shops and back when I need to." Then her face lit up in a moment of realisation, like a lightbulb had switched on. "I remember now. That boy in the photo lives in the flat next door. Always knocking on my door, he is."

"But you don't know him that well? You sure have a lot of photos of him."

She sat in silent thought for a moment as the unoiled gears in her head grinded around. Her expression changed to one of pained frustration. "All your questions are giving me a headache."

"Sorry, I didn't mean to do that. Let me talk for a moment," I said. "There's something I need to tell you. The boy that lives next door is called Logan, the one I mentioned before. He was my daughter's boyfriend. I have some sad news about him." I took a deep breath and prepared myself to replay the monologue I had gone over a thousand times. "I have information that suggests he has passed away. Yesterday he…"

"Good," she said, cutting me off. "Right little sod he was. Always bothering me. I told him to leave me alone, but he wouldn't listen.

"Oh," I said, taken aback. "I expect he was just making sure you were ok."

"Always bumping and knocking about next door too. You've wasted your time if you've come all this way just to tell me that. Won't catch me shedding a tear for that one. In fact, now you mention it, I ought to get rid of those horrible pictures."

I had anticipated and prepared for several different outcomes, but Mauve's blunt response was not one of them.

I was in the grips of a mind blank. "Umm... OK then," I eventually said. "I'm glad you're not upset. So... do you want to do a crossword?"

"Ooh that would be lovely," she beamed.

The human brain is a fascinating thing. For someone who couldn't recognise her own son's face, or remember that she had a son, Mauve's mind was an impressive vault of information that she recalled with ease. "Wispy, high-altitude cloud. Six letters," I said, scratching my head.

"That'll be cirrus," Mauve said.

"Yes, that fits. It makes the first letter of six down an R. That's the one that we couldn't get."

"What was the clue for that one again?" she asked.

"Equal-sided quadrilateral."

"Hmm. Still not sure with that one, me dear."

"Rhombus?" I asked.

"Ooh I think you might be right."

"Next one," I said. "Politician of Indonesian descent. Three and three. Must be Ava Lee. It fits, except I thought her parents were Thai, not Indonesian."

"No, it's Ana Eka. She's MP for D10. Ava's mother was Thai, but her father was Chinese."

"Really?"

"Yes."

"I've never heard that."

"Not many people know."

"Are you sure about that?"

"As shore as the sea. Before she was a politician, she was a professional gymnast. I remember watching her as a little girl. Competed for China in the 2008 Olympics in Beijing she did. Not that she was very good. Important parents is all. I was surprised she was allowed to be an MP with all the fuss about the Chinese doing this and that. Spying on us and such. Always in the news causing trouble, they were. But she got her British passport and that was that."

Hmm.

"You're a font of knowledge, Mauve," I said as I checked my watch, it was midday, "I've learnt a lot today, and I've had a lot of fun, but I ought to be going. My wife is coming to pick me up."

"Ok my dear."

"Perhaps I could visit again one day, if you wouldn't mind?" I said as I stood to leave.

"You can come any time you like. Don't go many places so normally here pottering about. Can't promise I'll remember who you are though." I was impressed with her frankness.

I bent down to give her a hug. "I know you thought Logan was a pain, but I expect he was just trying to be a good neighbour, so try not to think too badly of him. It might be nice to keep a few of the photos."

"Yes, I think I will."

"Bye Jeff."

I paused. "It's Jack."

"Oh, sorry dear. Bye Jack."

Zoe was waiting in the car at the same location she had dropped me off. I opened the passenger side door and slumped into the seat. An enormous sense of relief flushed the anxiety from my nervous system and my body turned dense, sinking down into the chair. But somewhere inside a niggling trace of guilt remained. My satisfaction with the outcome was selfish. I had gotten myself out of a hole, but Mauve had lost her son whether she remembered him or not. In a sense her obliviousness was beneficial to her. There is no grief like that of a mother whose child has passed before their time. I could see that in Zoe. At least Mauve was spared that pain. But I feared there was a remote corner of her brain that knew the truth and was suffering as it mourned undetected.

"Pinch me," I said to Zoe. "Tell me this is not a dream."

"This is definitely real life," Zoe said. "How'd it go?"

"She doesn't remember Logan as her son, just as a pain in the ass that lived next door. Something to do with a head injury that has taken away parts of her memory, or ability to recognise faces. I told her Logan was dead and she said good! She must have had Logan late in life. She's got a good fifteen years on us, minimum."

"Oh my goodness, that's so sad."

"Yes, it is. But at least I didn't leave a devastated old woman behind. She's a lovely lady. As mad as a box of frogs, but lovely. Seems independent enough so I think she'll be ok without Logan for a while, but we should keep an eye on her. I said I would go back some time and she was pleased with the idea."

"Wow. I'm shocked by your empathy. That's not like you."

"Hey, what do you mean?" I said, moderately offended. "I can be empathetic. I'm an emotional guy."

"Ha! Grumpiness doesn't count."

"That's rude."

"But seriously, it was a compliment. I meant *shocked* as in *impressed*. It was a kind thing to do."

"It's the least I can do given the circumstances. Plus, I… had fun."

"Oh yeah? Is this some old lady fetish you've recently developed? Should I be worried?"

"Funny. Just concentrate on the road will you."

CHAPTER 27

I had always thought that the Special Forces selection process would be the most demanding thing I would ever have to endure. A gruelling trial of lengthy marches up and down the mountains of the Brecon Beacons, carrying a bergen on my back that got heavier with every march. The pinnacle was a forty-mile solo hike, carrying twenty-five kilos, to be completed in under twenty-four hours. One guy died of heat exhaustion that day. Then came the jungle training phase in Belize, a long month in a hot, humid, and unforgiving tropical environment that pushed my survival skills to the limit. I was surrounded by things that wanted me dead, venomous animals and poisonous plants, even the smallest scratch could lead to a life-threatening infection. My feet began to rot in the permanent dampness of my boots and only intravenous antibiotics prevented the need for amputation of my toes.

The worst part was the Tactical Questioning phase, or Resistance to Interrogation. A mental challenge, not a physical one. Countless hours spent being forced to sit, stand, and lie in stress positions that required all my effort to maintain, whilst simultaneously being blindfolded and bombarded with the most horrific noises imaginable. Time became irrelevant and reality an abstract concept. I was threatened, insulted, and humiliated, but had to remain silent until enough time had passed for the operational information in my memory to become obsolete. The whole thing was hell. Some of the toughest men I had ever met cried. Some of the fittest died. In the end, nine of the one hundred and twelve soldiers that began the process were left standing. But I'd rather go through that all over again than face what I was having to deal with. I could manage physical exertion and resistance to interrogation as they both relied on factors within my own control. No matter how tired and broken you are, no matter how much you want to give up, you can always take one more step. After that you can take one more, and after enough 'one more steps' you will always find yourself at the finish line. An interrogator can inflict as much pain on you as they like, but they have no method of forcing you to talk so long as you have the will to keep your mouth shut. But the present situation was not in my control. I had minimal means of obtaining reliable information, I was enormously outnumbered and had no back up or senior authority for support. Worst of all, I was emotionally involved, and people close to me were in danger.

Fighting for my country was an honour. Fighting for my family was terrifying.

"Out of the question," I said. "There is no way it's happening."

"I'm not keen on the idea myself but there's no choice," Zoe replied.

"Going to the lab by yourself was one thing, but intentionally meeting those people face-to-face alone is insane. You said yourself they are willing to let millions of people die, so what are they going to care about one awkward woman who is getting in the way of whatever it is they are planning to do?"

"If I don't go then they will get suspicious, and we'll all be in danger. Me, you, and the kids. Better that I go and see what I can find out. Plus, if we are ever going to win this, at some point we are going to have to appeal to someone with the real power to put a stop to it, and for that we'll need evidence. I have an old dictaphone. I could record the meeting and try to elicit something that could be useful."

She had a point. "Ok, but I'm coming with you," I said.

"Impossible."

"Not to the meeting, but in the vicinity. You can take a radio in your bag so I can listen in to what's being said. If at any point it sounds like you are in danger, I'll come to get you out."

"You're forgetting about the armed guard."

"No, I'm not." I hesitated. "I also have a gun."

"What on earth? Where did you get that?"

"The other day when I was on assignment. That guy Pete who shot himself, he got the gun he used from a crate that was supposed to contain solar panels. I took one too. I don't know why. I regretted it at the time, but it's been useful."

"You haven't killed anyone, have you?" Zoe said with alarm.

"Only a dog that wanted to savage me to death." Zoe visibly relaxed. It felt like a good time to get it all out on the table, while she was in a good mood. "Actually... I have two guns." She didn't say anything but gave a look, not an angry one, more like disbelief. "I managed to acquire a rifle last night. Makes you wonder what kind of pharmaceutical company needs a weapons cabinet. But it's too big to be of any use today. That reminds me, it's in the garage. I'll put it in the loft before we go."

"Anything else you want to get off your chest?"

"I don't think so," I said.

"Thank God for that. We better get going. The meeting starts at three o'clock. I'll ask next door to keep an ear out for Zach. Cora is having a sleepover at Ashley's."

I set up camp on the eastern edge of St James's Park, within a safe margin of the radio's three-hundred metre operational range, and a one-minute sprint to Zoe if things got dicey. A wrought-iron bench in a quiet corner of the park made a reasonable base for a couple of hours. It was secluded, but not suspiciously so, like I was hiding. I settled down and took in the surroundings. If it wasn't for the abandoned coffee kiosk, its walls thick with layers of peeling posters and graffiti, I could have been persuaded that I was stationed in the Serengeti. A row of white pelicans, prehistoric looking, with their curvy necks and long yellow bills, sat along the perimeter of a lake up ahead, while twenty more swam around on the green water. I half expected a lion to come prowling out of the untamed, sandy-brown vegetation and stalk across the parched grass that was desperate for a drop of rain.

I unzipped my bag and reached inside to take out a radio. The hard metal surface of the Desert Eagle brushed against the back of my hand. It was an enormous risk to bring a weapon out in public and I needed to avoid prompting any kind of confrontation. It could lead to me being searched and then I'd have to do something that I'd rather not. Zoe and I had gone over the logistics on the journey. She had a two-way radio in her bag with the transmit button taped down so that it constantly broadcasted a signal that would be received by my radio. The microphone on Zoe's radio wasn't very sensitive and so it needed to be placed close as possible to the person speaking. If her bag was placed on the floor between two chairs, I would only be able to hear Zoe and the person she sat next to, so she needed to choose her seat wisely, assuming there was a choice. She was to speak in a way that conveyed as much information as possible but without sounding too contrived, like using people's names in full instead of her/she/they, and repeating information spoken by people that would be out of the radio's range. If she considered herself to be in danger, she would use the phrase "Can we take a break for five minutes?" Best-case they would agree, and she could move to somewhere safer. Worst-case I would move in to extract.

I adjusted the volume on the radio so that I could hear what was happening. The only sound at that moment was the clip-clop of heals on hard flooring. A door creaking open and clunking shut. A chair scraping across the floor. A thud.

"Hello Zoe." A faint crackle of mystery voice.

"Olivia," Zoe replied. She had chosen her seat well.

There were a few minutes of background chatter that I couldn't make out. Then Oliva spoke again. "Yes, there was an arson attack at the facility last night. One male was killed trying to flee but it is believed that he had at least one accomplice that managed to get away. They targeted a building that is used as a waste storage area, but we believe the fire was a distraction as the accomplice took a weapon from the security room. Investigations are ongoing but the most likely motive was to obtain firearms. There was no damage to inventory so we can continue as planned."

It was excellent news. No indication that they knew who was involved and taking the gun had thrown them off the scent of our real reason of being there, not that they would notice two missing vials. But arson as a distraction to obtain firearms was a nice little theory all tied up with a bow. And no mention of Stuart's involvement. I prayed he was ok.

Then Zoe spoke. "I would like to understand what you mean by *continue as planned*. I hope you can forgive my reaction on Wednesday. I was taken off-guard by the sudden change in direction. I was under the impression that we were phasing the roll-out to gather further safety data."

"The passion and pride you have for your work is undeniable, Zoe. No need to apologise," Olivia said. "The new plan is all about maximising uptake. But it means making some difficult decisions. The safety of this drug is not where we want it, but the rate of adverse reactions needs to be weighed up against the benefit of having a fully treated population. The concern is that if we take too long there will be greater awareness of potential side effects and increasing numbers of women will refuse the drug."

"I see," Zoe said. I could imagine the colour of her face and hoped she was managing to keep her feelings concealed.

"I understand that perspective. But that means we would be taking away women's right of bodily autonomy."

"*We* are not doing anything beyond providing data and recommendations. Your safety recommendation is clear, as is the uptake projection put together by my statisticians. The decision is Alvina's to make as what she sees to be in the country's best interest, and she has done so. This is on Alvina's shoulders, not yours."

"Understood," Zoe said. "A couple more questions for clarity, if I may."

"Of course."

"The treatment I developed has a limited shelf-life. How have you managed to stockpile so much inventory in advance?"

"Our chemists have made a few tweaks during scale-up to extend usage period." It was a quickfire but vague response.

"Any changes to the product need to be validated to ensure no impact to safety or efficacy."

"We have done so."

"May I see the data?"

"No. You'll have to take my word for it."

"Alright," Zoe said. "Second question, what's the criticality of having a fully treated population that it weighs so heavily on the balance to warrant hundreds of thousands of potential deaths? It's not like we are dealing with a contagious, life-threatening pathogen."

"That is relevant to phase 2."

"Which is?"

"On a need-to-know basis," Olivia said bluntly. "But that is a nice segue into the late addition to the agenda. Alvina, shall I leave this one to you?"

I screwed my eyes shut and placed the radio to my ear, but I couldn't hear anything further being said. An old man wearing a woolly beanie hat and a long, beige trench coat appeared out of nowhere and sat next to me, a little too closely. He had a musty odour about him, not dirty, but like he needed airing out. "Hello son," he said. "Lovely day, isn't it?"

"Hi. Yes, it is nice," I said, in a short response. I didn't want to be rude, but I couldn't take my attention away from what was being said in the room.

He peered at me through squinted eyes, and then at my radio. I could see him puzzling over my presence. "I love to come for walks around here," he said. Autumn is my favourite time of year for it. The trees turn such a wonderful golden colour. Then around February or March, when the daffodils and crocuses pop out. A lovely sea of yellow and purple." This time I ignored him, but he continued. "The pelicans have been here for four-hundred years, you know. Should be fifty of them around somewhere, although I expect numbers are dwindling these days. Gifted by the Russian Ambassador in 1664."

Zoe's voice crackled through the radio. "You can't do that!" she said.

That? What use is *that*? I instructed her to convey as much information as possible. Not just *that*. She began saying something else, but the old man started talking again.

"They say Charles II used to come down here and —"

"Look," I interrupted. "I don't mean to be rude, but I'm kind of in the middle of something. Please would you go and sit somewhere else?"

In a swift manoeuvre like something out of a martial arts movie, the guy swished open his trench coat, pulled out an eight-inch knife, slid up next to me and jabbed the blade into my ribs, almost puncturing the skin. I grabbed hold of his hand to force the tip of the knife away from my body, but he was much stronger than he looked. His hand was large with calloused knuckles and with an up-close perspective it became obvious that his grey stubble told a lie about his age.

He wasn't an elderly man, perhaps a few years older than me, but he was weathered, like he had seen his fair share of suffering. Deep lines in his leathery skin formed crows-feet around his blue eyes. "What are you doing here?" he said in a gravelly voice.

Zoe's voice again. "What about the rest of the team?"

"I'm not doing anything," I said. "Just sat enjoying the sun."

"Who is that on the radio?" the man asked.

"I don't know. I think I'm picking up a crossed channel. I brought this to stay in contact with my daughter. She's out running around the park. She'll be back in a second." My hand that was not trying to release the pressure of the knife inched towards the open end of my bag.

"Don't give me that. A man sat on his own, within spitting distance of government buildings, listening to a two-way radio. You're up to something."

In one movement, I shoved the man's weapon-holding hand away from me at the same time as pulling out the Desert Eagle, aiming it at waist height into his gut. He looked surprised, but in an impressed kind of way. A moment passed as we sat like two aged stags locking horns, grandstanding before engaging in combat. An incredible tension flowed through our connected limbs.

"Tell me what you are doing here, or you won't be walking away from this alive," he said.

"That's a bold statement for someone with a gun aimed at them," I replied.

He laughed. "I could have that off you in less than a second." He wasn't bluffing, or at least he believed it. "If you were going to kill me you would have done it by now."

Zoe's voice came through the radio again. "You'll have to drag me kicking and screaming!"

"Who is that talking on the radio?" the man asked.

"That's my wife."

"She in there?" he nodded towards the Whitehall office buildings.

"Yes."

"What's her name?"

"Zoe," I said. The tension between us instantly dissipated and the knife fell to his side.

"Zoe Wilson?" he said, his eyes wide open.

I was filled with a mix of intrigue and apprehension. "Yes, how do you..."

"So that makes you Jack."

"How do you know all this?" I said, more forcefully this time.

"Zoe is not supposed to be at the meeting."

"Can you tell me what's going on?"

"She is in danger."

"Why?"

"There is an explosive device in that meeting room set to go off at any minute."

I studied the expression on his face. Stared through his eyes into the depths of his soul. He was telling the truth. My heart momentarily stopped. "How do you know?"

"Never mind that. Can you contact her through that radio?"

"No, I can only receive her signal. How did a bomb get into the room, and how do you know?"

"I have contacts."

"Call them and get them to stand down."

"I can't, and even if I could... this is too important."

"Sod this," I said, as I slung everything into my bag, stood up, and sprinted toward the park exit at the southeasterly corner. I found myself on a wide, main road which, on the right, vanished off into the distance in a convergence of trees that lined the pavements. Ahead and to the left was the perimeter of the cordoned off area that contained the government buildings. Fifty metres down, the security checkpoint was occupied by the same giant as the previous occasion. I crouched down behind a parked car and reached into my bag. I put on my baseball cap and pulled it down to cover my face. Then I took out the gun and shoved it down the back of my trousers. I marched towards the checkpoint. The armed guard in her black SWAT gear was standing tall in a commanding position, with a small semi-automatic machine gun held diagonally across her chest pointing at the ground.

Her day was about to get as exciting as it had ever been.

Hidden by a bus shelter, I whipped out the gun and fired two shots into the windows of the small hut at the security gate. The guard leapt out of her skin then crouched to the ground, covering her head as the thundering gunshots reverberated around the tall buildings. The glass of the security hut windows exploded into a shower of diamonds that twinkled in the sunshine as they scattered all over the ground. The guard scanned around from her crouched position like a stalked doe, obviously unsure whether to stand and fight the invisible enemy or to flee for her life. I willed her to run. She eventually chose a third option of diving for cover in the hut. She must have hit a panic button as the streets were suddenly filled with the penetrating sound of alarm bells, activating a few seconds apart around the vicinity.

That was not part of the plan.

I stood to make my move across the perimeter when people began filing out of the buildings. They were relaxed and chatting to each other and moved over to congregate under a tree in a landscaped area of the square garden. It was the opposite of what they ought to be doing in the event of a potential terrorist threat but presumably thought the alarm was a fire drill. The entrance to Zoe's building was on the adjacent parallel street, so I didn't have direct visibility to tell if they were also vacating. All I could do was pray that they were, as far too many people had amassed outside for me to risk an extraction. I considered my next move: stay and wait for Zoe to show up or hightail it out of there and meet her somewhere safer. Both scenarios relied on her making her own way to safety which I didn't like but couldn't avoid.

Before I could decide, the sound of the alarm bells was drowned out by an almighty explosion in the buildings in front, generating a shockwave that shattered the nearby windows and sent the congregated office workers bolting for shelter, screaming whilst spilling out into the streets and hiding behind cars or crouched behind walls. The air filled with the smell of war, smoke, dust, explosive residue. My stomach dropped. I scrambled through my bag for the radio to see if I could determine Zoe's location, but when I pulled it out all I could hear was the crackling hiss of the dead signal.

CHAPTER 28

Three at the dog. Two at the hut. Five of seven.

I checked the magazine of the gun. One round remained, but there should have been two. I scratched my head. I might have started with six. I couldn't remember. Either way, with one round remaining, the risk of carrying the gun outweighed its usefulness. I needed to find Zoe. I wasn't ready to contemplate anything other than her being alive and well, but finding one individual amongst the hundreds of people that were milling about, leaderless and directionless, was near impossible. And before going any further, I needed to deal with the cold steel problem in my hand.

Then I had an idea.

The lake in St James's Park was twenty metres through the park entrance behind me. I retreated through the chaos into the park, slid myself in amongst the bushes and let the final round off into the air. Its roaring boom sent everyone scattering. I wiped down the gun as best I could and launched it into the centre of the lake where it landed with a deep splosh and sank to the bottom like an incriminating rock. I exited the park and headed back to the street, which the gun shot had left deserted. Broken glass crunched underfoot as I jogged towards where Zoe would have exited the building. A handful of people remained under the tree in the garden and several more were ambling through the streets, but nobody that I recognised and none that were my wife.

"Zoe!" I shouted, my voice echoing off the high walls in

the eerie silence. "Zoe!"

I rounded the corner on to the road with the office entrance and was confronted with a scene of absolute devastation. Smoke and dust filled the air. Glass and debris covered the ground. The stretched, black car that had picked us up from the train station lay diagonally across the road and flipped on to its roof, the driver's arm hanging out the window, grazed to the bone, having left a red smear across the tarmac. A woman in a red dress was folded in the middle like a ragdoll, impaled on the black railings that surrounded the building. My mouth filled with vomit as I saw a lifeless body with brown hair and wearing a black suit lying face down on the pavement, legs and arms bent unnaturally like a mistreated toy.

Please God, no!

I raced over, skidding to a halt through the fragments of glass. "Zoe!"

I rolled the dead weight of the body on to its back. Dark brown eyes were unresponsive and stared straight through me like I was invisible. Her face was burnt, bloodied and barely identifiable, but my heart skipped as I realised... it wasn't her. I closed the stranger's eyelids and brushed down her dusty clothes to send her on her journey with dignity.

Behind me a guttural, gurgle caught my attention. The driver of the car was alive, strapped upside-down to the chair of his inverted car by his seatbelt. Blood streamed from his mouth and his face was covered with dozens of small cuts. The arm that was reaching out the window was bent in three places and his forearm was loosely attached to his elbow by a mess of exposed tendons and ligaments. His skin had begun to pick up a greyish hue with amount of blood lost to the pool that was collecting on the inside of the car roof. I pulled on the door handle and heaved as the top of the door scraped open against the concrete. I reached in and released the seatbelt, sending the driver falling like a sack of meat and landing with an agonising groan. He grunted and moaned as I dragged him out of the car.

"Jack?" a call from behind me. Zoe stepped through the door to the building under the arm of a younger woman with blonde hair, helping to support her weight as the younger girl hobbled along beside her.

"Oh, thank god," I said as I rushed over, wrapped my arms around her and squeezed. "I thought I had lost you." I patted her down, inspecting her, checking for signs of injury. Both Zoe and the blonde girl were covered in dust and soot, but despite the girl's limp, they appeared unscathed.

"Stop fussing, I'm fine," she said. "Can you give me a hand with Jenny?"

I wrapped Jenny's other arm over my shoulder and the three of us staggered down the stone steps to street level. Jenny winced as she put weight on her right leg and had a small patch of blood seeping through her tights on her right knee which trickled down her shin. "Are you ok?" I said. "What happened to your leg?"

"It's nothing serious," replied Jenny. "I tripped as we were coming down the stairs."

I looked across to Zoe. "This is a clusterfuck. There are other people involved. I don't know who, but this guy came up to me in the park and...". My speculating was interrupted by the growing sound of a vehicle approaching, the unmistakable gruffness of a diesel engine that was getting closer rapidly. Then an old white transit van screeched around the corner in a cloud of black smoke. It came to a halt in front of us and the side door slid open.

"Get in!" It was the man from the park bench. Jenny smiled and led us forward.

"Wait a minute. I'm not getting in there," I said.

"It's ok Jack," Zoe replied. "I think they are on our side. I'd be dead if it weren't for Jenny."

I hesitated, studying the man's blue eyes as he leant out

the van, holding out a welcoming hand. I turned back to the driver of the overturned black car. "What about him?"

"He's not our problem," the man replied.

"Yes, he is," I said. "Your explosion caused this. He's going to bleed out. I'm not going to leave another man to die. Not this time."

"Fine, bring him in. My wife has some basic medical training. But you're wasting your time judging by the state of him."

The driver screamed in pain as I tried to get him to his feet. He was unable to stand. I bent down, lifted him up on to my shoulder and carried him into the side of the van. I sat him on the edge and the mysterious man grabbed him from under the armpits and pulled him inside as I lifted his feet. I leapt in after and slid the door shut. The van pulled off and the four of us that were sitting up steadied ourselves against the rusty, white walls as we lurched and bumped around. We were sitting on a grimy plywood floor, stained with engine oil that saturated the air with its sickly odour. The windows in the rear doors were painted white and let through the slightest amount of light, giving a mustardy glow that just enabled us to see each other's faces. I looked around, waiting for someone to say something.

"Somebody better start talking," I said, as I released the buckle of my belt and whipped it out through the loops of my trousers. I tied it in a loop around the bloody stump of the driver's partially severed arm. The driver groaned as I pulled it tight in a makeshift tourniquet. "So?"

"My name is Tobias Beck," the man said. "You can call me Beck. And this is my daughter, Jenny."

"And?" I said.

"We are part of a small group that has concerns about government activity. You just ruined our only hope of putting an end to whatever they are planning."

"I... what you talking about? You almost blew up my wife!" I said.

"Zoe wasn't supposed to be in that meeting," Jenny said. "She was added at the last minute when Olivia Sharp requested the shutdown of the labs."

I looked across to Zoe. "That is what they called you in for? They are shutting you down?"

"Yes," Zoe replied. "They've pulled our funding and are reallocating resources to a new project. Said we have fulfilled our purpose."

"You have, haven't you? You've achieved what you set out to do?" I said, not concentrating on what I was saying as I applied pressure to the driver's open wound.

"Except we know that's not what they are planning on using," Zoe said.

The stress of the situation was making me agitated. "Where do you fit in to this?" I said, looking at Jenny.

"I work with Alvina, as an assistant. I got a job there six years ago to support the movement."

"And you?" I said to Beck.

"We'll get to that, Jack," he replied gently. "I can tell you're shaken up. Sit back, relax, and enjoy the journey. All will become clear in time."

There wasn't much to enjoy about jarring around in the cargo hold of a ramshackle transit van, but I leant back on the wall and let the vibrations judder their way through the back of my skull. Beck shuffled across to sit next to Jenny and put his strong arm around her like a cloak of protection. He removed his beanie hat and ran his hand through thick locks of wavey, silver hair. The knife wielding maniac I had met in the park had transformed into a doting father who tended to his child's injured leg. Jenny, despite being in her mid-thirties, played every bit the wounded toddler, head nestled into her father's side and winching when he got close to touching her wound.

A shard of pain penetrated my chest as memories of tending to Grace poured out. Dabbing the grazed elbow of a little girl who had fallen off her bike. Rocking her to sleep when she was crying with a fever. My arms locked around her like impenetrable armour on that supermarket floor. I watched Beck comfort Jenny. The pain gave way to emptiness. Then envy. Then sadness. I stifled the tears that welled in the corner of my eyes. I wasn't going to cry, no matter how much I wanted to. Not there. Zoe obviously sensed what was going on inside my head as she cuddled up next to me.

"Come here," she said as she rested her head on my shoulder. "She would be so happy to see you back to yourself, you know."

"Perhaps. But I left it too late, didn't I?"

"What happened to Grace wasn't your fault. You need to stop beating yourself up."

I didn't want to talk about that any longer. "So, what went on in your meeting? From what I heard we are no clearer on what's going on, other than there is a phase 2."

"That's about the gist of it. That bitch Olivia is cagey as hell. All this *your pride is undeniable* stuff is pretentious bullshit. But whatever they're up to can't be any good. There is evil in that woman. You can see it in her eyes. She's loving the power and Alvina just goes along with it. Would be interesting to know what dirt Olivia has on her."

"So, you think Altior is pulling the strings?" I asked.

"That's the way it comes across."

"And your lab is being closed? What does that mean for you?" I said, trying not to sound too pleased about it.

"They can't close the lab as its owned by the university, but funding for the project has been withdrawn immediately and further self-funded research in the area is forbidden."

"Forbidden? Isn't that a bit shady?"

"Very. But shady sums the whole thing up."

We had been moving for around an hour and a half when the vehicle slowed and began to shake from side-to-side like a raucous fairground ride.

"We're here," Beck said. "Sorry, the track to the house is a bit bumpy."

"Just a bit," I said, as I leaned forward, steadying the car driver who was rolling around on the oily floor.

The van eventually came to a stop and Beck sprang to his feet and pulled open the door. "Welcome to HQ," he said. "It's no palace, but we are safe here. Make yourself at home."

I stepped out of the van on to a dusty, cracked mud floor, like it had previously been waterlogged and dried out. We were on a plot of land about an acre in size. The boundary was marked by a two-rail fence made of gnarled, twisted wood. Beyond the fence was mature woodland of fir trees with rolling hills visible in the distance through sporadic gaps. Within the boundary, the garden was wild. Tall clumps of brown grass sprung up to waist height like little explosions in freeze frame. A handful of apple trees that were beginning to bear their small green fruits formed an orchard at the far end of the plot. A derelict barn with corrugated iron roof took up most of the right-hand side and the left was dominated by the main dwelling, a two-storey farmhouse with textured, white rendered walls and a thinning thatched roof that exposed rafters in places and was partially covered by a blue tarpaulin that flapped in the breeze. The noise of the diesel engine wound down with a rattle, and we were enveloped in dense silence. I listened for signs of civilisation but could only hear what sounded like chickens clucking in the barn.

"This is a nice peaceful spot," I said to Beck. "Where are we?"

"It's better that you don't know," he replied.

"The problem is I have a fourteen-year-old at home by himself so if we are miles from home then we'll need to get going."

"Ah, Zach," he said with a knowing smile.

"Yes, but..."

"We're around fifty miles, roughly south from where we started. Not much more than an hour from where you live."

The driver side door of the transit opened and closed and a woman in her late fifties stepped out. She wore urban camo trousers, black boots, and a black vest top. Her shoulders and biceps were lean and defined, and she wore grey hair in a shoulder-length plait. She strode towards Zoe and I with friendly confidence and offered a firm handshake. "Pleased to meet you Zoe, Jack. I'm Isabella. People call me Bella."

Beck walked over and kissed Bella on the cheek. "Nice driving darling," he said.

"I do the best with the tools I have," she said with a scornful eyeroll toward the van.

"Hey," Beck said. "Don't knock old Betty. She's done two-hundred K and she'll do a hundred more."

"Let's get our driver friend inside," Bella said. "He seems rather poorly." Then she looked at Beck. "Fetch us a drink will you Toby? Something strong."

This time I went straight in for the fireman's lift. It must have been agonising for the poor guy, but I figured it was like pulling off a plaster, best to get it over and done with quickly. Easy for me to say with my arm securely attached to my body.

Bella led us around the back of the house to a set of double doors in the ground which she heaved open to reveal steps leading down to a basement. She went first and switched on the lights. "Watch your head as you come through," she said. I descended one step at a time into the basement and ducked my head as I reached the doorway. I couldn't stand full height, so I waddled along hunched over. "Put him down over here," Bella said, patting an old, threadbare faux-leather sofa. I placed him down as gently as I could but a crunch in his rib cage led to a distressed yelp. Bella checked over his head, face, and neck, lifted his shirt and manipulated his legs before concentrating on his arm.

"Are you a doctor?" I asked.

"No, but I spent some time in the medical corps when I was younger so was surrounded by them for a while. Saw some stuff and picked a few things up," she said as she bent down to inspect the underside of his injured arm. "Can't tell what internal injuries he has, other than an obvious broken rib or three. Cuts are mostly superficial, no sign of major head trauma, but this arm is a real problem. There's no saving it. It's going to have to come off at the elbow and I'll need to cauterise the wound to stop the bleeding."

The man hadn't spoken a word but must have understood what was being said as his eyes opened wide with an expression of sheer horror.

Zoe arrived at my shoulder. "I don't suppose you have any anaesthetic and antibiotics?"

"Nope," Bella replied. "I have a bottle of vodka and a blow torch."

Beck came down the stairs with a bottle of spirit, followed by Jenny clinking along with a tower of stacked glasses. Beck took the glasses and poured an inch of colourless liquid into each, then passed them round. Then he gave the remaining half bottle to the patient. "Here you go, you poor bugger. Cheers everyone." Beck downed the liquid in one go. The man on the sofa took a large gulp from the bottle causing him to cough and splutter all over his blood-stained shirt. Then he took another and laid his head back and closed his eyes.

"I'll give that a minute to kick in before I get to work," Bella said. "Toby, why don't you take our guests to sit down."

I was glad of the suggestion as I had no desire to watch what was about to happen. Beck gave a summoning wave, and we followed him to a round, wooden table in the corner of the basement. It was the first time that I had paid any attention to the surroundings. The basement was a wide, open area that spanned the full footprint of the property with the low hanging ceiling being supported by a grid of block pillars. A single lightbulb illuminated the centre of the room with warm light that diffused into blackness as it faded toward the walls, giving the rectangular room a circular quality. The space was filled with old farming machinery and wooden crates stacked up in orderly piles. The reassuring hum of a generator came from one of the corners where the light couldn't reach. The corner we were heading towards, however, was an oasis in the darkness. Mini floodlights brought the basement walls into artificial daytime. The scene in front of us was like something you'd expect from a murder investigation, with boards covered with photos, newspaper clippings, maps and hand-scrawled notes. There were large pictures of Alvina and some of the other main government figures, and another section dedicated to key players at Altior. Zoe's name was written under a section headed 'Project Theia' and beneath her name was written the names of all our family. Grace's name had a red line through it.

"What's Project Theia?" I whispered to Zoe.

"It's the code name for the development of the cure," she replied.

"What does it mean?"

"Theia was Gaia's daughter. Goddess of vision and brilliance."

"Who came up with that?" I said.

"I did."

"How modest of you," I teased.

Beck pulled out one of the four wooden chairs. "Sit down guys," he said after sitting down himself. The wooden chair scraped across the damp concrete as I pulled it out and sat opposite Beck. He sat in a confident pose with his elbows on the table and fingertips pressed together in front of his lips. Large veins snaked up his bulky forearms. I was now certain of my suspicion. Beck was ex-military too. The way he carried himself, his physique, his skill with weapons, it had to be the case. Zoe and Jenny joined us and sat opposite each other on the adjacent chairs.

"Let's get it all out on the table, shall we?" Beck said. "Who wants to start?"

For some inexplicable reason, everyone looked at me. "What?" I said. "Seven days ago, I was a depressive househusband whose mundane life would reach peak excitement at finding fresh carrots at the supermarket. Every day since has been a nightmarish adventure that you couldn't make up. I'm the one that needs answers!"

"We may have some answers for you, Jack," Beck replied. "But I don't want to tell you things you already know. Let's start with the virus that caused the Gaia, and how the government might be involved."

"Well," I said. "If you had asked me a week ago, I would have said the origin of The Gaia was unknown and a feminist political party capitalised on the dwindling male population to get into power and enact their insane policies. But now I know from Zoe that attempts at developing the cure were intentionally delayed, I suspect there may be more to it than that. Taking advantage of a situation is one thing, but actively preventing a way out suggests something else."

"Ok," Beck said. "And I assume you have heard of Altior?"

"In the last few days," I replied. "One of the most outrageous things to happen this week was that the British Prime Minister was standing in my kitchen. She explained to me that Altior is a private company that helps fund and build infrastructure in return for some beneficial treatment that she was curiously vague about."

"Anything to add Zoe?" Beck said. "You've been closer to

this than most?"

"Nothing factual, but I have some theories," Zoe replied. "I have been working on projects aimed at developing a treatment for The Gaia for many years. Some were genuine dead ends. Others, as soon as we started showing signs of success, something would push us off course. Head researchers suddenly falling ill. A fire in the laboratory. Or as with the case with the Paris collaboration, funding was blatantly and openly removed at a critical moment. So, no matter what the origin of The Gaia, Alvina obviously likes things the way they are, but wants to give the impression that we are trying to do something about it."

"OK," Beck said. "We're on the same page with more recent events. But sounds like you're missing some of the backstory. Are you aware of Alvina's Chinese heritage?"

"Only recently," I said.

"Ava Lee," Beck continued, "originally Yuanling Li. Her mother was a prominent Thai politician. Her Chinese father, a senior figure in the CCP." He pointed at photographs on the board. "Ava studied politics at Oxford and applied for UK citizenship on conclusion of her studies. During her time at university, she was an ardent feminist and was notorious for her activism, often causing major disruption in the capital. She got in trouble with the police on multiple occasions when marches she organised, both in Oxford and London, got out of hand. She later got into UK politics and started her own party."

"I can't say I'm surprised about the activism," I said, "but how is her background not common knowledge?"

"All references to it have been erased over time," Beck replied. "Her renaming as Alvina was part of it. It's easier to drop a surname than suddenly change one, even if it did only give a slight nod to her original name. You won't find reference to her father's nationality, or any connection to China for that matter, in any book printed in the last twenty-five years."

"Hmm," I said in contemplation. It was absurd yet also, at a stretch, plausible.

"Here is where it gets interesting," Beck said. "There is some evidence to suggest that the virus that caused The Gaia was developed by China."

"I don't believe it," Zoe chipped in. "Why would they do that?"

"The why is obvious. Destabilisation of a political enemy. Think about it. They have targeted males when the Chinese have a strong preference for sons. The condition they have chosen results in horrific disfigurement which goes against the Chinese values of keeping face and personal dignity. And this is the best part, any guesses on the Chinese lucky number?"

I suddenly felt a bit sick. "Eight?"

"Bingo!" Beck said. "So, Alvina didn't capitalise on The Gaia to get in to power, China intentionally distributed this virus to get her in to power, bring the country to its knees and allow Alvina to keep it there."

"Shit," Zoe said. "Which is why we haven't been allowed to progress with development of a cure."

"Indeed," Beck replied.

"How do you know all this?" I said.

"It's a combination of things," Beck said. "In a previous life I was in the Marines, a Captain in the 30 Commando Unit based down at Stonehouse Barracks in Plymouth. We specialised in intelligence and surveillance. I was one of the senior officers who did *not* accept the bribe of a cushy job in a dingey government office to keep me quiet when they decided to break us all up. We managed to maintain a small network of senior military figures who kept tabs on things in the dark. Obviously, we have no domestic resources to do much about anything but did have connections with some of our foreign allies who were useful for intel."

"Why haven't they done anything to help us? And how have you managed to make all these communications without being caught?" I asked.

"We have encrypted satellite phones that connect via systems that our government have no access to. Pretty much untraceable to them, unless they knew what they were looking for. Which they don't. Any help from other countries was strictly off the record. Just nuggets of information passed from previously held contacts. Don't forget, China is a huge part of the Global Alliance and so nobody is going to risk upsetting their utopia for our sake." He paused for breath. "But incoming comms have dwindled over recent years as our contacts have moved on. Jenny managed to get promoted from receptionist to Alvina's assistant and has been feeding information back directly since. Can you believe the background check they did as part of Jenny's promotion considered my position in the military as a positive thing? That's the calibre of the people we are dealing with. Unfortunately, the stupidest people tend to be the most dangerous."

"And where do Altior fit in to this?" Zoe said.

"Originally, we thought they were a financial gateway for China to help fund and implement Alvina's government policies but dressed up as a UK private enterprise to avoid suspicion among the public and other foreign interests. But more recently we think there may be more to it than that. They are becoming increasingly operational. How people are recruited into the organisation is a mystery. Most of them have no obvious foreign links."

Our conversation was interrupted by a scream so loud that it threatened to reduce the crumbling farmhouse to rubble around us. Then a burning, meaty odour wafted in our direction, like what I remembered grilled bacon to smell like, but less appetising. I knew what was going on behind me and I wasn't going to look. The expression on Beck's face, who had full view over my shoulder, said it all.

"Jesus..." Beck said, screwing up his face.

Zoe cut back in with a welcome distraction. "So, we are all up to date with distant and recent history. What comes next?"

"We are more in the dark here," Beck said. "For some reason they allowed you to finish developing the cure this time. But we know that they don't plan to administer it. That's as far as we got. Altior is a heavily siloed organisation, and no division knows everything about what's going on. Only those at the top. Which is why we decided to end this by taking them out. But now that's failed, and we are not going to get another opportunity."

"Wait a minute," I said. "You don't know what they are planning to administer in place of the cure?"

"No," Beck said.

I smiled. It was nice to be ahead of the curve for once. "Zoe?"

"I analysed a sample at the lab this morning and it matches a compound that we developed several years ago. It changes the male survival rate from one-in-eight to zero-in-eight. One-hundred percent mortality of male foetuses, essentially."

Beck was clearly taken aback by this revelation as he opened his mouth, but nothing came out for several seconds. "Incredible," he eventually said. "Where did you get this sample from?"

"The facility in D20. I managed to infiltrate last night," I said.

"Wait a minute. The fire at the drug factory, that was you?" Beck's face lit up like a child on Christmas Day morning.

"Yes, kind of." I wanted to give Logan his credit, but it was an unnecessary and complicated detail.

"Brilliant!" Beck shouted, slamming his palm on the table, and tipping his head back in a roar of joyous laughter. "You SAS boys never disappoint. Brilliant!" I felt embarrassed as a ball of pride swelled inside me, blocking my throat, and preventing me from saying 'thanks'. It had been a long time since I had received that kind of recognition. Then in a moment of realisation, Beck's expression turned stern. "One-hundred percent mortality? What are they up to?"

"We couldn't work that out either," I said.

Bella came to join us, wiping her hands with a blood-stained towel. "I've done all I can. It's quite a shock for the body to recover from. He has lost a lot of blood, but it's stopped. I'll cook him up some chicken livers for when he gets his appetite back. Get his iron levels up."

"Good job, Love," Beck said. "Let's take stock. In as little as seventy-two hours, women across the country will begin receiving drugs that could stop a baby boy ever being born again. From what Olivia said at the press conference, plans for distribution are already well advanced so we stand no chance of disrupting it physically. We could be talking about scores, or hundreds of treatment centres and we don't even know where to begin looking."

"What about your ex-military network? Can they help?" Zoe asked.

"We've dwindled to a group of seven, most of whom are now old codgers. Perhaps given enough time we could muster up some resistance, but nothing can be done in three days. The only hope of killing this now is to chop off the head, but following today's shambles the various players are going to be dispersed and with increased security. We don't even know where Alvina might be staying." Cracks in Beck's cool and confident demeanour broke open and drops of frustration began oozing out.

From behind me on the old leather sofa, a weak and croaky voice uttered its first words of the day. "I might be able to help with that."

CHAPTER 29

20:00 - Friday 8th June 2063

"The first cases of holo... holo... prosency were discovered in June 2023 in the Chelsea & Westminster Hospital, London. Alarm bells were sounded when four cases were detected in the space of one week... Dad! Wake up." Zach prodded my face as I lay on the sofa, battling my crippling exhaustion. As soon as I walked through the door after Bella dropped us home, Zach bounded up full of excitement, clutching a pile of books that he had brought home from the library as requested. He sat reading with his bent knees over my horizontal body. But his audience was not as attentive as he would like. "Come on, are you listening?"

"Yes of course I am. I was just resting my eyes. You were saying four cases in one week."

"Yes... it says... Cases began spreading to all corners of the country within six months. The virus had a low transmission rate, and the genetic alterations were triggered when a threshold viral load had been reached. This meant that the virus remained contained within the island of Great Britain, however extensive testing of foreign visitors to Britain was conducted by countries around the world and approximately fifteen-thousand infected tourists were returned to Britain for quarantine." Zach looked puzzled. "What does that mean?"

"I think it means that the virus didn't spread easily, and you had to spend a long time around it before it made you poorly."

"Oh," he said. "Shall I continue?"

"Does it say anything about where it came from?"

He flicked through the pages for a few seconds before settling on one. "Origins. The true origin of the virus remains a mystery, however the lead theory is that it jumped to humans from a domesticated rabbit. Genetic sequencing of the virus shows large sections of DNA consistent with viruses found in Leporidae species." Zach started giggling.

"What's so funny?" I asked.

"Rabbits are supposed to be good luck, not bad. It says in my encyclopaedia, the bit about the Chinese Zodiac."

"Excuse me?" I said, sitting bolt upright.

"The Chinese Zodiac. You know they have different animals for different years?"

"So, what's this year's animal?"

"A goat."

"What about 2023?" I was suddenly interested.

"Hang on," he replied. "Let me get my book." Zach toddled off and returned a minute later carrying a heavy textbook. "There are twelve animals. The order goes: Rat, Ox, Tiger, Rabbit, Dragon, Snake, Horse, Goat, Monkey, Rooster, Dog, Pig. 2023 was forty years ago. That means thirty-six years ago, would be the same as now, a goat, then count back four more…" Zach counted in his head and started giggling again. "It's the rabbit again." A rabbit-based virus in the year of the rabbit, a supposed lucky symbol. I didn't find it so funny. It could have been a coincidence of course, but it added weight to the possibility that Beck was not a deluded madman. Zach read from his book. "The rabbit is associated with good fortune and happiness. The year of the rabbit is considered a favourable year for things such as starting a new business or having a baby."

"A good year for having a baby? That's what it says?"

"Yep," he said. "We're both snakes."

"Pardon me?"

"In the zodiac. Both born in the year of the snake."

"In that case you better slither off into bed. Hissss!"

Zach ran up the stairs in fits of laughter and my heart glowed with warmth. Father and son bonding over something so morbid. Who would have thought? But my thoughts switched to other matters. I was so tired that I was beginning to question my own sanity and I needed an early night to be fresh for the next day. It turned out the car driver's name was Adam and saving his life had been a masterstroke. Thanks to Adam, the plan was clear, for stage one at least.

08:30 – Saturday 9th June 2063

A warm breeze blew in through the open window, sending the curtains flapping like tethered ghosts. The skies were an angry grey, and the air was saturated with moisture. It had that feeling of needing to rain. I left Zoe snoring and went downstairs as Cora arrived home from her sleepover. Zoe's words rang in my ears.

You need to find another way.

"Hey Cora," I said. "Could we have a chat?"

"What now?" she replied in her standard petulant tone.

"I'm not looking for a fight. I want to find a way where you and I can have some mutual respect and talk to each other like adults. That includes Zach too. We should be able to be kind to each other, even if we don't always agree on things. Being able to see things from other people's perspectives is an important part of growing up." I waited, giving her space to respond, but she sat in silence in her self-assured way. "I don't want to live in a house where there is fighting and shouting all the time. It's not nice."

"You won't need to worry about that for much longer," she said as she stood.

"Cora, please can you sit down? What do you mean?"

"I don't want to live with *you* that way either," she said. Something had changed. For the first time ever, I sensed a hint of hurt in her voice. Not the usual screaming and shouting, but genuine upset. I thought she was going to cry. Then she walked off and vanished up the stairs to her bedroom.

"Cora, please, come on!"

I slammed my hand on the table in frustration leaving my palm red and stinging. I couldn't understand what I needed to do to connect with her. Perhaps I had left it too late. Perhaps I had done things my own stubborn way for too long and driven her away for good. If I was honest with myself, the connection had never been there. Not like with Grace. With Grace, the love was always there. Unconditional and unwavering. Even during the difficult teenage years when she was screaming in my face. But Cora had been a difficult child ever since starting school and before that all she ever wanted was Zoe. We never had a chance to forge that bond that makes it possible to stay close when life gets tough. My palm throbbed with its own heartbeat as I sat with my shoulders slumped and my head hung low. Sorrow and shame built up to a critical pressure, bursting the dam that held the reservoir of guilt. I gave up. Surrendered. Capitulated. I couldn't do it anymore. I was so deeply sorry. Sorry that I had failed her. Sorry that I didn't know how to fix it. But mostly sorry for the question that flashed through my mind.

Never mind love, did I even *like* my own daughter?

No parent should question such a thing about their child. But her persistent defiance made it impossible to get close. Maybe, I thought, the best thing is to disconnect myself, reduce the emotional investment and let Zoe take control. Even if just for a while to see if things would improve with time. They couldn't get any worse, or so I thought.

A pair of warm hands squeezed my shoulders. "Why are you sitting here alone like Mr Grumpy Pants? Did I hear Cora?"

Zoe said.

I let out an audible sigh. "Yes, she's gone upstairs. Honestly, I give up. I tried speaking to her like an adult and she walked off. I know you see it as a rebellious phase but I'm telling you that she thinks females are superior to males. There is nothing I can do as there is zero respect. I need you to start backing me up more often."

"You're right. Let me have a chat with her later while you are out," Zoe replied.

CHAPTER 30

18:00 – Saturday 9th June 2063

The skies had opened. Six months of pent-up precipitation being unleashed on the earth's surface at once causing roads to become rivers. Zoe's little electric car was pelted with raindrops as I traversed the flooded streets of South London. The windscreen wipers were swiping back and forth in overdrive yet couldn't keep up with their task, causing me to slow to a crawl. The metallic drumming on the roof was so loud that Beck and I were speaking in raised voices to formulate our back up plan. The rain had made Beck's Plan A unfeasible. I was happy about that.

We were on our way to One Hyde Park. Once considered the most exclusive real estate in the world, home to the rich and famous with apartments selling for hundreds of millions of pounds, seized by the local authorities and place of residence for city officials and members of parliament. Our new friend Adam informed us that, at that moment, Alvina was staying in one of the penthouses. He had a keycard for the building, but not her apartment. Plan A had been an assassination, plain and simple. Playing judge, jury and executioner was not something I was in favour of, but Beck was convinced it was the only way of putting a stop to their plans. Adam informed us that Alvina was scheduled to host a drinks event that evening and was expected to be parading around on the balcony, sipping champagne in the sunshine. A rifle round to the head, fired from a concealed spot in Hyde Park which was overlooked by the apartment, would have been the extent of the effort. Crude but effective. However, the storm of the century made it unlikely that anyone would be outside, meaning taking a shot would be impossible without high-velocity, armour piercing rounds to penetrate the toughened glass.

The good news, as far as I was concerned, was that it made space for a more nuanced Plan B, which would mean going inside once the guests had left. Significantly more dangerous but with the possibility of acquiring useful intel. Afterall, we knew nothing of Olivia's whereabouts. I threw my hat in the ring as I knew Beck would go in all guns blazing. Instead, he would play overwatch from a distance and keep an eye on security.

We approached Hyde Park from the south via Sloane Street, lined with its grand four-storey town houses. Judging by the groaning and squirming, Beck's aged body was not having an enjoyable time being squashed down in the passenger footwell. There was no reasonable explanation for two middle aged men to be driving around alone in this part of town and we needed to avoid getting pulled over given the bolt action rifle and silenced pistol that were stowed in the boot. Collusion, possession of firearms, intent to kill. The punishment doesn't bear thinking about. We joined the park's three-mile perimeter road and drove anticlockwise, passing One Hyde Park on our right. First impressions on the exterior were a little underwhelming given the supposed exclusivity. A complex of four individual columns of glass fronted apartment buildings jutted forward towards the road. I assumed they were more impressive on the inside, and there was no questioning the spectacular location. Alvina was staying on the top floor of the first column, but as I slowed to steal a cautious glance, I saw no signs of life.

"I can't see anyone there," I said through my teeth like a ventriloquist.

"Is it still raining? Perhaps they are inside."

"It is easing up a bit. But none of the lights are on."

"Keep driving. Let's loop round and find a place to stop."

We continued around the circular road, hanging permanently leftwards, and entered the park on northern edge through Victoria Gate. Following the road south, we reached a small car park next to the bridge that crosses the mossy green waters of The Serpentine, the snake-like lake that winds its way through the centre of the park. The dense population of bushes and trees that enclosed the carpark meant that it was nicely secluded and not visible from a distance. Aside from a handful of dedicated joggers, the evening's downpour meant the park was deserted, which was good in one respect, but also meant our presence was more noticeable. Further eastward along the lake's shore, it would be possible to see the top of the One Hyde Park apartments over the treeline. I stayed in the car and let Beck stretch out his achy joints, mini binoculars concealed inside his jacket. I took out my crossword book and made sure it was visible from the outside by resting it high up on the steering wheel. I made an obvious effort of chewing on the end of the pencil. It wasn't much of a cover story, but the aim was to look less suspicious than sitting there alone staring into nothingness like a psychopath. Plus, it helped pass the time.

Muscle of the ribcage, eleven letters. An easy one. I N T E R C O S T A L.

After what seemed like only a few minutes the door opened, and a bedraggled Beck slumped down into the seat. His luscious silver hair was soaked, leaving it lank and sticking to the side of his face like a dirty grey mop. He shook his head like a dog coming out of a river, spraying me with rainwater.

"I'm glad you're back," I said. "I have one that you should be able to help me with. Old slang for a navy ship's cook. Two words, seven and eight letters."

"What the bloody hell are you doing?" he said. "You should be keeping an eye out."

"I was trying to blend in," I said.

"Blend in with what? I don't see any other crosswording middle-aged men sitting alone in cars."

"There's nobody about. Relax."

"Jeez, I had you down as a professional." He paused a moment. "It's Clacker Mechanic, by the way." He looked at me, clamping his lips shut, choking back a laugh that wanted to burst from his mouth.

"Bloody hell," I said. "I never would have got that."

"Clacker is pastry. You can work out the rest."

"Gotcha," I said, scribbling it down. "So? What's the news?"

"I think you are right. I couldn't see anyone there. There's no party happening."

"Perhaps we're early," I said, checking my watch. It was 19:15.

"I don't think so. You would expect some activity, some preparation for it at least."

"I guess almost being blown up yesterday could have forced her to change plans." I said.

"Yep. But assuming she is staying there, it makes your job easier."

"I thought this was a team effort?" I said, laughing. The grin was wiped from my face by the heavy, solid tapping of truncheon on glass. My head snapped around to see a police officer glaring through the window.

"Shit. Here we go," Beck muttered under his breath.

I wound down the window. "What is the purpose of your visit to the park?" the officer said, chewing gum. She had brown eyes and brown hair, both of which were mostly covered by a black baseball cap pulled forward over her face. She poked her head into the car and inspected the rear. She breathed a combination of fresh mint and stale coffee into my face.

"We are on our way back home from assignment in north London. Just stopped off for a toilet break," Beck said without the slightest hesitation.

"What assignment?" the officer replied with a hint of scepticism.

"Rubbish clearance."

The police officer glanced over her shoulder at her colleague standing behind, one hand resting on a taser that was hanging off her belt. "ID cards please."

My hand reached toward my pocket when Beck said. "They are in the boot."

This time my head snapped in the other direction. "Are they?" I said with glaring eyes and gritted teeth.

"Out of the car," the officer said, like she had lost her patience.

I unfurled from the cramped interior of the tiny car. The officer, wielding her truncheon, stepped backward and to the side, revealing a direct line of sight to the second officer who had the taser pointed square at my chest. I raised my hands to shoulder height.

"Both of you, get around to the back." she said.

We all edged towards the rear of the car. The second officer, a broad-shouldered lady with a square chin and hooked nose, stayed a five-metre distance away, easily enough for her to react with the taser if we tried to tackle her.

"Stand over there with your hands on your head," Officer One said, pointing to a spot on the ground two metres behind the car. She moved to the boot and searched for the release button with her hand. My heart was racing as I shot Beck a jaw-clenching *What are you doing?* glance. In return, he pointed at Officer One with his eyeballs. My gut knew he was about to do something, and I would need to respond. I gave him a subtle nod of acknowledgement. Then he made a loud whistling noise through his teeth. It was the signal to act. His right arm moved from being bent with hands overhead to full horizontal extension, without existing in any time or space in-between. A mini-binocular-shaped missile was released from his sleeve at Officer Two and struck her square in the temple. Her knees gave way, and she collapsed on the dusty ground.

My turn.

I ducked as I stepped forward, spinning with an outstretched leg, sweeping Officer One's legs from beneath her. She fell to the ground and dropped the truncheon, which I picked up. At the same time, Beck had covered the distance to Officer Two and had acquired her taser, which was pointed at Officer One. Officer One scrambled on to all-fours before she noticed her predicament. Beck knelt next to the second officer and checked for a pulse, all the while keeping the taser trained on its target.

"Don't worry," he said. "She's alive. There is no reason for anyone else to get hurt. But let's be clear, I will not hesitate to put fifty-thousand volts through you if you don't do as I say. Throw me your radio and take off your belt." She spat dirt from her mouth and regarded Beck with a look of disgust but did as instructed.

"Stand up please," I said. "Hands behind your back." I collected the radio and tied her hands using her belt. "Over to the car. Sit." I walked her over to the police car and opened the rear door. I untied her boot laces and bound her ankles together with tight knots, then shut her in the rear of the car. Beck had dragged Officer Two over by lifting her from under the arms and then folded her limp body in to the front passenger seat. Moving to the driver's side, I took the keys and yanked the radio, ripping the wire from its connection. "Now what?" I said, peering over the car roof at Beck. "We can't leave them here in plain sight."

"Release the handbrake," Beck replied. "We'll have to roll it in to those bushes."

I did as Beck said, pushing the car with one hand as I steered it with the other. Beck provided most of the momentum from the rear. The police car gained speed as it rolled along, then came to a halt as it cracked its way into the thick shrubbery, disappearing into a mass of leaves and branches. It wasn't invisible but was sufficiently camouflaged in the dying light and wouldn't be spotted by ignorant passersby. The officers' escape was hindered, but it wouldn't hold them forever.

"Shit. That was intense," I said, as we dashed back to Zoe's car.

"Yes. The genie is well and truly out of the bottle. We have to assume they will remember the plates on this car. If they run them, it will link back to Zoe. We need to act fast. I'll drive and keep the car on the move. You get in and do the job by any means necessary. The time for subtlety is over."

The circular road led us back in front of One Hyde Park. Beck slowed for me to jump out the car and then accelerated off into the distance. I cleared the four-foot, hedge-covered railings with a giant leap and landed softly on the grass on the other side, hidden behind a sculpture of two skyward-gazing, stone heads. I took a moment to assess the area. The ground floor of the buildings that made up the complex were empty retail units, vast glass frontages granting views to abandoned shops with bare shelving. Residential apartments began from the first floor but only a handful in each block showed any sign of occupancy from the outside.

With the coast apparently clear, I skirted my way along the hedge until I had the shortest distance to cover across the open garden to make it to the entrance to Alvina's building. I ran, ducking low, to a tree that marked the halfway point, then across the remaining space to the front of the building. With each step I took, Beck's silenced Glock pressed into the base of my spine as a reminder of things to come. The revolving glass door that secured the building's entrance began to spin as I swiped Adam's keycard, and I passed through into a lobby made entirely of hard, polished surfaces. Grey marble floors, white marble pillars and an expansive mirrored ceiling. Spiky gold light fittings hung in rows like glistening stars overhead. Exotic plants and flowers splashed islands of colour on the monochrome backdrop and the centrepiece, an enormous and curvaceous red sofa, sat invitingly in the middle. It was symmetry and precision defined. I conceded, it was impressive.

I headed for the bank of lifts, thumbed the call button, and stepped through the doors that opened. The doors slid closed without making a sound and I pressed the button for the top floor. As I ascended, I stared into the mirror that covered the back wall and took a moment to assure the sceptic that was glaring back at me that I was doing the right thing. The problem was that the sceptic was more convincing. Every kill I had made was sanctioned by a higher authority, was backed by reliable intel, and most importantly, was lawful. It struck me that I was intending to kill, no murder, another human based on the story told by a man I had known for twenty-four hours. Yes, his story was convincing, but there was a chance it was a series of coincidences. Perhaps he was using me to finish the dirty work he had failed, to satisfy an unknown grudge he bore. I had no idea. All I knew was the pain and suffering my family, and every other individual who had the misfortune of living in Britain, had to endure daily. How much of that was directly attributable to Alvina was up for debate. But I wasn't convinced she deserved to die, especially if it was Olivia pulling the strings.

I was still conflicted as the lift came to rest and the doors opened.

Holding the door open with my foot, I took out the Glock and peered around the corner, expecting to come face to face with at least one security guard, but I was alone. I padded down the plush, red-carpeted corridor to the single door that lay dead ahead, an imposing mahogany slab with gold inlaid trim and hand-carved architrave. I tried the keycard on the electronic lock but was rewarded with a flashing red light and a door that remained locked. I pressed my ear to the door but heard nothing on the other side, only my rapid breathing and my heartbeat thumping in my ears.

I gave a knock.

No response.

I aimed the Glock at the doorframe and released four rounds with a muted, high pitched, popping sound that was drowned out by the noise of splintering wood. The locking mechanism was sufficiently compromised for the heel of my boot to do the rest of the job and the heavy door flung open on its hinges with one hefty kick, crashing against the interior wall. I moved in, hugging the walls, pistol raised to eye-level, peering around corners, checking for threats. The gentle tapping of my footsteps on the polished oak of the entrance hall floor transitioned to silence as I crossed the threshold on to luxurious white carpet. The elegance and sophistication of the lobby continued to run through the interior of the apartment, but with a greater sense of naturalness and softness. Plump velvet cushions and floating silk curtains. A strong theme of wood, highly polished with intricate swirling grain, flowed throughout the space. I reached the point where the hallway opened into a cavernous living area when I heard the clink of glass.

"You don't need to hide. I won't bite... you know." It sounded like Alvina's voice, but the pacing and intonation was off. "Come on. Out you come," the voice said, like it was coaxing a cat out from under the bed.

I turned the corner, pistol outstretched, and found Alvina sat on a black, ring-shaped sofa, ten feet in diameter, sunk into the ground so that her chest was at floor level. Directly above, was a chandelier made from hundreds of foot-long crystal prisms that fired specks of rainbow around the room. The rain had picked up again, turning the floor-to-ceiling windows in to a gushing waterfall. In the centre of the ringed sofa was a glass table on which a decanter of whiskey stood three-quarters empty.

"I suppose you... you have come finish what you started, huh?" She was drunk.

"Sorry, I don't follow."

She made an explosion sound with her mouth and used her hands to gesture the same.

"That was nothing to do with me. My wife was in the room, remember?" I said.

"So... why have you come in here waving *that* thing around? Is there anyone that doesn't want me dead?"

"I don't know if I'll need this yet. It depends on what you say over the next few minutes." I was alert, surveying the room, trying to work out if the drunken mess in front of me was genuine, or part of a trap.

"Oooh... do you think I've been a naughty girl? Why don't you come and take a seat... right here next to me... and I'll tell you anything you want to know," Alvina said, patting the sofa. "Come on... let me pour you a drink." She reached out to take hold of a spare glass but knocked it over sending it rolling off the table. I picked it up and held it steady as Alvina's shaky hand poured, filling the glass past the brim and spilling brown liquid over the mirrored tabletop. "Here's to... what shall we drink to?" she said.

"I'm not here to celebrate. I want to know if you were involved in the virus that caused The Gaia."

"I might have played a small part... but that's all water under the bridge, right? A looooong time ago."

"Not the way I see it, Alvina. People are suffering day in, day out. Including the women you claim to represent."

"Well... you might have a point. Things didn't turn out as we... expected."

"What *did* you expect? If China's aim was to bring the country to its knees, I'd say you have done a decent job of it."

"If China aimed to do what?" She let out a hysterical laugh. "Has your imagination been running wild again, young Jack? Although, I suppose I shouldn't be so surprised that a primitive male would seek to fulfil his biased presumptions rather than look at himself to find the truth. In case you haven't noticed, I have tried my best to distance myself from my past. I'm surprised you managed to find out." She paused. "Let me tell you something about China... what do you think happened when my parents found out they were having a baby girl? Huh?"

"I don't know."

"Yes, you do. They had an abortion. In fact, when that one didn't work, they were so adamant that I wasn't what they wanted that they tried again. That's right, as a female, I had to survive two attempts to bump me off to make it on to this planet. The fact that I'm here is a miracle, so you should bear that in mind when you judge me, as the universe has already passed its judgement."

My head was spinning. Beck was wrong.

"So, fill me in. What was it all about?" I said.

"Saving the country from impending doom. You think it's bad now, if I hadn't come along, none of this..." she moved her arms, pointing at the walls and ceiling, "...would be standing. Have you ever heard the term 'Napoleon Complex'?"

"No."

"Sometimes called Short Man Syndrome? Its condition attributed to people of short stature who strut around being aggressive and domineering to compensate for their physical shortcomings. Before I was PM, Britain had become a right little Napoleon. Unable to let go of the influence they... we, once had in the days of the British Empire. Still thinking we were a major player on the global scene, sticking our nose into other countries' business, picking fights with regimes who would squash us like a fly it if wasn't for our big brother looming across the pond. But even the US got fed up with policing the world. I guarantee we would have provoked a response that we would not be able to defend against if I hadn't come along."

"How noble of you," I said.

"But it wasn't only that. The whole patriarchal capitalist system was past the point of failure without anyone realising it... or wanting to admit it. Everyone including the collective taxpayer was drowning in unsustainable debt, but nobody knew to whom. Where had all the money gone, Jack? I'll tell you where, Banks, Hedge Funds and Corporations, all headed by men, stuffing their bulging pockets at the expense of everyone else. Even the wealthy middle classes, who used to be so defensive of their precious economic system, came to realise that when they were bleeding out their tax pounds yet couldn't see a doctor when their snotty-nosed offspring were ill. The country was crumbling around their ears! At least I'm honest about the way I run things. The previous governments did nothing but look after themselves and their corporate chums, and then scatter a few crumbs to the wage slaves and tell them to be grateful. Which would you prefer, huh? Huh?" I wasn't sure whether she was expecting me to respond. "Believe me, if we had managed to avoid nuclear obliteration, civil war was a certainty within a decade. Who knows where the country could have ended up. You ought to be thanking me for coming to the rescue. You men had your turn and you fucked everything up!" She paused, appearing deep in thought. "But we didn't mean it to get this far."

"Who's we?"

"While I was studying at Oxford, I met a dear friend. Penelope Sharp. Penny was a brilliant scientist, a virologist, who also happened to be married to a hedge fund billionaire. An odd choice of friend for an anti-capitalist you might be thinking, but she shared my feminist philosophies and was using her husband's vast wealth to do good in the world. She was working on a controversial but potentially groundbreaking approach to medicine, using transmissible viruses as a treatment for genetic defects, like a self-administering vaccine that could work its way through the population without direct intervention. It would be revolutionary for the developing world who couldn't access medical care. All self-funded by her private research organisation, Altior. One of the conditions she was trying to eradicate was cleft palate. It was a common defect that especially impacted children in developing countries as access to treatment was limited. But during her research she accidentally stumbled across something else."

"Let me guess, The Gaia."

"Yes. One night after a few too many glasses of wine she joked about unleashing it on the country. How it would give us the opportunity to shift the balance and install a state of real equality. Not a token gesture of having a few more female CEOs or paying actresses and sportswomen the same as their male counterparts, but a world in which women were truly equal. For weeks after, I couldn't get the idea out of my mind. I ended up convincing myself that not only was it a good idea, but it was morally the right thing to do as reparations for the centuries of discrimination that women had endured. Penny didn't take much persuasion. She was confident she would be able to develop a treatment to reverse the effects within a few years, and we would choose an appropriate time to put things right. But ten years after the virus was let loose, she had still not managed it. Then she fell terminally ill and her young protégé took the baton."

"Olivia. But she didn't share the same intent as her mother," I said in a moment of realisation.

"There is an evil in that woman like I have never seen. Believe it or not, there was some good intent behind mine and Penny's actions, regardless of whether they were realised. But Olivia... she is something else... she just wants to watch the world burn. And I can assure you, her ambitions are big."

"I appreciate the honesty, but why are you telling me all this?"

"I'm tired, Jack. I've spent my life doing what I could to stay in government, trying to right my wrongs with the tools I had at my disposal. Some of that has required sowing the seeds of division. Divide and conquer, as it were, as a distraction. Let the people fight amongst themselves rather than realise the failure I had become. But doing so while managing Olivia's ever-increasing demands has become exhausting. She is the only person who knows what her mother and I did and has been threatening to go public. I can't take any more. I need it to be over. So why don't you put that gun to good use and put me out of my misery."

"That explains the drunken stupor."

"Don't get all judgey with me, mister. Come on. Shoot me."

"If Olivia is the real bad guy here, I don't have much to gain by incriminating myself."

"They won't do anything to you. Not *Mr Jack Wilson*. You are too important to their plans. Do it. Shoot me!"

The windows shook with the explosion of thunder that resonated through the building. Alvina lunged forward, trying to reach the pistol that was sitting in my lap. We grabbed hold of it simultaneously and she fell on top of me, trying to wrestle the gun out of my grip. My legs kicked out as I fell backwards on to the sofa, smashing into the table and knocking the drinks over. Her face was inches from mine. Potent alcohol breath fumed into my nostrils. Folded skin surrounded eyes that gave a window deep in to her soul.

"Come on Jack. It's time for you to be the man you know you can be. End it."

I could see her desperation, her fatigue, her burning desire for conclusion. I struggled to free my hands and then… suddenly… she was still. The weight of her body on mine tripled. A sharp intake of breath. Eyes stretched wide with a grateful emptiness. She had pulled the trigger. I rolled her sideways and she slumped on to the floor, clutching her stomach with a gurgling sound in the back of her throat. A crimson patch soaked her blouse and bloomed outward from her belly button until all that existed was red.

I knelt beside her and took hold of her head in my hands. "Alvina. Stay with me."

"Thank you," she said.

"Where can I find Olivia?" I said as I shook her, trying to keep her conscious.

"Olivia will find you," she said, and her head fell to the side like a limp doll.

CHAPTER 31

Tumultuous gusts and slanted rain gave way to indigo skies with pin-prick stars, like the world had been cleansed of a malevolent force.

I knew in my gut it was just the eye of the storm.

We thundered down the motorway towards home. Beck sat in astonishment as I recalled the events of the previous hour, stroking his grey stubble as he listened.

"What does she mean, Olivia will find you?" he said.

"I don't know. But Olivia already told Zoe that she had served her purpose. And it's only a matter of time before those police officers make the link. We are all in danger. I need to get home asap."

"Yes, instead of taking me home, I'll come with you," Beck said. "Let's collect your family and you can all come to my house while we work out the next step."

We continued in silence for a while, the cognitive machinery in both our heads churning, moving pieces of the puzzle, trying to make sense, trying to fathom what might happen next. Alvina had only confirmed what Beck already knew, albeit with a different motive, but something about hearing her say the words had ratcheted the stakes ten-fold. The ramifications were enormous.

I pulled up outside the house and darted inside. Zoe wasn't in the kitchen. I moved to the living room. "Zoe?" Still no sign. A tense mass of dread began to build inside me. They had already got to her. I shouted up the stairs. "Zoe? Are you here? Zach? Cora?". I ran upstairs. Our bedroom was empty. Then I heard a noise coming from Cora's room. I burst in to find Zoe and Cora sat on the bed reading a book. The tension dispelled.

"Oh, you're back," Zoe said. It took a second for her to register the blood that covered my shirt, hands, and arms. "Oh my god, what have you done?".

Cora screamed and pulled the duvet up to her face.

"It's ok, it's not mine," I said. "Where's Zach?"

"He's in his room," Zoe replied. "Why?"

"It's not safe here. Gather whatever you need for the night and go downstairs. Beck will explain while I get cleaned up. We will stay the night at his house."

"I'm not going anywhere," Cora said.

I looked her straight in the eye. "Just this once, you are going to do as I say." I held her gaze until she turned away.

"Fine."

I got in the shower and scrubbed Alvina's blood from my body. Orange water pooled around my feet and spiralled down the plughole, the final traces of her being expelled from this world. Once the water had run clear, I got dressed, bagged up my clothes and met the others downstairs. Zoe was sat with her head in her hands, disbelief written all over her face.

"We can't stop this on our own," she said. "We need to call for help."

"Who do you have in mind? And how?" I replied.

"You said you had a satellite phone, Beck," Zoe said. "Can't we call one of your foreign contacts? Surely they would do something now we have all this confirmed."

"Cross-border comms dried up a long time ago. We have been speaking to ourselves for years," Beck replied.

Zoe's face brightened. "I've got it. If we can get to the lab, I can get an email message to the team we worked with in the us. They could get a message to the authorities. In fact, our data archive has a computer. It's underground with one way in and out. We could hole up there until they send help."

"If they send help," I said.

"It's not a bad plan," Beck said. "We don't have many other options."

"Better grab some snacks," I said. "We could be there for a few days."

The journey to the university campus took less than half an hour. We parked the car and Zoe led us across a grassy square with winding paths flanked by knee-height hedges. A huge spherical water feature sat in the centre, moonlight gleaming of its surface and the gentle trickling of water deafening to my heightened senses. Up ahead was a magnificent red brick building that resembled a church, with large arched windows and delicate pointy spires. The pitch of the slate roof increased above the main entrance and angled directly upwards into a clock tower that reached into the clear night sky. The clockface showed midnight, and the gloomy sound of the bell struck twelve, as an unwelcome reminder that we were running out of time. I walked alongside Zach with my arm over his shoulder. He was wearing bright blue pyjamas and flipflops, carrying a small rucksack. He gave a gaping yawn.

"It's Sunday, Dad. I'm tired," he said.

"I know, pal," I replied. "Once we get inside you can get your head down for some sleep."

Zoe and Beck walked together up ahead. Cora lagged behind alone, wrapped up in a pink dressing gown. She stared at the floor, deep in thought. The door to the building was heavy panelled oak with a large brass knob. Zoe scanned her security pass, but the door remained locked. She tried again with the same result.

"They've removed my security access!" Zoe said. "They have no right over university matters. Someone must have been leant on. When I find out who has done this, heads are going to roll."

"Let's worry about staying alive until morning for now," I said. "Is there another way in?"

"I have a key," Beck said, pulling out his Glock.

Zach's eye widened to saucers. "Cool!"

"Put that away," Zoe snapped. "That door is over two hundred years old. We'll go around the back."

The rear entrance was a standard double door that Zoe was happy for Beck and me to put through with a hefty and coordinated barge of the shoulder. The doors flung open into a wide corridor that formed a cross, with the old oak door at the front dead ahead of us, and an intersecting corridor that ran left to right, halfway up. Doors leading to offices and small classrooms intermittently broke up the dark panelled walls that ran up to the vaulted ceiling high above. Footsteps on terracotta tiles echoed as we walked along under the scrutiny of the oil-painted faces that glared down on us from on either side.

"Who are all these people in the paintings?" Cora asked.

"They are past professors from the different departments," Zoe said.

"There sure is a lot of men," I said. "Shouldn't these have been taken down and burned?" I was only half joking.

"This is a place of enlightenment," Zoe said "We don't believe in erasing the past. We believe it should be front and centre to learn from and track progress against." Judging by the lengthy list of names inscribed in gold lettering on a wooden plaque, progress wasn't the right word. They had swung from one extreme to the other.

We turned left at the junction and then left again, through a door and on to the landing of a set of solid stone steps that led to the underground archive. The windowless room was cool. The musty odour that characterised the rest of the aged building was concentrated by the lack of ventilation. Rows of floor-to-ceiling bookshelves housed vast amounts of information meticulously catalogued in textbooks, folders, boxes of loose paper and various formats of computer disks. Every shelf on every rack was divided up and allocated a location number. At the far end of the room was a bank of four wooden tables, each with its own lamp, one blue fabric sofa, and a metal frame desk that was home to an old computer.

"You kids go and lie down on the sofa over there," I said. "Try to get some sleep." Judging by the synchronous yawn they both let out, I didn't expect that to be a problem.

"Don't get comfortable just yet," Zoe said. "If they have removed my security access then my computer account may have been restricted too." She sat down at the metal desk and tapped a few keys. "Ah, great. I'm in."

I settled the kids down who both fell asleep within seconds. Then Beck and I shunted one of the heavy shelving units in front of the door and joined Zoe around the computer monitor.

"What am I going to tell them?" Zoe said. "I'm beginning to wonder why anyone should care."

"Just lay it all out as simply as you can," Beck said. "You can tell them that we have proof, but that our lives are at risk."

Zoe composed an email, addressed it to a handful of people in the US that had been working on the collaboration, and then hit send. "And now we wait," Zoe said. "It'll be outside working hours in the States. There's a chance someone might pick it up from home but if not we're here for the next eighteen hours at least. Suggest we get some rest."

Sleep came easier than expected but was cut short by the rattling of the handle on our barricaded door.

CHAPTER 32

The dinginess of the windowless room provided no hint of the time of day. My body ached from lying on the hard floor and my arm tingled as the blood rushed back into it. I sat up and glanced across at Beck who was alert and had his index finger pressed vertically against his lips. I rubbed my eyes and checked my watch.

06:12.

Zoe had always been a heavy sleeper. I crawled across and nudged her to wake her up.

"Zoe, there is someone at the door. We need to check your email to see if there has been a response," I said.

Zoe whispered. "Who is it?"

"I don't know, but we don't want to let anyone know we are here until we are sure it's safe."

"Hello?" a voice shouted, followed by the sound of something heavy hitting into the door.

Zoe leapt to the PC and frantically tapped the keys. "There is a reply!"

"What does it say?" I said.

"It says... We have flagged this up to the authorities. They will send help. Sit tight and stay safe."

"Yes!" I said, suddenly wide awake and buzzing with excitement.

"How did they get here so fast?" Zoe said. "It's a nine-hour flight."

"Let's find out," I said. "Wake the kids and stay back out the way."

Beck and I made our way down the centre channel of stacked up papers towards the door.

"Hello? Is anyone in there?" The voice again. Female. This time I detected a European accent.

"Yes," I said. "I'm here. Who is this please?"

"We are representatives of the Dutch government. Our ministers received an urgent SOS overnight from their American counterparts. We have armed soldiers and a helicopter to take you to safety."

A surge of optimism poured into my heart. "It's ok Zoe. I think it's them!" I called to the back of the room.

Beck gave me a slap on the back. "Thank God it's not the French," he said with a smile. "Don't think I could live with being rescued by a Frenchman. Help me shift this thing."

We pulled at the shelf that blocked the door, metal legs scraping against the floor. I reached for the door handle and turned. The door opened an inch and then slammed into my face as something heavy hit it from the other side. The world turned black as I stumbled backward and fell to the ground. The earth tilted and turned through water-filled eyes. Blood streamed from my nose. I looked across to Beck for help, but he was standing in surrender with his hands in the air. A black-clad police officer stepped into the room, sub-machine gun trained on Beck. Then another, scanning the corners of the basement room before aiming at me. Then a female face I recognised. It took a moment to recall the name through the fuzziness in my head. Then, as a pair of green eyes glared down on me like I was filth, it came to me.

"DCI Steele," I said to myself.

"I'm off duty. Call me Catherine," she said. "I always wanted to be an actress when I was younger. I would have been good at it, don't you think? The Dutch accent is particularly difficult to master."

Behind her followed a fourth figure, the gaunt and pointy features of Olivia Sharp.

"Isn't this a nice cosy family get together?" she said. "And who is this? Let me guess, old Uncle Bob?"

Beck said nothing.

"Are you sure you brought enough back up?" I said defiantly, nodding at the two weapon-wielding soldiers.

"Don't worry, there are plenty more upstairs guarding the front and the rear. Escape is impossible so you can save your strength. We need you in good condition. Why don't you go back and join the rest of your family? Nice and slow."

I got to my feet and sidled my way backwards to where Zoe and the kids were sitting. Beck did the same. Zoe was sat on the sofa shielding the children.

"Ah Zoe," Olivia said. "I wish I could say it's a pleasure to see you, but truth be told, I'm looking forward to never having to see your arrogant, self-righteous face ever again."

"Arrogance suggests a lack of substance, Olivia," Zoe replied. "I think we both know that's a label much more fitting yourself."

Olivia threw her head back in a laugh that indicated anger over amusement. "You really do rate yourself don't you, Zoe. Here was me, being all merciful, about to end your existence and let you die with a modicum of dignity. But I can't bring myself to do it. I will not allow you to be a martyr. You will die knowing the true extent of your pathetic failure." She turned to face me. "How many children do you have, Jack?"

"Three, well two," I replied.

"No..." Olivia said. "You have two children with Zoe. What about the others?"

"I don't know what you're trying to say but I've never

—"

"Calm down, I'm not suggesting you have been sleeping around. But you have been a regular sperm donor for some time, have you not?"

"Right, yes, I have."

"So? How many children do you have? Have a guess."

I did some basic mental maths. "Four hundred."

"Way off," she replied. "A smidge over eight thousand. And on that basis, how many sons that have survived until birth?"

"Must be around five-hundred."

"Wrong again, Jack," Olivia said. "Four-thousand three-hundred." Everyone stood in silence. "Do I need to join the dots for you? Here we have a man whose genetics can overcome the effects of The Gaia. Is it purely coincidental that the wife of this man is the person who claims to have invented the cure for The Gaia? Or is it more likely that she has been drip fed information to lead her blindly to exactly where we wanted her, like the useful idiot she is?"

The colour drained from Zoe's face to the point of translucency. "The team in Chicago weren't real," she said, telling herself as the lightbulb finally popped. "But we had video conferences and…"

"Oh, they're real, but they work for me," Olivia said. "A part of our expansion project. I wish you could be around to see what remarkable things we have planned across the pond. But sadly, that's not going to be the case."

"Why go to the lengths of developing a cure that you have no intention of using?" Zoe asked.

"Phase two relies on the public taking their medicine, but they are growing increasingly sceptical of what Alvina and her government say and do. We needed the trusted face of an esteemed scientist to reassure everyone that everything is going to be ok. Despite your many flaws, you did a decent job on that stage during the press conference. You came across genuine."

"That's because I was being genuine, you stupid bitch!" Zoe said. "How dare you use my reputation as a means to instigate your evil."

"I'm not evil, Zoe. As a woman surely you can see the benefits of a female led society. We just need to iron out the flaws that Alvina didn't foresee. Even I must accept that men are crucial for us to survive as a species. They just need to be placed under more effective control. The older generations are not as compliant as they need to be and the younger ones, well, we are making progress with the education system but for some reason mothers remain oddly attached to their sons when it comes to putting them to use. Believe me, we have tried other things. We put drugs in the drinking water to stop the production of oxytocin, you know, the love hormone, to make mothers that bit less attached to their repulsive boys. But it just made everyone confrontational and had no effect on the mother's relationship with the child. Seems there is something beyond hormonal chemistry when it comes to the mother-son bond. So, more drastic measures were required."

"How can you have such little empathy towards children?" Zoe said. "What if you were to have a son? Would you be happy to see him sent off into slavery?"

"Me? Oh, I can't have children. That's my own genetic anomaly that I must bear. You probably think that's made me bitter and twisted. But you're wrong. I've been put on this earth for a greater purpose than mere reproduction, to add more bodies to an overpopulated planet. I'm here to reverse the damage done to humanity caused by the negligence of men. To take us forward to a more enlightened period where women are in control." Olivia's voice was full of passion. She looked up through the ceiling, towards the gods, clenching her fists.

"Ha!" Zoe laughed. "You're no messiah. You're just a narcissist with a chip on her shoulder."

"Picture it," Olivia said, ignoring Zoe's insult. "Thanks to a compound you accidentally developed, every baby born into freedom is a girl. I suppose I ought to thank you for that one at least. There would be no such thing as crime. No rape. No domestic abuse. No armed robbery. No dick-measuring, sabre-rattling politicians, starting wars to grab land and build empires. Wasting precious resources on building bigger bombs and faster missiles. Threatening to vaporise their fellow human beings. The world could be shaped to ensure women flourish in peace. Meanwhile, thanks to your beloved husband, we can precisely control the birthrate of men to do the necessary tasks. We happily farm animals into servitude, so I don't see what the difference is. We will eventually reach a point where they know no different. And they will be well treated."

"So that's the purpose of the enormous dormitories you're building? Men farms?" I said.

"I wouldn't use those words, but essentially, yes," Olivia replied as she turned back to face me. "Anyway, that's enough chit chat. Let's get what we came for. Catherine?"

Catherine Steele whipped out a pair of handcuffs. "You've made our job rather easy, Jack," Steele said. "We considered dragging you in last week after the shooting at the hydrogen plant, but we weren't ready until Zoe had stood up in front of the country to share her good news. But since then, you have been a busy boy, haven't you? And thanks to your daughter, we have all the evidence we need to do whatever we want with you. What an upstanding citizen you have raised. You should be proud." She looked at Cora and beckoned her over. "Come." Cora scanned the room and attempted to stand up from the sofa, but Zoe pulled her back. "I said, come!" Steele repeated more forcefully as a machine gun pointed in Zoe's direction. Cora stood and shuffled over next to Steele, who put her arm over Cora's shoulder. "Why don't you tell your dad about what you found? It's ok, you won't get in trouble."

Cora's eyes sought every part of the room except my

face. "My teacher said we should watch out for things that are strange and report them... I found a bullet on the bathroom floor."

Damn it!

The round I'd ejected from the chamber. I hadn't miscounted after all.

"Brave girl," Steele said, pulling Cora closer. "That's right Jack, Cora found a fifty-calibre bullet in your bathroom, just like the ones that were used to murder innocent people that day at the plant. We know you didn't have anything to do with those killings, but the bullet is identical to the one that killed a guard dog during an arson attack at a pharmaceutical facility, and the ones fired at the scene of the terrorist attack on a government building a few days ago. I'd say that puts you in pretty hot water." She lifted the cuffs. "Arms out."

I looked at Cora with my heart in pieces. Another part of my life that had been carved out and discarded, leaving me hollower still. There were no bounds to what they would take from me. But as I knew well, some actions had unintended consequences. It was once said that there is nothing more dangerous than a man with nothing to lose. And I was getting damn close to having nothing to lose. Besides, Alvina's words finally made sense.

They won't do anything to you. Not Mr Jack Wilson.

They needed me to fulfil their plan. They wouldn't kill me.

I was suddenly filled with the courage of indifference.

"Arms!" Steele repeated.

"Yeah, I don't think so," I said. I took my chance and lunged for the closest armed police officer. I was inches away, then...

"Shoot him!" Olivia's voice boomed in the confined space.

CHAPTER 33

I heard the silenced pop and felt the impact at the same time. I spun, then slumped hard on the floor. Then came the pain. An incapacitating agony that erased all external reality. I closed my eyes with all attention on the lump of lead that sat uninvited in my shoulder. I was not of this world. Then I heard something. A ghostly voice from another dimension.

"Jack!"

And another, younger voice.

"You said you wouldn't hurt him!"

Then a cry of somebody else in pain

"Argghh!"

Then...

"Shoot him again!"

A heavy impact on the same side into my collar bone. My nervous system was being sympathetic. The pain barely registered. In fact, if anything, it pulled me back to reality. But the sensation of bone breaking was unmistakable.

The world began to rematerialize around me. As my vision restored, I looked up to see Olivia holding Zach up by his hair. He kicked and thrashed with his legs as she dragged him along.

"Have it your way," Olivia said. "There is a fifty-percent chance this one will carry the same gene and I'll take great pleasure in extracting it from him. Harvesting stem cells from bone marrow is one of the most painful medical procedures there is. Awful shame about the shortage of anaesthetic. And if we don't have any luck with this one there are four-thousand others that we can track down." She moved backwards towards the door, pulling Zach along by his hair. "If only you Wilsons would learn to toe the line, your lives would be so much easier. If you hadn't been so determined to kick up a fuss at every possible opportunity, you might still have your eldest daughter alive. Grace, wasn't it? That warning shot was obviously too subtle for your ignorant little brains. Never mind, at least you will soon be reunited." She paused, then shouted at the armed police. "Don't leave any of them alive."

Zoe collapsed in a hysterical heap against the sofa. Beck slid his back down the wall and fell on to the ground. I couldn't have moved if I had wanted to. We had reached the endgame. We had fought hard, but we hadn't won. I braced myself for the final blow.

I hoped it would be quick.

Then I saw Cora's face, as red as pure, crystallised fury. Arms thrust straight down by her sides. Fists clenched. Like a little stick of dynamite with half an inch left on the fuse. Primed. Ready to explode. Then it came.

"Get your hands off my brother!" she screamed as she threw herself, rugby tackle style, into one of the police officers. She didn't have the mass to take the officer down, but it was enough of a distraction for Beck to react.

He didn't hesitate.

He was on his feet within a second, covering the distance to the nearest officer, the one that Cora wasn't hanging off, in a swift, fluid motion that resulted in a weighty uppercut to the underside of her chin, snapping her head backwards and generating two clear inches of fresh air beneath her feet. Before she had landed, he had hold of her weapon and had double-tapped two rounds in the other armed-officer's head. He turned back to the officer that he had floored, who was writhing around on the ground like a tortured earthworm, and put a bullet in each knee. Then he rotated one-eighty on his heels into a kneeling crouch and aimed down the centre aisle, through the middle of the shelves that led towards the door.

Cora kicked the newly headless officer's weapon towards me. I leant forward, scraped it up with my good arm and sprayed a shower of rounds into Steele's back as she tried to flee. She hit the deck and skidded along on her front. Then, with a clear line of sight, Beck took out both of Olivia's ankles with the two best shots I had ever seen with a close-range weapon. She crumpled in a shrieking mess, clutching at the bloody stumps on the end of her legs and releasing Zach who got to his feet and ran back to safety. He jumped on me, and I winced in pain as he wrapped his arms around me.

"My little one-in-eight," I whispered into his ear. Then Cora jumped on us both. Then Zoe. One big tangle of pain-inducing love. It was excruciating, but I never wanted it to end.

"Sorry to break this up, but we have more trouble to deal with upstairs," Beck said. "Jack, can you stand?"

"I think so," I said as I pushed myself up off the ground with my left arm. The blood leaking from the bullet holes in my shoulder formed slick black patches on my dark blue t-shirt and red lines that branched down my arm. I tied together the arms of my jacket into a makeshift sling to support my injured arm and picked up the SMG with my left. "Now what?"

"An unknown quantity of armed targets and the disadvantage of lower ground," Beck said. "That's what. We are going to need to take this quietly and hope to catch them off-guard. Zoe, take the kids and wait at the back of the room. One of us will come back for you when it's clear."

Beck and I made our way towards the stairs, stepping over Steele's corpse and tiptoeing around the red liquid that flowed from it like a macabre lake. Just beyond, stretching along the floor in a wavy skid mark, was a bloody trail that led to Olivia lying prone and trying to pull herself along on her elbows, grunting with every movement. Beck lifted her and propped her sitting up against the wall.

"You're dead men," Olivia hissed through gritted teeth. Her eyelids flickered as she fought for consciousness.

"We'll see," Beck said. "Just make sure *you* stay alive." We crept up the stairs to the small landing. The door exiting to the corridor was closed. I peered through the small square of glass in the door and saw four more armed police officers, alert and ready for action. One of them spotted me through the window and the wooden door was suddenly shredded with a torrent of machine gun rounds.

"Back up! Back up!" I shouted as the darkness of the landing was punctured by columns of light that burst through the door. We reversed back down the stairs. "Shit. We're sitting ducks."

"It's not going to be easy for them to make it down these stairs either," Beck said. "It won't take long before they realise that they'll have to gas us out. Then we're screwed."

"Better make sure they know she's alive then," I said, nodding towards Olivia.

"Good point," Beck replied.

Olivia screamed out in pain as Beck applied pressure to her ankle with the bottom of his boot. "Bastard!" she spat.

I leant against the wall. The dark wet patches on my t-shirt had spread to cover most of the right-hand side. I started to feel lightheaded.

"I don't have the luxury of time here," I said.

The constant emotional rollercoaster of defeat followed by victory followed by defeat had become exhausting. We needed a way to stay on top, but the odds were stacked so heavily against us, there was no apparent way out. Charging the stairs meant certain death. Staying put, the same, but slower. What was needed was a miracle.

I had never believed in God, or divine intervention. But I believed in karma. Do enough good in this world and eventually it will come back around. It will come in peaks and troughs. There will be times when bad fortune piles on in heavy doses, and it will feel unfair beyond measure. But keep on being a good person and by the end, it will pay off. I honestly believed that. But stood there, slumped against the wall, with my life flowing out of me, I was feeling short changed. Perhaps karma felt differently about the things I had done over the course of my life. Things that no man should do to another, in a perfect world. But knowing the world wasn't perfect, I had always thought that history would judge me kindly. I was on the right side. One of the good guys. Perhaps there is no such thing as *the right side*, or *good guys* and *bad guys*. Maybe it's just a bunch of guys with different opinions who decide to shoot each other instead of talk. They say these moments of revelation come to those close to death. For the first time ever, I came to question my entire reason for being.

Beck moved next to me, as if sensing what was going on inside my head. "You know, Jack," he said. "It's been a lonely fight over the past couple of years. Jenny and Bella have been amazing, but it's not the same, if you know what I mean."

"I do," I replied.

"I know we have only known each other for the blink of an eye, but if we make it through this alive, I hope we can keep in touch."

"Me too."

"If we don't survive, then know this: it will be an honour to die by the side of a man of your calibre." Beck's shovel-like hand smacked on to my left shoulder and squeezed.

"Thanks. That means a lot," I said. And it did, especially from a man like Beck. More than he could ever know.

His words dredged up a strange sensation. An irresistible urge to survive. To fight to protect my family. To fight for a way of life that worked for everybody. There were such things as good guys, and I was sure I was on the right side. I shook the fog from my head and looked at Beck. "Let's do this."

He checked his watch. A red light blinked like a strobe, colouring his face from under his chin. "Give it a few minutes."

"Why?" I said. I wanted to act while the adrenaline was pumping.

"You'll see."

The words had barely left his mouth when an earthquake struck. A catastrophic crashing sound rumbled overhead. The door at the top of the stairs flew off its hinges and a shockwave of burning gas funnelled down the narrow stairway, causing Beck and me to dive on the ground for cover. I cried out as I landed heavily on my injured side.

Beck lifted his head and flashed a wonky grin. "You alright over there?"

"Just about," I said. "What was that?"

"Overprotective wife. Never lets me out of the house without a tracker."

"How romantic. Now can we go?"

"Yes, lets. Zoe, kids, come on. Stay close but stay back. Jack, you lead. I'll bring our friend."

Beck hoisted Olivia over his shoulder, and we all edged up the stairs in single file. At the top I peered into the corridor. The bodies of armoured police officers lay strewn on the ground. Orange flame licked at their corpses like a merciless creature enforcing its justice. At the point where the two corridors crossed was the skeleton of a large vehicle engulfed in fire. One of the bodies lying on the floor groaned and rolled over on to its back, triggering a spray of bullets from somewhere hidden that thumped into its chest.

"I think it's clear," I said. "Let's go. Cover your nose and mouth."

We slid through the smoke-filled corridor towards the burning vehicle. I kicked lumps of debris out of the way as rows of grey-haired men gazed down stoically, their faces blistering off their canvasses as fire climbed the walls. We reached the crossroads and turned left, towards the front entrance where a shadowy figure holding a weapon stood proudly.

"Really?" shouted Beck from the back of our line. "Did you have to blow up old Betty?"

"Never mind Betty," Zoe said. "Look what you've done to my building!"

The shadowy figure laughed. "I was hoping for a bit more gratitude than that."

As we got closer to the exit the smoke thinned to reveal Bella's sooty face, beaming with an accomplished grin. "Ignore them," I said, putting my arm round her. "I'm very happy to see you."

"Nice to know someone appreciates me," she said. Then she spotted my injuries. "That's nasty. Jenny has one of their vehicles running. I expect there is a first aid box in the boot."

Beck pushed past to the front of the queue and curled his free arm around his heroic wife, giving her a forceful kiss. "You are a wonderful woman, Isabella Beck. But what took you so long?"

"Your tracking signal vanished around midnight. We came to your last known location but couldn't see any sign of you. We had started the journey home when it popped up for a few seconds. I guessed you were in the area but must have been in a shielded room."

"Or underground," he said. "We came back to ground level but were forced back down by the police you took care of." He paused. "I still can't believe what you have done to my van. She was my first child."

"Forget that heap of junk," Bella replied. "We've got our hands on a major upgrade." She pointed with her thumb behind her to a row of black, seven-seater SUVs with tinted windows and shiny chrome wheels. "Come on kids," she said, waving to Cora and Zach. "I bet you've never been in a car like this. Why don't you jump up front, young man?"

Zach didn't need telling twice. He sprinted over the passenger side, pulled the door open and climbed in. "Cool!" he said with a radiant grin as he regarded the cockpit's arrays of screens and coloured lights.

Zoe and Cora squeezed into the rear two seats. Bella found the first aid kit and sat next to me in the middle row. Beck moved to the rear of the car and deposited Olivia into the boot.

"Shit," he said, as he climbed in next to Bella. "She's dead. She was Exhibit A. How are we going to convince anyone of what's been going on without her testimony?"

"Puh!" Bella said. "She wouldn't have said a word. There has been a development on that front anyway. Yesterday evening while you were out, the comms radio crackled to life. Old General Fleetwood had received a message from the French. That Atkins family that died in the car accident a few days ago, turns out they were done away with by someone that wanted to keep their secret hidden. Their French relatives have demanded a full investigation. The uncle is a famous academic." She turned her head to face the rear. "The French authorities are keen to speak to you about your interactions with the University of Paris, Zoe."

"Professor Aubert," Zoe said.

"That's the one," Bella replied. "They are sending a boat to collect us at Dover. We'll be put into quarantine when we arrive in France. But they are willing to listen. Floor it, Jenny, before any more trouble arrives."

CHAPTER 34

17:30, Saturday 22nd September 2063

The British summer heat lingered on into the later months, but the sunlight faded earlier each day, as it had every year before. I winced as I cast the line one final time, sending the lure flying through the air and sinking into the river with a splash.

"How do you get it so far, Dad?" Zach said.

"Far? That's nothing. Wait until my arm is better, I reckon I could get it to that tree over there," I replied, pointing into the distance.

"No way," Zach said.

"Way."

I rested my head back in the green deckchair and let the last of the sun's rays soak into my skin. The soft trickle of running water and the clicking of the grasshoppers induced a feeling of absolute contentment. There was nowhere else in the world I would rather have been.

"I think I've got one!" Cora said as she leapt to her feet. "I have, I have, Dad. Please can you help? Quick! Before it gets away."

I jumped up and helped Cora reel in her catch. "That's it, not too quickly or you'll pull the hook through its mouth. You grab the net and bring him in."

"Whoa, it's massive," Zach said, having abandoned his station. "What is it?"

"I think this one is a Brown Trout," I said. I unhooked the fish from the line. "Here you go, Cora. You can hold it."

Cora squealed as the strong fish flipped and flapped in her hands. "Eww, It's all slimy!"

"Pop it back in the river then," I said. The fish jumped out of her hands, landed with a splosh, and swam away to safety. "Alright, that's enough for today. You win catch of the day, Cora."

"Yay!" she said, thrusting her arms into the air and doing a little jig.

Zach looked disappointed. "Can we come again tomorrow?" he said.

"Tomorrow is your turn to go and spend some time with Mrs Duggan," I said.

"Oh, but she wants to do crosswords all the time and I'm no good at them."

"No buts. It's important, and she looks forward to it." I leant in for a whisper. "Plus, I think you're her favourite."

Zach gave a little smile. "Okay then."

"Right, let's get this lot packed up." I folded the deck chair, collapsed the fishing rods, and set about picking up our litter.

"Dad?" Zach said as he packed up his bag. "Do you think you will get another job when things go back to how they are meant to be?"

"I already have the most important job in the world, don't I? Looking after you two."

"I guess," Zach said.

"Besides, mum is going to be so busy with her new job I don't think I'd have the time."

"What is she doing now? We see even less of her than before," Zach said.

"That won't be forever. She is working with a special team from other countries to help put in place a new government. But once the emergency situation is over, she will have more time for us. Until then, we need to do what we can to support her. It's very important work."

"Do you think she will be Prime Minister one day?" Cora asked.

"You never know," I said. "But even District Representative is an important job."

"I'm still going to be a fisherman," Zach said.

"You'd be a hungry fisherman because you never catch anything," Cora teased.

"Hey!" Zach replied.

"What about you, Cora?" I said as we began to push our way back through the towering grass. "What do you want to be when you grow up?"

"I think I'd like to be a politician like mum," she said. "I'd make a rule so that everyone has to be nice to each other all the time and everyone is treated the same, no matter who you are."

"That's a lovely ambition," I said. "I think you'd be the best politician ever."

THE END